Praise for

Fiction Hye
Myers, Bill 953-

"A prolific pioneer of Chr...
audio drama, and who kn...
write a crisp, express train ...atic
settings and action, and, a ...inise I wish I'd thought
of—and he succeeds splendidly! Two thumbs up!"

—Frank E. Peretti, on *The Voice*

"Strong writing, edgy . . . replete with action . . ."

—*Publishers Weekly,* on *The Face of God*

"I couldn't put *Fire of Heaven* down. Bill Myers's writing is crisp, fast-paced, provocative . . . A very compelling story."

—Francine Rivers, author

"With the chill of a Robin Cook techno-thriller and the spiritual depth of a C.S. Lewis allegory, this book is a fast-paced, action-packed thriller."

—Angela Elwell Hunt, on *Blood of Heaven*

"Now this is innovative. Bill Myers has played a great game of 'what if?'—creating a compelling story of grace triumphing over judgment . . . A bold new twist on an age-old theme. *Blood of Heaven* is an enjoyable and provocative read. I wish I'd thought of it!"

—Frank Peretti, author

"The always surprising Myers has written another clever and provocative tale." —*Booklist,* on *Eli*

"With this thrilling and omnious tale Myers continues to shine brightly in speculative fiction based upon Biblical truth. Highly recommended." —*Library Journal,* on *Eli*

"Myers weaves a deft, affecting tale." —*Publishers Weekly,* on *Eli*

"*Soul Tracker* provides a treat for previous fans of the author, but also a fitting introduction to those unfamiliar with his work. I'd recommend the book to anyone, initiated or not. But be careful to check your expectations at the door . . . it's not what you think it is."

—Brian Reaves, *Fuse* magazine

"The prolific Myers steadily plugs along offering competent novels such as this one, which provides glimpses of heaven while exploring the darker side of the supernatural. As usual, Myers fans will not be disappointed."

—*Publishers Weekly*, on *Soul Tracker*

"Thought-provoking and touching, this imaginative tale blends elements of science fiction with Christian theology."

—*Library Journal*, on *Soul Tracker*

"Myers strikes deep into the heart of eternal truth with this imaginative first book of the Soul Tracker series. Readers will be eager for more."

—*Romantic Times* magazine

"Bill Myers's novel, *The Seeing*, compels the reader to burn through the pages. Cliff-hangers abound and the stakes are raised higher and higher as the story progresses—intense action-shocking twists!"

—TitleTrakk.com

"An entertaining novel, Bill Myers's *The Seeing* is a great reminder of spiritual warfare and the impact of choice and is reminiscent of Frank Peretti's *This Present Darkness*."

—IDealinHope.com

"[*When the Last Leaf Falls* is a] wonderful novella . . . Any parent will warm to the humorous reminiscences and the loving exasperation of this father for his strong-willed daughter . . . Compelling characters and fresh, vibrant anecdotes of one family's faith journey."

—*Publishers Weekly*

Bill Myers

The Voice

A NOVEL

NEW YORK
BOSTON
NASHVILLE

Copyright © 2008 Bill Myers

FaithWords
Hachette Book Group USA
237 Park Avenue
New York, NY 10017

Visit our Web site at www.faithwords.com.

Printed in the United States of America

First Edition: April 2008
10 9 8 7 6 5 4 3 2 1

FaithWords is a division of Hachette Book Group USA, Inc.
The FaithWords name and logo is a trademark of Hachette Book Group USA, Inc.

Library of Congress Cataloging-in-Publication Data

Myers, Bill
    The voice / Bill Myers. — 1st ed.
        p. cm.
    ISBN-13: 978-0-446-69799-6
    ISBN-10: 0-446-69799-0
    I. Title.
    PS3563.Y36V65 2008
    813'.54—dc22   2007030665

Design by Ralph Fowler

For Bobby Nordlund . . .

A young man after God's heart.

The Voice

"... He lifts his voice, the earth melts."

—Psalm 46:6 NIV

Prologue

Fredrick Fussle expected to hear the voice of God.

Not this.

After years of research, the meticulous collection of data, the construction of mathematical models, and the building of a subterranean laboratory, he was sure they would hear something.

But not this.

"What is happening?" William Mayer, his assistant of six years, cried. The man's voice shimmered, warbled as if he was yelling through the pounding air of a giant fan.

"It's not sound!" Fussle shouted. "I feel it inside my head!"

But he did more than feel. As the energy radiated from the control rods encircling the lab, it saturated his brain, his very thoughts. Suddenly memories disappeared—not dissolved, but shattered. Fragments of past recollections flew apart, then came back together again.

Together, but different.

Re-formed.

Instead of the priesthood he had been a part of for fifty-four years, he remembered proposing to Dorthia Cutler over that dinner of veal parmesan and a bottle of Chardonnay '72 in Vienna.

But only for a moment.

Now he recalled exchanging vows with Sylvia Horton at a lakeside wedding he never had. Well, never had until then. Instead of the pleasantly plump brunette he'd spent half his life with, he was now married to that saucy blonde he'd nearly left her for . . . but apparently had left her for.

"Shut it down!" he shouted. "William, shut it—"

But it was no longer William standing at the console. Now it was some tall, gangly geek he never saw before, but had seen— for the past eighteen months he and the kid, Gerhardt Muller, had worked side by side on the project.

"Gerhardt, shut it down!"

His assistant didn't move. He stared at Fussle like a total stranger. He was a total stranger.

But he wasn't.

The concrete floor pitched violently, throwing Gerhardt to the ground. It rolled like the floor of a carnival funhouse gone berserk. Pitching and rolling. Melting and reshaping.

Then melting again.

Light exploded. Blinding. Piercing. It filled the room with its sound—or was it the sound filling the room with its light? Not only the room, but their minds.

Not only their minds, but their realities.

A swelling wave of concrete lifted Fussle and tossed him to the ground. He tried to shout but he no longer had a voice. At least not his own. The light-sound had absorbed it, overpowered it. His vocal cords vibrated, but with the same light blazing through the room.

He began to crawl on his hands and knees toward the control console. At least where he knew it used to be. But it was impossible to know anything for certain. Just as it was impossible to see because of the light and sound.

The floor was soft and gooey, wet putty. He gripped it and pulled himself forward, lifting one knee from the muck and *then the other, until finally his shoulder struck something soft. The console.*

Grateful that it was mostly solid, he grabbed it and pulled himself to his feet.

The reset button was on the other side, just to the left—if the console's reality had not changed.

He staggered around to the front.

Memories of children he never had filled his head. His heart ached over the recent loss of his oldest to leukemia.

He groped the controls, the posts and switches, pleased they were still as he had designed them—though they now felt like gelatin.

Another pulse of light-sound exploded from the control rods. Fussle cried out as he clung to the console, as the same light-sound roared from his throat.

The wave quickly passed and the memories of his children disappeared. At least those children. Now there were others . . . gentle Kimberly, Samuel with the birth mark on his cheek . . .

Until, at last, he reached the reset button and hit it.

One

CALIFORNIA

"Hi. It's me again."

Charlie Madison turned from the counter and pretended to be startled—though he'd been aware of her presence from the moment she'd entered his store. *Know your surroundings*—that had been part of his training. And old habits die hard.

"Oh, hey there." He cleared his throat. "So how's the guitar coming?"

She flashed him a killer smile. "Great. Well, except for my fingers." She stepped closer and held her hand out to him. "The strings are really doing a number on them."

Charlie looked at her fingers. They were long and graceful, except for the small, white blisters on three of their tips.

"You were right," she sighed. "I shouldn't have started off with steel."

"Yeah"—Charlie cleared his throat again—"they can be tough."

"Yeah, they sure can be."

A moment of silence followed.

She nodded. "Yup, they sure can."

More silence. He knew he should say something, but words weren't exactly his specialty, particularly in situations like this. He coughed slightly. "Looks like you really went at it."

She cocked her head up at him, rich chestnut hair falling on some very lovely shoulders. "I don't do many things halfway."

He swallowed, somehow guessing the fact.

She continued. "Maybe I should, you know, switch to nylon strings. At least for a while."

He nodded. "Maybe."

More silence. Was it his imagination or had she moved closer? And the perfume. He hadn't noticed it before, but it was quite nice.

She shrugged. "Of course, I don't know the first thing about restringing or anything."

"You could bring it in, I'll do it."

Her face lit up. "You'd do that for me?"

He glanced away and swallowed again. The petite beauty had been in his store a handful of times over the past two weeks. And each time he got a definite vibe from her, which he definitely liked . . . which he definitely had to cut off. By the looks of things, there was no time like the present. More coolly, he said, "It's a service I offer all my customers."

If she noticed a drop in temperature, she didn't let on. Tossing back her hair, she smiled. "Thanks."

He retreated behind the display counter and found a row of harmonicas to rearrange.

She followed him. "So, when can I bring it in?"

He leaned farther into the case. "What's that?" His voice sounded small and hollow inside the glass enclosure.

"My guitar. When can I—"

"Oh, any time. Store hours are—"

The front door to the shop flew open, slamming into a tower of Fender amps directly behind it. In the opening stood a young girl, twelve, maybe thirteen—backpack, strawberry hair, earbuds hanging over the top of a green sweatshirt, and eyes darting in all directions.

Charlie pulled his head from the case. "Can I help you?"

Spotting him, she raced toward the counter. "He's right behind me!"

"What? Who?"

"Hide me!" Her voice was nasal, the consonants so soft they barely existed.

"Who are you? What—"

She saw the back room behind the drum display and started for it.

Charlie reached across the counter and grabbed her wrist. "What are you talking about? Who's after—"

"Let go of me!" She struggled to get free. "Let go—"

He held tight. "Who are you?"

She spun toward the door, her hair flying, then to the back room, then to Charlie, all the time trying to pry loose his hand. "He followed me from the bus station! You gotta—"

"It's all right," a voice boomed from the doorway.

Charlie turned to see a stout man in a navy-blue fleece jacket. The left side of his face had a scar that included a bad eye. The girl didn't seem to hear and continued struggling until she followed Charlie's gaze to the door.

"Who are you?" she shouted. "Where is the guy who was—"

"I'm Special Agent Boler."

"What's going on?" Charlie demanded.

The man reached into his jacket and flashed a badge. "FBI."

"Where is he?" the girl cried. "Where's the guy who—"

"He won't be bothering you now."

"He followed me from the station, he—"

"I've got two agents outside. One in a car across the street."

Charlie looked out the storefront window. It was true. Two men had moved into position at opposite ends of his shop.

"You're safe now," Boler said.

"What's going on?" Charlie repeated. He turned to the girl. "Who are you?"

"Who am I?" Even with her nasal speech, there was no missing the attitude.

"The Lutzers' daughter," Boler explained.

"What?"

"I'm Jazmin," the girl said, shaking loose her hand.

"Who?"

"Jazmin Lutzer," the agent answered. "Your sister's child."

Charlie stood speechless. He knew Katie had a kid ten or so years ago. Even remembered it being a girl. But that was another lifetime ago, before he killed his family. Before he stopped returning calls and answering letters.

Loud banging on the back metal door refocused his attention.

"Sounds like someone wants in," the woman said.

Agent Boler motioned them toward the street. "Everybody outside."

The banging stopped, followed by the pop of a gun. And another.

That was all Charlie needed. He wrapped a protective arm around the girl and herded her toward the front door.

"You too, miss!" Boler motioned the woman to follow.

For a brief second Charlie wanted to swing by the cash register and grab his gun. But since it was unregistered and since he was in the presence of a Federal agent, he thought better of it.

They stepped out into the bright sun.

"This way!" The agent took the girl by the arm. "The car is across the street!"

Two more pops echoed from inside the store.

The woman ran down the street toward her pickup as Charlie, Agent Boler, and the girl crossed to a Jeep Cherokee.

Boler yanked open the rear door on the driver's side. "Get in!"

They piled inside—the girl first, Charlie second . . . just as a bullet struck the left front fender.

"Down!" Boler motioned. "Get down!" Turning for cover at the rear of the Cherokee, he reached under his jacket to produce a boxy MAC-10 machine pistol.

Charlie saw it and stiffened.

Another shot glanced off the bumper with a *thud-zing*.

Instinctively, Charlie pushed the girl to the floor, covering her body with his own.

"What are you doing!" she cried. "Get off me!"

The passenger door behind them was still open. He twisted, reaching for the handle. That's when he saw the shooter inside his store—ten feet from the door, near the horns display. Latin, Middle Eastern, it was hard to tell in the shadows.

The two agents outside had dropped below the window. They were pressed against the wall, inching their way forward.

But they weren't agents. Charlie knew that now. Feds travel in ones and twos, seldom in threes and fours. He cursed himself for being so stupid. Then there was Boler's gun. The FBI use Glocks, though the older guys still hang on to their Sig 228s or 226s. No way do they use MAC-10s.

"Get off me! I can't breathe!"

He rose slightly and glanced out the Cherokee's back window. Boler was crouched near the bumper, pulling back the slide of his gun, chambering the first round. The final clue. Americans, from cops to Feds, chamber their first round as soon as they slam in the magazine. Not these boys.

More shots. This time from Boler or whoever he was.

Charlie had seen enough. He rose from the girl and pushed her toward the opposite door.

"Ow!"

"Get out!"

"That hurts!"

He reached past her and opened it. "Go!"

"What are—"

He continued pushing until she tumbled out onto the curb. She swore, rubbing her elbows, immediately checking for scrapes.

He joined her side and made a quick assessment. Boler was at the back of the car, preoccupied with the gunfight. The driver was around the front also firing. Their best option was the hardware store behind them.

"Come on!" He grabbed the girl's arm and pulled.

"You're hurting me! You're—"

He dragged her into the store. Her turquoise flip-flops slapped against the worn oak flooring as they ran. The place smelled of dust and oil.

"Let go of me!"

They passed long wooden bins of nails, rows of PVC pipe, copper pipes, and electrical hand tools, until they arrived at the lawn mower repair section in back. He kicked open the alley door and, still holding her arm, dragged her back out into the sunlight.

Omar Atmani stopped shooting. He couldn't risk hitting the girl. The Mossad agents, absolutely. Killing as many of those dogs as possible would be fine sport.

But not the girl.

He had watched her uncle, surprisingly agile for an older man, open the car's door and escape into the hardware store. He'd even said a prayer for their safety. But they would only be safe a moment—only if Omar kept the others occupied by drawing fire, by distracting and preventing them from giving chase.

He resumed shooting, taking no particular aim as he made his way back through the shop. Any second the two agents in front would storm through the door. How he wished he could be there when that happened. He hadn't anticipated they would know the girl would run to her uncle. And he would have preferred sticking around to take out the entire unit as a reward for their diligence.

But that was not the assignment.

Besides, he expected others to be circling the store, preparing to block his exit.

He fired three more bursts before returning to the back room—not without bumping into a drum set, sending the snare and cymbals crashing to the floor. The noise had barely faded before a metal canister, the size of a water bottle, bounced through the front door. Recognizing it, he spun around and clenched his eyes. A deafening concussion filled the room. Light, brighter than the sun, exploded behind him. It would last only a second, enough time for the agents to enter and take him.

But Omar was already racing for the alley door.

By the time they finished scouring the room he would be long gone—down the alley, preparing for the next step.

"Where are we going?" Jaz did her best to match her uncle's quick strides while keeping a careful eye on his lips. "Slow down, will you!"

He gave no answer.

"Excuse me?"

Still no answer.

"*Excuse me!*"

Talk about lack of verbal skills. They were a good three blocks from the store before he finally spoke. "I don't know what you're doing here, but those men are serious."

"Oh really," she said, making sure he caught her sarcasm.

"Really. And the sooner we get this cleared up and get you back home, the better."

"Can't."

"Can't what?"

"That's the deal. Great, I think I'm getting a blister. Can we slow down, please?"

"Deal?"

"Pleeease . . ."

"What deal?"

"They took them."

"Took who?"

"Kidnapped."

"Kidnapped *who*?"

"Who do you think? Mom and Dad."

He slowed to a stop and stared at her. More like glared. Well, at least she'd gotten his attention. "They took them last night. It was pure luck that I snuck out to see Brad—don't tell Mom, she'd have a cow. Where's your car, anyway?"

His cold gray eyes burrowed into her skull. "Who kidnapped them?"

"The guys who wanted the Program."

"What guys? What Program?"

"Where's your car?"

"*What guys?*"

"You don't have to yell."

He repeated, more evenly, "What guys?"

"The guys those other guys are trying to save me from. Why'd we run away, anyway? They were only trying to help."

He turned and she couldn't see his answer.

"Excuse me." She reached over and grabbed his arm. "Excuse me!"

He turned back and she caught the last phrase. ". . . who they claim to be."

"*What who claim to be?*"

Again he turned and again she grabbed his arm. "I can't hear if you don't look at me."

He turned back to her. "What do you mean, you can't hear?"

"I'm deaf, remember?"

The look on his face said he didn't.

"Oh, brother. What *do* you remember?"

"Sorry, I—"

"Forget it. Where's your car?"

He glanced up the street and answered.

"Excuse me!"

He turned back and spoke slowly, with exaggeration. "I . . . said . . . I . . . walked."

"I . . . am . . . deaf . . . not . . . an . . . idiot. How far's your car?"

"The house is 1.3 miles away."

"*Miles?*"

"During that time you're going to brief me on everything that's going on."

"One point three miles? Did I mention I'm getting a blister?"

He looked down to her flips-flops, then the rest of her. She wasn't sure what he gawked at, but she sucked in her stomach just in case he was checking out her flab, which everyone said she didn't have, but which of course she knew better.

He reached for her backpack. "Here, let me—"

She turned it away from him. "I've got it."

"No, let me—"

"I said, I've got it."

He shrugged and started forward.

She readjusted the pack and scrambled to catch up. "Shouldn't we go to the police or something?"

He turned and answered. "Why didn't you?"

"Mom said not to." She tossed back her hair, hoping to gain some relief from the sun. "She's like, 'If something ever happens, go to Uncle Charlie.'"

He gave no answer.

"You'd know what to do."

Another no-answer.

"You do, right?"

More silence. What a surprise.

The blister between her big and middle toes grew hotter. But she vowed to keep quiet. And she did—two, maybe three minutes—until she couldn't take any more.

"How much farther, now?"

Nothing.

She blew the hair from her eyes. "You know, you can really be rude sometimes."

He turned right and picked up their pace, starting down a dusty road winding around the yellow-brown hill of dry grass.

"And mean."

If he was paying attention, he didn't let on.

He walked faster. She had to practically run to keep up. "Rude and mean. Did anybody ever tell you those are not your most attractive features?"

And *still* he gave no response—though she noticed he was starting to give the muscles in his jaw a workout.

🐜 🐜 🐜

return 2 coup, re-check eggs.

Omar Atmani reread the text message to make certain he understood. Then he stepped from the late-model Volvo, walked to the railing of the bridge, and discretely dropped his cell phone into the sprawling Santa Clara River. It slipped into the water and disappeared.

He had another dozen in his glove compartment.

He climbed back into the car and headed to Highway 126, toward the 101 and San Luis Obispo. The three-hour drive would put him there early evening and, though exhausted from thirty-six hours of no sleep, he'd drop by the Cal Poly lab and carefully search it one last time.

He wasn't crazy about the girl slipping away, but at least they had the parents. Not only had them, but if everything went according to plan—he glanced at his watch—they were already on board the yacht and heading for international waters.

The whole thing was easier than he'd anticipated—except for capturing the girl. Still, she wasn't entirely necessary; just a way of putting pressure on the parents should they refuse to cooperate.

But they would not refuse.

He reached for the bag of red pistachios on the leather seat beside him. Tearing the plastic open with his teeth, he poured only one into his mouth. Methodically, he rolled it from side to side, clicking it, enjoying the taste of the salt. He did not bite down, not yet. He would make the bag last until he arrived at the college and called the Cell.

The Cell . . . great men of God, every one of them.

He and Abdul al-Midhar met as engineering students at the University of Washington. Both grew up in the Philippines under the Salafi tradition with its strict moral codes. A quick kinship grew between them as they shared their dreams, their homesickness, and the bigotry they faced daily for their literal interpretation of the Qur'an. Within months three more entered their little circle—one from Pakistan and two from Malaysia. Four months later two brothers from Egypt joined. They met in Omar's cramped apartment, sharing meals and stories from home, while criticizing the Western immorality with its corrupting movies, decadent music, loose women, and of course, insatiable materialism.

Nearly twelve months passed before Abdul invited the venerable Yazid bin al-Shibh to one of their meals. As a member of the mysterious and legendary *Jemaah Islamiya*, he had been involved with the famous nightclub bombing in Bali, as well as more current acts he could not divulge. The stories he shared of other young men's bravery, their self-sacrifice, and their absolute commitment to Allah seemed to emphasize how empty the lives of Omar and his little group had become.

They invited him again, and yet again, his stories capturing their hearts. It was on the third visit that he presented the challenge:

"If one seriously believes the Qur'an, one simply cannot ignore the call to *jihad*."

The group exchanged glances. Omar spoke up, politely reminding him, "The Qur'an also calls for tolerance. *There is no compulsion in religion*," he quietly quoted.

Abdul agreed with his friend, reciting the Basmalah: "*In the Name of Allah, the Compassionate, the Merciful.*"

"Yes." Yazid nodded. "But you are taking the truths out of context, my brothers."

"I am taking them at face value," Omar said.

"Then how does one reconcile the verse: *Fight against such of those who have been given the Scripture as believe* not *in Allah nor the Last Day . . . ?*" Yazid took a sip of his thick, black coffee, all the time holding Omar's eyes.

Omar knew the verse well. Like the others in the group, he memorized the Qur'an as a boy. But to take such words, literally . . . And yet, was not Muhammad, himself, a great fighter and warrior?

Once again Yazid quoted: "*The only reward of those who make war upon Allah and his messenger and strive after corruption in the land will be that they will be killed or crucified . . .*"

Another point that could not be ignored.

The discussions continued off and on throughout the weeks—quotes, counterquotes, sometimes intense and passionate, but always with the understanding that it was the will of Allah and Allah alone they sought.

Yazid brought videos of the great *mujahideen* heroes, Abu Bakar Baasyir, Abdullah Sungkar. He quoted their speeches, showed photos and clips of their accomplishments. These were men who had the same desire to submit to Allah as Omar and his friends—but who had the courage and integrity to commit themselves entirely to the call.

Then came that rainy October evening in the midst of Ramadan, as they sat around the candlelit table breaking their fast. The air smelled of cooked meat, and scallions.

"Abdul? Omar?" Yazid asked. "You are engineering students, are you not?"

"Yes," Omar answered, passing him a plate of flat bread, "you know that we are."

The man took the bread and dipped it into the hummus. "Then please explain to me, if you don't mind, how men who use logic every day in their studies cannot see it in their own lives."

"What do you mean?" Abdul asked.

"There are laws and forces in the physical universe that cannot be altered—gravity, inertia, leverage, torque. You use mathematics and computers to calculate their impact every day."

Omar nodded. "That is correct."

"What would happen if you decided to ignore just one of those laws?"

"What do you mean?"

"What if you were to ignore, say, gravity? What if in building your structures, for the sake of convenience, you chose to ignore that one single law?"

"We would have a catastrophe on our hands," Omar said.

Abdul chuckled. "And more than a few lawsuits."

But there was no humor in Yazid's eyes. "Are not the spiritual laws of Allah just as real as his physical ones?"

"Of course," Omar agreed.

"And yet, forgive me, my friends, but you choose to ignore them. For the sake of 'convenience.'"

Omar glanced down to the table, feeling his ears grow warm.

Yazid said nothing more but waited until he looked up. More quietly he continued. "Let me ask you . . . if you were to go on ignoring those physical laws, could you continue to call yourself an engineer?"

Omar shook his head.

"And if you continue to ignore the laws of Allah and his prophet, can you continue to call yourself a follower of Islam?"

There was no sound except the repetitive *drip, drip, drip* from the outside rain spout.

Yazid looked about the table, his deep brown eyes flickering in the candlelight. "The world is falling into the hands of Satan, my brothers. And those who see this, yet sit back for convenience, are they any less guilty than those who openly oppose Allah?"

More silence, longer this time.

Finally Ahmed Sufaat, one of the Egyptians, cleared his throat. "But, instead of destroying the system, can we not work to change it from within?"

Yazid turned to him and asked only one question. "As you enjoy the comforts of its sins?"

Ahmed did not answer. No one did.

Yazid sighed wearily and looked beyond them to the watery lights outside the window. "No . . . I am afraid the shadow cannot be straightened when the rod is bent." Another moment passed before he turned to the group. "And you, my brothers . . . you have the skills and the knowledge. More importantly, you have the command from the prophet himself. *You* are the ones called to straighten the rod."

Omar stared through the Volvo's windshield, remembering the meeting. Even now he felt the draw of that night, the power of Yazid's challenge. The call of Allah.

The pistachio's salt was gone. With his tongue, he found the split in the shell and bit, cracking it open. Rolling down the window, he spit out the shell. He glanced at the odometer, quickly multiplying the number of nuts in the bag times the length to eat each one, then dividing that into the miles he had to travel.

He would make this one last twelve more miles before he finished chewing it and took the next. That was the discipline necessary to make them last. That was the discipline necessary to accomplish his mission.

* * *

"Your mom was into mathematics," Charlie argued. "Not acoustics."

The girl answered wearily, " 'Everything is mathematics.' "

They continued down the dirt road circling behind the hill.

"Aren't we there yet?"

Charlie saw no need to answer. They hadn't covered that much distance in the thirty seconds since she'd last asked.

"Excuse me?"

He turned and started up the hill, wading through tall, dry grass that smelled of the heat, roasted oats, and dust.

She struggled to catch up. "How far have we gone anyway?"

"Two miles."

"I can't see you."

He turned to her and repeated. "Two . . . miles."

"*Two miles?* I thought you said it was 1.3. Isn't that what you said, '1.3'?"

"I said my house was 1.3—"

"I can't see—"

"I said my house was 1.3 miles. We're coming to it from the rear." He brought them back on topic. "Why do they want it?"

"What?"

"The formula?"

"Do you have sunscreen at your place? Anything over thirty-five."

"Why?" he repeated.

" 'Cause I got real fair skin."

"Why do they want the formula?"

"You mean the Program?"

"The Program."

"So they can hear God."

"Hear *what*?"

"Not what. Who." She looked to the sky, shielding her eyes. "In twenty years everyone's going to have skin cancer, thank you very much deplenished ozone layer." She lowered her hand and gave another sigh. "When is industrialized America going to wise up?"

"About?"

"Global warming."

"What's that got to do with hearing God?"

"Nothing."

"Then what—"

"It's why I need sunscreen."

Charlie took a deep breath and continued climbing in silence. As they approached the top of the hill, he slowed to a stop.

"So are we close?" she asked.

He stooped down and pushed through the grass. The girl joined him. A warm breeze rolled up over the hill. They were only forty miles from the Pacific, but by the time the wind blew across the Santa Clarita Valley to the tiny community of Fillmore, it had plenty of time to heat up.

Below them sagging rooftops came into view, followed by broken fences, a chicken coop or two, and the remains of at least two gutted cars where front lawns had once grown. This was Fillmore's low-rent district, and Charlie liked it just fine.

"Which one's yours?"

He ignored her question and searched the dusty street until—there it was, the Jeep Cherokee, one block from his house, its gleaming blackness definitely out of place amidst mud-coated pickups, minivans, and sun-faded Hondas.

"You have AC?"

He peered west, against the sun, searching the yard of a small house to their right. His house. The one with more exposed wood than peeling paint. Everything looked normal. He continued his search, forcing his eyes to move slowly across the adjacent yards until, there, in the backyard of a neighbor, lay a man on his belly. He was hunkered down behind two rusting fifty-five-gallon burning barrels, his rifle aimed at Charlie's back porch.

"They say you're supposed to have eight glasses of water a day, but if I did that I'd be peeing the whole time. Mom's always going, like, 'You have to drink your water,' but I got a bladder the size of . . ."

He continued searching until he spotted a second man on the opposite side, hiding in the shadows of a neighbor's carport. That was enough. Charlie eased back. When he was clear he rose, turned, and started down the hill.

The girl ran to catch up. "Where are we going? I thought you lived down there."

He continued toward the dirt road.

"Excuse me. *Excuse me!*"

Three

Lisa's pickup slid around the corner. Through the glare of a dirty windshield, she spotted the man and his niece. He heard her and turned, placing a protective hand on the girl's shoulder. For a moment it looked like they were going to bolt. But checking Lisa's decked-out F-310 leaser, he must have figured she was no threat. Instead, he simply directed the girl to the side of the road.

Lisa pulled up and stopped, a cloud of dust following her and briefly enveloping them.

"You guys okay?" It was a stupid question, but she didn't have another.

The girl chirped a cheery, "Hi!"

The man peered through the dust beyond her.

"What's going on?" Lisa asked. "You need a lift?"

He turned to her with those same gray eyes that always left her a bit unsteady whenever she visited his store.

"Sweet," the girl said as she started for the truck . . . until his hand on her shoulder brought her to a stop.

"You shouldn't get involved in this." His voice had a quiet strength, nothing like she remembered at the store.

"In what?" She pushed back her hair. "What went on back there? And where's the FBI? I thought they were—"

"They're fakes," the girl interrupted. "They were trying to trick us." She looked up at the man and shaded her eyes from the sun. "Isn't that right?"

"Trick you?" Lisa asked. "Trick you how? What's going on?"

"You don't want to get involved."

"I'm a big girl. I can decide what I want and don't." She was able to hold his gaze until he turned and looked up the hill beside them.

"So do you need a lift?" she repeated.

The girl squinted up to him. "C'mon, Uncle Charlie, my foot's killing me."

He looked down at her foot, considering, then nodded her toward the truck.

"All right!" She raced around to the door, yanked it open, and climbed into the back of the extended cab. "Does this thing have AC?"

"I'm supposed to bring it in next week," Lisa replied.

The man checked the road one last time, then crossed around the truck and entered.

"I'm Jazmin," the girl said from the back, "with a *z*. But you can call me Jaz, like the music, well, sort of."

"I'm Lisa."

"How do you do?" she said, offering her hand. "I'm deaf."

Lisa shook it, not exactly sure how to respond.

"And this is my uncle Charlie. You don't mind me calling you that, do you? Uncle Charlie, I mean?"

"Fine," he answered quietly as he looked out the window.

"What? I can't hear you if you don't look at me."

He gave the slightest nod as he continued checking out the hill.

"I'll take that as a yes."

"Those guys at your store?" Lisa asked. "If they're not FBI, who are they?"

"It's a long, boring story," Jaz said, "but basically they want to kill me."

"Kill you?"

She nodded.

"Why?"

"'Cause of the Program."

The man turned and examined the road in front of them. "If they wanted to kill you, they had more than enough opportunity."

"You're not looking at me."

He turned to her. "They don't want to kill you."

Lisa frowned. "I don't understand."

He turned back to the hill. "Can we talk somewhere else . . . a little less public?"

"Sure." Lisa put the truck into gear. "Why don't I drop you off at your place? You can call the sheriff and—"

"It's the first place they'll look," Jaz said. "Right, Uncle Charlie?"

He nodded.

"Oh," Lisa said. "Well, then . . . I suppose I could take you directly to the sheriff's."

"Not yet," he answered.

"Not until we know who to trust," the girl explained.

" 'Who to trust'?"

"How 'bout your place?" Jaz asked.

Lisa turned to her. "I'm sorry, what?"

"Your place. They'd never think to look for us there."

"Actually"—Lisa cleared her throat—"I don't think that's such a—"

"*Go!*" Charlie shouted.

Lisa turned and saw two men charging down the hill. "Where—what should I—"

"Go!"

She hesitated.

Charlie reached his foot over to the accelerator and stomped on it.

"What are you—"

Tires spun and they shot forward.

Lisa grabbed the wheel, hitting the brakes. "Are you nuts? What are—"

"Let off the brake!"

"No! Take your foot off the—"

"Let off the—"

The passenger window exploded. Jaz ducked and screamed.

"Let off the brakes!"

Another round glanced off the hood directly in front of them. Lisa removed her foot and they fishtailed down the road.

"I got it!" she shouted, stepping on his foot, trying to get to the accelerator.

He wouldn't budge.

"Move!" She kicked at him with no result. Using one hand, she tried to physically remove his leg. Then she began punching it, once, twice, until they hit a rut and bounced into the air.

"Look out!" Jaz screamed.

They flew toward a giant boulder, barely hitting the ground in time for her to yank the wheel and miss it.

"Let me have it!" she shouted. "I know how to drive! I—"

"Trade places!"

"What?"

"Trade—"

Another shot punctured the back window.

"What's happening?" Jaz shrieked.

He moved across the seat, sliding under Lisa.

"What are you—"

"Trade places!"

She gripped the wheel tighter, but he slipped under and forced her up until she was on his lap.

"Will you— Stop it! Stop—"

"Watch out!" Jaz screamed.

Lisa looked up, saw the curve, and barely negotiated it in time.

The man heaved her up and over the console. That's when they both saw the Jeep Cherokee slide around the corner in front of them. He yanked the wheel from her hands and cranked it to the left. They flew into a 180—throwing Lisa the rest of the way over the console and crashing, butt-first, into the passenger seat. She swore, pulling in her legs as he accelerated.

"Where are we going?" she shouted.

"To drop you off."

"Drop me off? This is *my* car!"

"I apologize for that."

"*Apologize?*"

"I said you didn't want to get involved."

"This is my car!"

"I'll let you know where we leave it."

"This is my car. I'm not *leaving* it anywhere!"

They raced through a stop sign, continuing to pick up speed.

"Uncle Charlie?"

He gave no answer.

"Turn left up there!" Lisa yelled. "I live two miles down that road!"

He looked into the mirror.

She twisted around and saw the Cherokee behind them.

She turned back to see the intersection quickly approaching. "That's the road to my house! Turn here! Turn left HERE!"

They shot through the intersection and bounced onto pavement.

"What are you doing?"

Still watching the mirror, he answered. "You don't want them visiting you."

The Cherokee bounced onto the blacktop in pursuit. As the dust cleared, Sheldon Houser, a.k.a. Agent Boler, saw the pickup more clearly.

"Call our *sayan* at DMV!" he shouted from the front seat. "Find the address for license number"—he leaned forward and squinted, making sure he had it correct—"3WUC-528."

"Through my cell?" Harold Milkner yelled from the backseat.

"Just give the order. Have them call back on mine!"

"Got it."

The pickup took a sharp right.

The young driver beside Houser, Jerry Iserson, followed, tires squealing.

"Stay with him," Houser ordered.

"They've changed places!" Iserson shouted. "Madison is behind the wheel!"

Hearing the concern in the youngster's voice, Houser assured him, "He's good, but not that good." At least that's what he hoped. At least that's what Intel concluded: *"Too crippled to be a threat."*

And by "crippled," they were not referring to his body.

Houser had never met the man, though their paths nearly crossed in Beirut. Once a member of the U.S.'s elite Delta Force, Charles Madison's reputation for intelligence and bravery had been legendary . . . until he caught religion from his wife and was ruined. His resignation sent ripples throughout the community. Rumor even had it the Assistant Joint Chiefs of Staff paid him a visit, asking him to reconsider. But there was no reasoning with him. He was done with the violence and killing. He had "seen the light," become a "new man." Unfortunately, the Syrians, whose noses he'd bloodied eighteen months earlier, were not so quick to forgive and forget. Their point was made clear by the gruesome murder of both his wife and young daughter.

Now Charlie Madison was only a shell of the man he'd once been—no good to his country . . . and no good to his God.

Houser would have little joy in taking him out. Nevertheless, if he got in the way, he'd have to be removed. It was not their custom to shed blood unless blood was first shed, but Harold Kellerman, director of *Ha Mossad, le Modiyn ve le Tafkidim Mayuhadim,* better known as the Mossad, insisted that this was a matter of national security, involving the survival of Israel.

Those were his words . . . and the ones Houser questioned three months earlier in the director's private apartment just north of Tel Aviv . . .

"With all due respect, sir."

"Yes?"

Houser chose his words carefully. "I am not certain how a simple recording, *if* it even exists, can bring down a nation."

A male secretary entered the room with a tray of coffee, milk, and sugar.

"Ah, here we are," said Director Kellerman, a gaunt man in his sixties. He reached for a cup and saucer. "And if Intel is correct, you still take yours black?"

Houser smiled as he reached for the remaining coffee. "Yes, sir, Intel is correct. They always are."

The director took a sip. "Let us hope so, Sheldon Houser, let us hope so." He waited a moment as the secretary stepped from the room and shut the door. Then, leaning forward, all pleasantries faded. "You are certainly correct about the *if*. At this moment we are uncertain the recording even exists. But *if* it does, *if* the rumors are true, and *if* the couple has somehow captured the voice of God Almighty—then, according to the Bureau of Scientific Affairs, it will take little effort to develop a voiceprint."

"A voiceprint?"

"Like fingerprints, every voice is different. We, each of us, have specific patterns . . . frequency, wavelength, amplitude, syntax, multiple of harmonics."

"And you believe the same is true for . . . God?"

"If he is a specific entity with a specific personality, then he would have a specific voice."

Houser struggled to hide his skepticism. He didn't succeed.

Kellerman said, "The Scriptures are full of God speaking—Abraham, Moses, Samuel, Gideon, Elisha, Ezekiel . . ."

"So why would such a thing be a threat? If they did have this voiceprint, why would—"

"Suppose it is not accurate."

Houser looked at him.

"Science is not always an exact . . . science. What we take as fact today is often disproved tomorrow. Suppose the pattern of speech does not align with the pattern of speech written in Scripture?"

Houser frowned. "Audible voices and written words—they're two separate things."

"No. Words, rhythm, even syntax can be easily compared."

Houser studied the director's face. "You're not giving me the entire picture."

The older gentleman spoke evenly. "I am giving you all you need to know."

Houser took the cue and backed off. Returning to the director's reasoning he asked, "If the Scriptures were actually disproved, what is the harm?"

Director Kellerman looked down at his coffee.

Houser continued. "Other than freeing ourselves of superstition and the tales of old women."

More silence.

He'd said too much. Still, he'd never been shy about voicing his beliefs . . . or lack of them. For Sheldon Houser, God started dying in Dachau—in the photographs of suffering faces, smoking furnaces, the mass graves where his "chosen" were piled up like so much refuse. His death throes continued when Houser's father, his best friend in the world, was cut down by a sniper during the Six-Day War. And the Almighty's last breath was drawn two years ago, when Houser's wife, along with eight other civilians, was murdered by a suicide bomber at Harrods Department Store in Tel Aviv. He was shopping with her, only a dozen yards away, when the explosion ripped through the store, throwing twenty-two of its deadly nails into her chest, her neck, and her beautiful face. He raced to her side, not feeling the ruined flesh on his own face or the loss of his eye. He dropped to his knees before the bloody mass that had once been her head. He cried for mercy, trying in vain to stop the bleeding as her life slipped through his hands . . . as God finished dying.

No, a personal God did not exist. And, if he did, he did not deserve Houser's respect, let alone his worship.

Director Kellerman looked up from his coffee. "I am well aware of your beliefs, Sheldon Houser. Nevertheless, the existence of our nation is based upon the words of God in the Holy Scriptures. If such words were proven less than authentic . . . then I'm afraid any claim we have upon this land would be useless. We would lose our support from without, and our will to survive from within."

Houser understood perfectly. Belief was irrelevant. It was merely a tool used by the politician. All politicians. Arabs, Christians, Jews. They were all the same. And if Israel needed a God to justify her existence, then he would do what was necessary to protect that God.

The screeching tires drew his attention back to the truck before them. It was turning hard to the left, tires smoking, completing another 180.

Iserson hit the brakes. "What is he doing?"

The truck finished its turn. Gravel spit from its tires as it lurched toward them.

"Block the road!" Houser yelled. "Force him off!"

"He'll hit us!"

"Block the—"

"The pickup is twice as heavy. He'll destroy—"

"Now!"

Iserson cranked the wheel to the left, forcing the rear to slide forward as they skidded to a stop. Now the Cherokee filled the road.

The truck raced toward them, gaining speed.

"Sir?" Iserson questioned.

Houser didn't answer. He knew the man wouldn't hit them. He no longer had the heart.

The truck was fifteen yards away. He could see Madison's face. And Madison his.

Ten yards.

"Sir?"

"Stay."

Iserson obeyed. He was that loyal.

They braced for impact, but it was unnecessary. Madison suddenly threw the pickup to the right, bouncing off the road and into the dirt. But only for a moment. Having passed them, he hit the accelerator and continued. The tires caught and shot him back onto the pavement behind them.

Without waiting for orders, Iserson quickly turned and began pursuit.

Houser's BlackBerry chirped and he pulled it from his pocket. "Yes."

The voice was brisk and hushed: "Registered owner: Fox Ford Motors."

"It's a lease?" Houser asked. "You got a name, address?"

"Yes, it's leased to a Lisa McCoy . . ." The voice dropped out.

"Hello? I lost you. Hel—"

". . . 3457 Ramona Drive, Fillmore, California."

Houser reached for the vehicle's GPS and entered the data: "3457 Ramona Drive, Fillmore . . . Lisa McCoy?"

"Yes, and . . ." Again the voice dropped out.

"Hello?" Houser plugged his opposite ear. "Hello, are you there? Hello?"

No response.

Angrily, he shut off the BlackBerry.

Iserson continued to accelerate. "It's two miles away!" He motioned to the screen.

Houser stared at it, then turned to the youth. "Slow down!"

"Sir?"

"Slow down. Let them get away."

Iserson glanced at the screen. "But, the turn, it's just—"

"I know. Let them pull ahead. Make them think they've lost us."

"And then . . ."

Houser leaned back into his seat. "And then we shall pluck him as a ripe fig."

Lisa stuck her head out the passenger window, looking back. "Where are they?"

"We've lost 'em," Jaz yelled.

Charlie scowled into the mirror. It made no sense.

"Good!" Lisa drew inside. "Go on back to my place, then *please* tell me what's going on!"

Charlie watched the mirror. He didn't know who they were, at least by name. But their guns and actions proved they were professional.

"We're coming to my turn again," Lisa said.

There was something wrong. They'd called his bluff, proven their superiority. Now they should be pursuing, wearing him down until he quit.

But *they'd* quit. Why?

"Do you have any aloe vera at your place?" Jaz asked. "I think I got a sunburn."

They knew who he was by name, and the girl. They'd made the truck. They probably even knew—

And then he had it.

"My turn's here," the woman said, "to the right."

He slowed, but instead of turning right, he turned left.

"No, *right*. My house is to the—what are you doing?"

He finished the turn and picked up speed, again checking the mirror.

"What are you doing? I live back there!"

The girl joined in. "Uncle Charlie? *Uncle Charlie?*"

"We're not going to your place," he said.

"What? Why not?"

He didn't answer.

"We've lost them," she argued. "They don't know where I live, they don't—"

"They have the make and model of your truck. Most likely the license."

"What does that have to—" She came to a stop. "And if they're FBI, they'll be able to—"

The girl had leaned forward to read their lips. "They're not FBI."

"Right, but whoever they are, they could find my address."

Charlie nodded.

"Where are we going then?" Jaz asked. "We still heading to Cal Poly?"

"Cal Poly?" the woman exclaimed. "Isnt' that in San Luis Obispo?" She didn't sound pleased. "That's 150 miles from here!"

"I'm sorry."

"You're sorry? *You're sorry?*" She raked her hand through her hair. "You're not even heading the right direction. This takes you to L.A. You should be heading—"

"I know."

"You know?" She was sounding like a parrot. "Then what on earth are you—"

"We have to go to Burbank, first."

"Burbank!"

"To the airport."

"We're flying?"

"No."

"Then, what? That's an hour's drive in the wrong direction!"

"I know."

"*You know?*"

He nodded.

"*You know?*"

He drove in silence—figuring it best not to add any more fuel to the fire.

Four

"You just can't steal a car!"

"Actually, it's more like a loan," Uncle Charlie said as he stood scanning Parking Lot B directly beside Burbank Airport. "A short-term trade."

"But . . . but . . ."

"What about this one?" Jaz called from two cars over.

"A Civic?" Lisa cried in distress. "You'd trade my F-310 for a Honda Civic?"

"It's a pretty color."

"Look for something with more room," Charlie said. "It's a long drive."

"Gotcha." Jaz spotted a midnight blue SUV and half skipped, half galloped toward it . . . while doing her best to keep an eye on the conversation between Lisa and Charlie.

The woman was definitely on the cranky side. Not that Jaz blamed her. Having your truck hijacked and left in the big city while stealing another is bound to make you a little moody. Even though, earlier, Uncle Charlie did his best to explain.

"Her parents are in danger," he said.

"I under—"

"She's in danger."

"Yes, I understand."

"People will be looking for her. And *you*."

"What people?"

"I'm not . . . sure."

Lisa swore and looked out her window at the passing countryside.

He tried again. "Whoever they are, they'll be searching for your truck."

"You think?" she fired back.

"But not at the airport. It's the opposite direction from where they suspect we're heading."

"They suspect we're heading to San Luis Obispo?"

"I'm not sure. But the parking lot is huge. It'll be days before they realize your truck is abandoned. In the meantime, we grab another car, drop you off, you report your vehicle stole—"

"Whoa, whoa, whoa . . . 'Drop me off'? You don't think they're going to ask me questions? You don't think your friends with the guns will be waiting?"

"That's a possibility."

"A possibility? *A possibility?*"

The two continued fighting like that all the way to the airport, with only one time-out, when Charlie found a pay phone and made a quick call. Of course, the bickering didn't matter to Jaz. She just stuck in her earbuds (her version of "Do Not Disturb"), closed her eyes, and enjoyed the vibrating hum of the tires against asphalt.

Now, thirty minutes later, she was cupping her hands against the tinted window of the luxury SUV. "Check it out," she called. "Monster stereo, leather seats, and look, a TV!"

Uncle Charlie joined her.

She looked up to him. "What do you think?"

He gave a slight nod.

"You gonna hot-wire it?"

"You've been watching too many movies."

"What's that supposed to mean?"

As usual, he didn't answer. He glanced around to make sure no one was near. When he was satisfied, he stepped back to the car beside them, an old Taurus. He wrapped his left hand around his right fist and slammed his elbow back into the Taurus's passenger mirror.

Lisa looked up startled.

He hit it again. This time the entire unit broke off and fell to the ground.

Lisa raced to him. "What are you doing?"

He scooped up the mirror, checked the screws sticking out of its base, and raised it to the SUV's driver window. Gripping the base tightly and pressing his weight against the window, he forced the point of one of the screws against the glass and slowly pulled it down.

Lisa winced at what must have been an awful screech.

He repeated the process, making the scratch deeper. And then again.

Jaz watched with interest.

Lisa with alarm.

He started another line, perpendicular to the first, scratching it three times, until he'd formed a small cross. Then he set the mirror on the ground, untied his boot, and pulled it off.

"Now what are you doing?" Lisa demanded.

Without a word, he slipped the boot over his right hand, glanced around the parking lot one last time, then quickly smashed his fist through the center of the cross.

Lisa's startled look said he must have set off an alarm. Jaz put her hand on the fender and felt its vibration. Meanwhile, Charlie, whose arm was still inside the car, dropped his boot and unlocked the door. He opened it, checked under the dash, and popped the hood.

Jaz stayed at his heels as he strode to the front of the vehicle and lifted the hood. Within seconds, he'd traced some wires and gave a tug. The vibration stopped. Lisa's face relaxed, but only a moment.

"A car," she cried. She dropped down, grabbing Jazmin's arm and pulling her until they were both out of sight.

Charlie turned and watched as the car continued along the rows toward them.

"Get down!" Lisa frantically motioned. "Get down!"

But he didn't. Instead, he waited until the vehicle pulled to a stop directly beside them.

Lisa groaned in dismay. "Oh, brother . . ."

Jaz peeked around her to see a hot-looking muscle car. She watched as Charlie strolled up to the driver. She couldn't tell what they were saying, but it looked like they knew each other, because the driver, some sketchy greaseball about Charlie's age, handed him a weird mechanical thing. Charlie took it and walked back to the SUV.

"If you want, you can get up," he said as he entered the driver's side. A good point since they were now in plain sight of the man.

As nonchalantly as possible, Lisa rose. She gave a casual nod to the guy then turned to Charlie and hissed, "*What are you doing?*"

Instead of answering, Charlie attached the mechanical thing to the steering wheel, gave a couple jerks, and the whole ignition popped out and hung from the steering column.

Turning to Jaz he explained, "*Now*, we hot-wire."

Lisa could only stare. "One of your friends?" she asked.

Without a word, Charlie headed back to the driver and returned the tool.

"Well," Jaz sighed, "at least he has one."

★ ★ ★

"I don't like this," Bernice Wolff muttered. She pressed the number on her cell phone designated only for Lisa Harmon/McCoy calls. "Hm-mm, no sir, don't like this at all." Glancing at the computer, she drummed her purple porcelains on the old, metal desk. For the umpteenth time, Lisa's phone rang and for the umpteenth time her voice mail kicked in. Bernie slapped the phone shut and returned to her computer, its screen framed by a dozen yellow Post-it Notes.

It had been a lousy idea from the start. Except in extreme situations, the Bureau frowned on putting agents into deep-cover situations with members of the opposite sex. But Lisa, who had been her protégé and best friend for the past five, almost six years, assured her this was one of those exceptions.

"The man's a wall," she'd said as they pored over his files in the cramped conference room. "Impossible for anyone to get to."

"But you can?" Bernice said.

"I have more of a chance than the rest of the team—particularly the guys." Lisa pulled a black-and-white photo from his folder. "And look at my resemblance to the wife." She slid it across the worn table. "That was taken six weeks before the murders. We could be sisters."

Bernice studied it. She was right about the similarities. Same eyes, button nose, determined chin. "And you think the similarities will help?"

"They sure won't hurt," Lisa said. "Remember Ted Kaczynski? His biggest protection was his isolation." She took a swig of Diet Coke. "I'm telling you, if someone can get inside this puke's head and gain his trust, our job is done."

Bernice had to agree. If Charles Madison was the Postal Bomber they'd been pursuing the past eighteen months (and evidence certainly seemed to be piling up), then finding a crack in his psyche and getting inside it would be the best line of attack. Still, it took another meeting before she finally caved to Lisa's persistence. That's when the two of them paraded together into Special Agent in Charge Harold Petersen's office and convinced him that Lisa Harmon was the one for the job.

But now . . .

As her contact agent, Bernice noticed a problem as early as Lisa's second phone report—a softening toward the man.

"I don't know, Bernie," she said. "We may have the wrong guy."

"Not according to the evidence, girlfriend."

"I know, but there's a kindness here, underneath the shell, I mean. One of those 'still waters run deep' kinda guys."

Of course, Bernice called her on it. And, of course, Lisa laughed it off. But as the reports continued to come in, no amount of laughing or denying removed Bernie's suspicions. She was too good a friend not to see it.

Then, last Tuesday, three weeks into surveillance, Bernice broached the possibility of pulling the plug on the operation and bringing her in.

"What are you talking about?" Lisa argued.

"Do you or do you not find him attractive?" Bernice demanded. "It's a simple question—yes or no?"

"Bernie . . ."

"Yes or no?"

"I'm a professional. Even if I did have feelings, which I'm not saying I do, I can put them aside. You know that."

Bernice let out a heavy sigh.

"Trust me on this. He's damaged goods. And yes, maybe I feel a little sorry for him, but—"

"Just like you felt sorry for that bad boy rock-and-roller?" Bernice asked.

"That's completely—"

"Or the biker, what was his name?"

"This is a job; you know I know the difference."

"Right. I also know you got a thing for bringing home stray puppies."

"Come on, Bernie, it's not like I'm sleeping with him or anything."

"I should hope not!"

Lisa chuckled. "Is that FBI policy or your Pentecostalism showing?"

"You're changing the subject."

"I'm telling you, Charles Madison is not our guy. Yeah, he's got a few scars, and yeah, he's not the biggest fan of the government, but there's a decency about him that—"

"Lisa . . ."

"And we're connecting. To pull me now, that's a month's work down the drain. A month closer to another bomb going off and more killings. Trust me on this. I can handle it. I *can* handle it."

And somehow, against her better judgment, Bernice believed her.

She was too good a friend not to.

But now . . .

According to the information on her screen, NSA had intercepted a phone transmission by a Mossad *sayan* working DMV. It was incomplete and lasted only seconds, but it relayed the Fillmore address the Bureau had rented for Lisa's assignment.

And now, for whatever reason, Lisa Harmon (a.k.a. Lisa McCoy) was not answering her phone.

Charlie raised his head so Jaz could see his mouth in the rearview mirror. "Say this voiceprint of God thing is for real."

"Oh, it's for real," she said. "Are we going to hit a pit stop soon? I gotta pee."

"We just stopped in Santa Barbara."

"Yeah, like twenty minutes ago."

Charlie said nothing. But not the girl.

"It's a scientific fact that women's bladders are 30 percent smaller than men's—mostly 'cause of all that reproductive stuff down there." Turning to Lisa, she asked, "You haven't, like, had kids yet, have you?"

"Uh, no."

"I think I'll probably adopt. You know, stretch marks and everything. Do you have a bikini? That's a stupid question, with a body like that. How many?"

Charlie stole a glance into the mirror. In many ways the girl looked like her mother at that age. Chattered like her too. And when she wasn't irritating him with her incessant talking, she was confusing him with her logic. It seemed every time he was about to catch up to her loopy thinking, she changed subjects and left him standing in the dust.

Not that his other passenger, Lisa (she'd never given her last name), was much better. But at least there was a genuineness to her. She was obviously hiding some things—who wasn't—but beyond that he sensed a trueness. He still wasn't sure why she insisted on coming along, and he'd done his best to discourage her. But she'd dug in and he knew nothing would make her change her mind. The woman had substance and strength, even when she was hopping mad. That and her trueness reminded him in so many ways of—

He tried pushing the thought out of his mind. He had not gone there in months. But now . . .

Brenda had been strong like that. When she set her mind on doing something, she did it. Whether it was enduring the weeks, sometimes months, of silence when he was out of the country, or whether it was the pursuit of her newfound faith in God—if it called for her stepping up, she stepped up. And don't even try to pull the wool over her eyes. The daughter of a North Dakota farmer, her motto was: "You can't fool the weather and you can't fool the land, so don't try to fool me."

And he never had.

It was this same, no-nonsense approach that eventually brought him back to his own childhood faith. Not the modern God-is-my-errand-boy stuff, but a deeper faith, one that called for radical changes in him, in them.

Ever since he was a kid he wanted to make the world a better place, to beat the bad guys. But as he began taking his faith more seriously, he began seeing that the bad guys really weren't the bad guys. They weren't the enemy—just prisoners of the enemy. Prisoners of a different war. And if he could help win that war, if he could set those captives free . . . well, maybe he wouldn't have to go around amputating the diseased parts of the human race. Maybe he could find ways of healing them.

At least that's what he told himself when he retired from Special Ops and decided to prepare for the ministry. Talk about a change in worldviews. And lifestyle. Still, if the two of them took everything they read seriously, they had little choice in the matter.

But the truth was . . . only Brenda had changed. For Charlie, it was a sham. Oh, he thought it was real enough, but eventually his hypocrisy won out. A hypocrisy that not only brought shame and disgrace to God, but destroyed his family.

He swallowed back the rising emotion, cursing himself for the self-indulgence, and refocused on the conversation.

"So tell me, Jaz," Lisa was asking, "why did Mr. Almighty wait so long to finally get around to talking to us?"

Jaz snickered. "More like, why'd we wait so long to get around to listening to him?"

Lisa laughed good-naturedly. "I did my part. Guess he wasn't in a chatty mood back then."

"Turn on the radio," Jaz said.

"Pardon me?"

"The radio." Jaz motioned. "Turn it on."

Lisa reached for the radio and turned on some head-throbbing rap music. "What do you like?"

"I'm deaf, remember?"

"Oh, right."

"I mean, I can feel vibrations and stuff, but my auditory receptor cells went MIA. Back when I was like six years old and ran the world's highest fever."

"Then why do you wear those?" Lisa asked, referring to the earbuds tangling from the top of her sweatshirt.

"They came with the iPod," Jaz explained. "I wasn't sure if I wanted black ones or white, but I think white's best, don't you? I like their 'elegant simplicity'—I mean since they didn't have purple or candy apple red."

Charlie stole a glance to Lisa who searched for a response. Jaz saved her the trouble:

"Now find a place that's *not* a station."

"A place that's not—"

"You know, some in-between spot that's all staticky."

Lisa nodded and tuned to a location with nothing but white noise. "Okay, now what?"

"That's it."

"That's what?"

"God's voice. Well at least 1 percent of it."

"One percent?"

"That's how much Cosmic Background Radiation most TVs and radios pick up."

Lisa exchanged another glance with Charlie. "Cosmic Background . . ."

"Yeah, CBR. The noise from the Big Bang—though we hate that name 'cause it wasn't big and it certainly wasn't a bang, since the entire universe was a singularity tinier than any atom and, as we all know, sound doesn't travel in a vacuum."

"Right." Lisa nodded.

Charlie cleared his throat. "What's this got to do with the Program your mom and dad created?"

"And me," Jaz corrected. "I helped too. It was like a family project."

"Okay. So . . ."

"So these two guys with crap for brains, pointed their radio telescope—"

"There's no need to talk that way," he interrupted.

"What way?"

"You know . . ." He searched for the word. "Potty mouth."

Jaz's eyes registered disbelief. "Potty mouth?" She turned to Lisa, mouthing the words, "*Potty mouth?*"

Lisa shrugged, suppressing a smile.

Not Jaz. "You're kidding me, right?"

Charlie said nothing.

" '*Crap*,' that's like a G-rated word."

"You heard what I said."

"Did anyone happen to point out that this is the twenty-first century?"

Charlie held his ground. "There is no need for little girls to talk like—"

"*Little girls?* I'm thirteen—well, next month."

"That's no excuse."

"I've got breasts and everything. I had my period almost a year—"

"All right, all right." He held up his hand. It was supposed to be in authority but it felt more like defeat. He turned to Lisa for support and once again caught her hiding her amusement.

Quickly sobering up, she turned back to the girl. "Go ahead, what about these guys?"

"Anyway, these poo-poo brains . . ." Jaz turned to Charlie and asked, "That's okay, isn't it?"

He ignored her.

"Anyway, they accidentally recorded the CBR back in 1965. Didn't even know what they had till some other guys pointed it out."

Charlie glanced into the mirror, waiting for more.

"So, there's like these tiny fluctuations, you really can't hear them or anything. People thought they were from gravity or something, but they're not. And if you run them through a computer, you start to see, like, a pattern."

"A pattern?" Charlie asked.

"Which actually corresponds nicely with the superstring theory."

Again Charlie exchanged glances with Lisa. This time Jaz saw it.

"Oh come on now, you do know about string theory?"

Neither answered.

With a heavy sigh of frustration, she explained. "Instead of the standard fifty-seven (and counting) subatomic particles that are the building blocks to our universe, lots of physicist types, including myself, believe that they're all vibrations of just one thing—these tiny, tiny, tiny little strings."

"Vibrations?" Charlie asked.

She nodded. "And the frequency of their vibration determines what type of matter you get."

"Frequency of vibration," Lisa repeated. "You mean like notes? You're saying the universe is made up of notes?"

"Bingo."

Charlie tried not to scoff. "Everything's a note?"

"Exactly. Now that also means we gotta have nine dimensions—the three we see and about six others surrounding us that we don't see. But, of course, that's small potatoes."

"Of course," Lisa agreed.

"How does this fit in with God's voice?" Charlie asked. "With your parents' Program?"

"I'm getting there."

Charlie took a breath and waited.

"After about a gazillion tries we found this pattern starting to make sense—mathematically, I mean. 'Cause like I said, everything comes down to mathematics, even our voices."

"So what happened?" Lisa asked.

"We discovered that the pattern could actually be translated into a voice—with exact frequencies, harmonics, and modulations and stuff."

"What's it say?" Lisa asked. "I mean, are there actual words?"

"It can be turned to words, yeah. That's what the Program does."

"So what does it say?" Charlie repeated.

"When we play it back, we hear only one phrase."

"Which is?" Lisa asked.

Jaz sat back in the seat and dramatically folded her arms.

"Well?" Lisa said. "What's the phrase? What does it say?"

"It says . . . 'Let there be light.'"

Five

"He's kinda cool, isn't he?" Jaz asked. "For an old fart."

Lisa stared at the water as it ran over her hands in the wash basin. It had been a risky decision to travel with the girl and her uncle, but the opportunity was too good to pass up. Not only was she working her way deeper into his head, but she'd personally witnessed him stealing a car, which would be enough to put him away, or at least get a search warrant. Then there was the matter of the men in the Cherokee impersonating FBI agents, the shoot-out in the store, the kidnapping of the girl's parents, and, of newest interest, this voiceprint of God business. Apparently she'd stepped into something far more complicated than the Bureau even imagined. That plus all the law violations made it a dereliction of duty for her *not* to stay with them.

At least that's what she told herself.

"Hel-lo?"

She glanced to the girl, one sink over. "I'm sorry, what are we talking about?"

"Uncle Charlie."

"He seems like a nice man."

Jaz snorted.

"What does that mean?"

"You like him. I can tell."

"I what?"

"Come on, you can talk to me. It's just us girls."

Lisa turned off the faucet and crossed to the dispenser where she pulled out a paper towel. "Please . . ."

"He's really not that old, you know."

Lisa shook her head and began drying her hands, a bit too vigorously. "Like I said, he seems a nice man, but definitely not my type."

"So why are you coming with us?"

"Why am I coming with you?"

"If you don't like him."

"I told you. I'm not particularly fond of going home and finding bad boys with guns sitting on my sofa."

Jaz snorted again.

"So until we get this all sorted out, I think it's best—"

"Bovine feces."

"I'm sorry?"

"He may buy that crap, but not me."

Lisa looked at her. There was a lot that amused her about this kid, particularly her honesty and attempts at being mature—she'd recently given Lisa a business card with her e-mail address "to stay in touch." But she was not crazy about her attitude . . . or her "insights."

Jaz grinned. "I see the way he looks at you."

Lisa wadded the towel into a tight ball and tossed it toward the garbage.

"And the way you look at him."

She missed the bin by a good foot.

Jaz giggled. "Don't worry, I won't tell."

"Listen, I'm not sure where you get your—"

"And if you want to get a hotel room, I won't say a word." Jaz broke into a side gallop toward the exit.

Lisa started after her. "Jaz . . ." She stepped into the blinding sun. "Jaz, that's not—" and collided into Charlie.

"You guys all right?" he asked.

"Yeah, we're fine." Jaz grinned. "Aren't we, Lisa?"

Lisa shot her a look then glanced up to see the man carefully studying her.

"Yeah." She brushed past him. "Fine." They headed toward the car. "We were just discussing this voice of God business."

He said nothing and followed.

"If it's true, if her parents really have developed a Program, then why on earth is it such a concern to everyone?"

They arrived at the SUV and he opened the doors for them. Jaz climbed in first, but not before giving Lisa a knowing look regarding his chivalry. He shut their doors and rounded the SUV to his side as Lisa turned to Jaz, making sure she understood the subject had been changed. "Why do *you* think that is?"

"Why do I think what is?" Jaz asked.

Charlie entered the vehicle.

"Why are the bad guys after your parents? I'd think everyone would be tickled pink that there's finally some sort of proof of God's existence."

He started up the vehicle.

"Oh, that's an easy one," Jaz said.

"Enlighten me."

Charlie pulled out and a moment later they were on the freeway as she explained. "We've got a partner, over in Switzerland, Uncle Fredrick. No offense, Uncle Charlie, he's not really my uncle or anything, actually he's a Father, isn't that what you call priests?"

Charlie nodded.

"Anyway, he's, like, been working with them on analyzing these rock formations and stuff."

"Rock formations?" Lisa asked.

"Right, from places on earth where God spoke. You know, according to the Torah and the Bible and stuff."

"And—"

"The molecular structure of those rocks is just a little different. They've been pushed around and rearranged."

"You're kidding."

"Nope. And what's even weirder is that these molecular ripples, that's what we call them, they all have the same pattern. A pattern that lines up exactly with the pattern of the voiceprint."

"The '*Let there be light*' thing," Lisa said.

"Right, only they're different words. Same voiceprint, different words."

There was a moment of silence. Finally, Charlie asked the obvious. "So you're saying . . . God's voice is recorded in some of those rocks?"

Jaz nodded. "But it wasn't until Thursday that Mom and Dad finally worked out the Program to play them back."

"A Program to play back the voice of God?"

"Pretty cool, huh? You know in the Bible where Jesus gets baptized and everything? Where God's, like—" She lowered her voice and quoted, "*This is my beloved Son*?"

Lisa nodded. "Go on."

"Well, Uncle Fredrick sent us different rocks from different places around there and with my folks' Program, we could actually see the phrase . . . and hear it."

"Hear the voice of God?" Charlie repeated.

"That's incredible. And that's what the bad guys are after?" Lisa asked. "This Program?"

"Yeah . . . I guess."

"Why?"

"I think . . ." Jaz hesitated.

"Go ahead," Lisa said.

"Uncle Fredrick sent us some other rocks. Some place where a New Testament guy got *knocked off his horse* . . . and a voice from heaven wants to know why he's persecuting him."

"That would be Paul," Charlie said. "The book of Acts."

Lisa looked at him in surprise.

"That's right," Jaz said, "you were going to be like a preacher or something?"

He shifted. "Or something."

Lisa continued to stare. In all the background checks, she'd never read anything like that.

"Anyway," Jaz continued, "there's this one major little problem."

"What's that?" Lisa asked.

"The voice that speaks to him from heaven says he's, like, Jesus."

"Why's that a problem?"

"Hel-lo? Are we paying attention here? The same voice that says, 'Let there be light,' is the same voice that talks to Saul—"

Charlie finished, ". . . and claims to be Jesus Christ."

Jaz folded her arms and sat back with satisfaction.

Lisa nodded, thinking. "I guess that could upset some folks."

"Oh yeah." Jaz sat back up. "Big-time. And there's like one other problem. Even bigger. Remember Mount Sinai?"

"Where Moses got the Ten Commandments," Lisa said.

"Right. We got some of those rocks from Uncle Fredrick too."

"And?"

"I mean from *every* place on that mountain and then some."

"What did you find?" Charlie asked.

"Nothing."

"Nothing?" Lisa asked.

"Nada."

"I don't understand," Lisa said. "If this voiceprint thing is accurate, but none of the rocks on the mountain have that pattern, then that means . . ."

Jaz finished her thought. ". . . God never spoke to Moses."

Six

It was early evening when the elevator doors rattled open to reveal the basement floor of the Clyde Fisher Science Building at Cal Poly. Charlie stepped out first to make sure everything was clear. When he was satisfied, he gave a nod and they followed.

"We work down here 'cause it dampens some of the sound," Jaz explained.

Lisa nodded. "I see."

" 'Course it's nothing compared to Uncle Fredrick's place in Switzerland. His is *really* underground. Ever been to Switzerland?"

"No, I—"

"I have. Twice."

"It must be nice."

"Did you know women can go topless on their beaches? I'm not really sure I'd want to. What about you?"

"Well, I really—"

"Not that I'm ashamed of my body or anything. Brad, he's like my boyfriend, he's always going on like I have a great one."

Charlie gave her a look.

"What?"

He knew he should say something, he just wasn't sure what—which had pretty much been his contribution to the last several hours of their conversation.

"You said your uncle has a lab?" Lisa asked.

"He's not really my uncle."

"Right, but—"

"It's in a tunnel. Their government's got 'em all over the place, 'case they go to war or something. They even got an underground hospital."

"Yes, I think I've read something about—"

"Not that it's any better than ours."

"What?"

"The lab. There's no such thing as a sound-free environment. Even the earth makes noise. Did you know the ocean waves have a frequency of once per every six seconds?"

"No, I—"

"They're so low and powerful that they vibrate through the whole planet. Sometimes when I lay asleep at night, I swear, I can actually feel them."

They continued down the hallway, Charlie hoping for a moment's silence, though suspecting the odds weren't in his favor.

"Here we go." She brought them to a stop before a windowless door that could just as well have passed as a storage room . . . except for the push-button combination lock.

She reached for it but Charlie grabbed her hand.

"What?"

"Let me do that."

"But it's a secret."

"It's safer if I do it."

"No one's supposed to know."

"I promise I won't remember."

"How can you promise that?"

"At my age, it's not that hard." Charlie smiled at his little joke.

She tilted her head, not getting it. So much for humor.

"I'll turn my back," Lisa offered.

Jaz hesitated, then agreed. "Okay."

Lisa turned as Jaz rose up on her toes and whispered into Charlie's ear, "0909."

He nodded and reached for the lock.

"That's my birthday," she explained.

Again he nodded and entered the code.

"We would have added the year, but there was, like, no room—unless we added the last digit, but that would be confusing 'cause—"

There was a faint *click*. He turned the knob and pushed open the door. Jaz tried to step ahead of him, but he blocked her. Before she could protest, he raised his finger to his lips for silence.

She frowned, but agreed.

He stepped over the large doorsill and onto a hard, rubber floor. Immediately overhead lights blazed on. He reached for his gun then cursed himself for leaving it back at the store.

"Motion sensors," Jaz explained.

He relaxed slightly. If she was right, there was a good possibility no one was inside. A possibility, not a certainty. Either way, they'd definitely announced their presence.

He scanned the room. It was twenty by thirty feet with two padded doors at the back—one open, the other closed. To his right was a mixing console with computers, a handful of monitors, and two large speaker columns in front of it. Before him set a black lab counter with steel brackets, holders, and more monitors. Five to six portable baffles on wheels were strategically placed throughout the room. Like the walls and the ceiling, they were covered in black, foam-like fins that stood out at least six inches from the surface. Then there was the sound. It was like wearing earplugs on the firing range. Not that it was muffled, there was just no reverberation. Any noise was immediately swallowed up and absorbed.

For the most part, everything looked in order . . . except for the desk in the far corner. Its drawers had been opened and dumped on the floor. Stacks of papers were pitched and tossed, and the door to a nearby filing cabinet had been left open.

"Is it safe?" Lisa asked from the doorway.

He gave a slight nod.

Jaz entered the room and did a pirouette. "Welcome to my world."

Lisa followed. "Pretty impressive. Who exactly funds all this? The University?"

Jaz turned back to her. "Sorry, what?"

"Does the college fund this?"

"Yeah, right," Jaz scoffed. "Like they could afford half this stuff."

"Then—"

"The DOD."

Charlie turned to her. "The Department of Defense?"

"Some of it, till Dr. Reynolds left. But Uncle Fredrick knows some—" She spotted the desk. "Oh, great," she said and started for it.

Charlie watched as she walked to the papers. She stooped down to take a look. He waited until she glanced up. "Is anything missing?"

"With this mess?" She shrugged. "Who knows."

Lisa approached, still on topic. "Why would the Department of Defense be interested in this sort of work?"

Jaz smirked. "You're kidding, right?"

Lisa shook her head.

Rising from one pile of papers and moving to another, she said, "Ever hear of acoustical warfare?"

"A little, sure."

"Like the stuff they have that'll fry your brains?"

"The stuff that *who* has?" Lisa asked.

"Our government." Jaz kicked at the stack of papers and looked around. "The good ol' U.S. of A."

Lisa chuckled. "Sounds like someone's reading too many blog sites."

"It's true," Jaz insisted. "They're also working on junk that controls your body and the way you think." She headed across the room to the mixing console.

Charlie's attention was drawn to the two doors across the lab. Particularly the closed one. He started toward it.

"You mean like Vietnam," Lisa said, "where they played loud music to disorient the enemy."

Jaz snickered. "No, I mean like sound lasers, sonic weapons, seizure-inducing frequencies, *and* mind control. Not to mention stuff that can wipe out half the world."

"I see," Lisa said, obviously trying to avoid sounding condescending.

Charlie arrived at the closed door, staying as close to the wall as possible.

"You think I'm making this stuff up?" Jaz said. She fiddled with the switches on the mixing console.

Charlie reached for the door's knob and slowly turned it.

Lisa answered, "I'm just saying not everything you read on the Internet is true."

When he could move the knob no farther, he threw open the door and quickly pulled back. There was no response except for two overhead pin spots that came on, lighting a small recording booth.

Startled by his action, the girls stopped talking.

He entered the booth. It contained only a music stand, a

mic stand, and a stool. Like the walls in the lab, it was also covered with black foam fins.

He glanced to the ladies, indicating all was clear.

Lisa resumed. "Even if such a thing was possible, our government wouldn't fool around with mind control."

"Hel-*lo*? And what reality are we living in?"

In his typical thoroughness, Charlie checked behind the door.

"We're the good guys," Lisa reminded her.

Satisfied with the booth's safety, Charlie stepped back into the lab . . . where a body suddenly leaped at him from the other booth. It hit him and they staggered into the door. He gasped at the rapid kidney punches, felt a sharp, boney fist drill his temple. They fell inside the first booth, dragging down the music and mic stands—Charlie seeing stars before he hit the floor.

♪ ♪ ♪

Sheldon Houser was not pleased to have lost the girl. Or Charles Madison. He had misjudged the man and had wasted valuable time waiting outside the woman's house. Now they had to make up that time. Night was falling as they raced north on the 101 Freeway. Iserson, the driver, rolled down the window to enjoy the smell of the ocean and fog, memories of home on the Mediterranean.

They were good men. Houser liked them all. Cohen, the well-oiled machine who let nothing stop him, Meier, the perpetual prankster. But it was Jerry Iserson he found the most interesting . . . and infuriating.

The kid wasn't Orthodox, but Conservative—the next worse thing. And it made for some lively banter.

"How can a university graduate of the twenty-first century still believe there is a God?" Houser had recently challenged him at a Holiday Inn bar.

Iserson's response was equally blunt. "How can a man who claims to be so wise, *not* believe?"

Houser leaned toward him. He wasn't drunk, but definitely had a buzz. "Because I've seen this God lie, I've seen him break covenant. I've seen him torture the very people he's supposedly chosen."

Iserson didn't bat an eye. "And for that you would deny him?"

"You wouldn't?"

"Since when is it God's job to make me happy? Show me one verse in all of Scripture where he is commanded to do so."

"He has a responsibility!" Houser was on his feet before he knew it. He felt Cohen's hands easing him back onto the stool.

Iserson waited until they were no longer the room's center of attention. Waited, but did not back down. "Now you sound like the Christians." He smiled, though there was no amusement in his voice. "Those who demand nonstop mercy so they can enjoy nonstop sinning."

"I don't need God to help me enjoy sinning," Houser replied.

"Amen to that," Cohen said, clinking his beer bottle with Meier's.

But Iserson didn't let up. "He has never been called to serve us. We have always been called to serve him."

Houser stared at the kid in wonder and disgust.

"We were created for *his* pleasure."

"And when he abuses that pleasure?"

Iserson focused on Houser's good eye and quietly quoted, "*Though he slay me, yet I will hope in Him.*"

"Well, I'm not going down without a fight."

"Some wrestle him their entire life."

"Though you might want to lose a few pounds first." Meier chuckled. "I hear he's in pretty good shape."

"We are his servants," Iserson repeated. "He is not ours."

Houser swore and turned away. He had no patience for such mindless devotion. Still, it was that devotion that made Iserson the most dedicated member of the team. If there was one person Houser could trust when the chips were down, it was the kid.

Inside the car, Houser's BlackBerry went off—faint cascading chimes indicating a text message. Only a handful of people had this number and, thanks to NSA's "*1984*" policies, no one was to use it unless there was an extreme emergency. He pulled the unit from his pocket and checked the screen. The message was a simple e-mail address. But the orders could not be clearer.

"Pull off," he shouted to Iserson. "Pull off now and find a pay phone!"

Iserson nodded and they took the first exit, Ysidro Road, just south of Santa Barbara.

Since obtaining phone numbers and addresses through 411 also carried certain Orwellian risks, they had to resort to a phone book. Three booths later they found one whose Yellow Pages had not been stolen.

Under a flickering fluorescent, Houser quickly flipped through the pages and discovered three Internet cafés. Ripping the page from the book, he strode back to the Cherokee, climbed inside, and entered the first address into the GPS. It was three miles away. Iserson dropped the vehicle into gear and they headed off as Houser entered the second address, then the third. The last was closest by nearly a mile. Iserson changed course and they drove toward it.

They dropped Houser off a half block away. It was a run-down section of town—surfer shops, thrift stores, and broken sidewalks. Just ahead was a twenty-four-hour tattoo place; its neon sign casting a red glow onto the foggy street.

Beside that, the Internet café.

He entered and was met with the smell of coffee and sandalwood incense. He approached a heavily tattooed kid who sat behind the counter reading a Japanese comic book. Over the drone of what could only be Bob Dylan, Houser explained why he didn't believe in credit cards.

The kid gave a noncommittal nod, took the twenty-dollar deposit (and an extra five for his troubles), and sauntered over to one of the keyboards where he entered his own code. When he was done, Houser thanked him. The kid mumbled, "No problem," and slouched back to the counter.

Houser rechecked the café. There was only one other patron and she was at the opposite end, near the door. He eased himself down in front of the screen. Pulling out his Black-Berry, he double-checked the saved message and opened a new account using that e-mail.

Once it was open and set, he typed a message to a completely different address:

Hannah:

i miss you more than you can imagine. what is the latest news?

love,
poppa.

He waited two, almost three minutes. He knew every second spent online was a second closer to being harvested, but he could not disconnect. Whatever information he was about to receive was too important.

Finally, at two minutes, forty-six seconds, a coded message appeared on the monitor.

Seven

Charlie's reaction was reflex. Despite the debilitating blows, he used the momentum of the fall to throw his assailant over him. He succeeded, but only for a moment before the man was back on top. Charlie raised his right hand, deflecting the next punch while dropping his left to the man's crotch and squeezing with all of his might.

The howl was boyish. Good. The assailant was young, less experienced.

Flirting with unconsciousness, barely able to see, Charlie judged the angle of the blows coming at him and thrust the heel of his hand where he suspected the face to be. He caught the side of a nose. Not a direct hit, but enough to feel the cracking cartilage.

Still gripping with his left hand, he raised his knee sharply into the softness of the belly. The howl ceased long enough for an *oof!* as wind rushed from the young man's lungs. His hand dropped to Charlie's, trying in vain to loosen his grip.

But where was the kid's other hand?

The answer came with another blow to Charlie's face. Harder than flesh or bone. A gun.

Charlie threw his free hand up and caught the arm just before it came down again. Holding it at bay, he followed the arm to the wrist, then the gun. He wrapped his hand around it. Their arms trembled, each trying to overpower the other as he groped for the fingers—more precisely, the index finger.

He found it and squeezed.

A shot fired—deafening at its closeness.

As he hoped, the kid panicked. What type of madman would fire a weapon when he had no control of it? Using the confusion, Charlie pulled the hand with the gun toward his own head, disorienting the kid even more, causing him to instinctively pull back—which was all Charlie needed. He reversed course, used the kid's strength to slam the hand and gun up into his face.

"FBI!"

He barely heard the shout. Still holding the crotch, he half-lifted, half-threw the kid off him. Adrenaline pounded as he began his own attack. He leaped onto him, striking him in the face once, twice—powerful blows, merciless— the animal he'd caged over the years unleashed.

"FBI!" The voice stood at the door. "FBI!"

He continued hitting the face—his vision and mind clearing enough to see the blood, the jet black beard and hair— igniting memories of his own family's slaughter. He relished the pain. His and the kid's. He would not stop. Doubted he could. Until a blow to his head toppled him off the boy like a rag doll. This time he did lose consciousness. Not long, but enough.

Opening his eyes, he stared up at Lisa. She stood in the doorway, holding her ID above her with one hand, while alternately pointing her Glock at him and the kid beside him.

"FBI! Put the gun on the floor!"

Charlie rolled his head to the side and saw the boy a yard away, still clutching his weapon.

"Put the gun on the floor!"

The kid didn't obey, and for good reason. The gun was eighteen inches away, pointed directly into Charlie's face.

"Put down your weapon!"

The youth was no fool. Blinking the blood out of his eyes, he kept the gun trained on Charlie . . . now, his hostage.

Or not.

"Shoot him!" Charlie croaked.

"Put the gun down!"

The kid's grip tightened. His voice was slurred from shredded lips and a broken tooth, but there was no missing his resolve. "Shoot me and he's dead."

"Shoot him," Charlie yelled. "Shoot him!"

But she could not. Protocol prevented her and the boy knew it.

Charlie swore in frustration.

"Get up," the kid ordered Charlie as he rose to his knees, still pointing the gun in his face. "Nice and slow."

Charlie scowled at Lisa, hoping by sheer concentration to force her into action.

"Now!"

Despite the throbbing of his head, and the pain in his side, he sat up.

"All the way," the boy slurred. "On your feet."

Charlie turned back to Lisa who still had her gun trained on the kid. "Shoot him!"

"Shut up!" the boy yelled.

Charlie wanted to attack, the animal still uncaged. Gun or no gun, he wanted to tear the kid's head off and shove it down his throat. But he would use the animal to his advantage, focus its rage. He'd make the kid sorry he ever lived. But at the right time.

The youth stood and waited as Charlie rose to his feet, wobbly, but standing nonetheless.

"Step out into the room." He motioned with his gun. "And you"—he nodded to Lisa—"lower your weapon or he's dead."

She looked to the kid, then to Charlie. He did all he could to will her to take the shot. But hostage safety had been drilled into the Feds' psyche from their first day of training. Slowly she lowered her Glock.

Charlie shook his head in disgust as he stepped out of the booth. The boy followed.

"Hand it to me." The kid nodded to Lisa's gun.

She hesitated.

"I said, hand the—"

The room began to rattle, a low rumble that Charlie felt more than heard. It shook in his gut. Not his stomach, but his intestines. His lower intestines. Suddenly he had the urge to go to the bathroom . . . a sensation that grew more urgent by the second.

He turned to Lisa. She felt it too.

And the boy? He was grimacing, reaching to his abdomen.

The sound increased, filling the room . . . and their bodies.

Lisa stooped over, looking like she was going to vomit. But it wasn't nausea. She was trying to control her bowels.

So was Charlie.

So was the kid. Still holding his abdomen, he reached out to the wall for support.

That's when Charlie moved. With a rage greater than any diarrhea, he spun around and slammed his forearm into the kid's face. The boy staggered backward as the gun slipped from his hand.

Charlie dove for it, but there was no competition. The others were too preoccupied. He came up with the gun and took aim at the kid who was bending over, crossing his legs, leaning against the door. Charlie rose and staggered past the boy to Lisa, who looked up at him, sick and confused. He grabbed her hand. She put up little resistance as he broke her grip on the Glock and took it.

Suddenly, the rumbling stopped. His gut still cramped, but the impossible pressure had ceased. He turned back to the kid, aiming both guns at him. "Who are you!" he demanded.

The kid said nothing.

Charlie stepped forward and hit him hard in the face with the butt of his own gun. The remainder of the bloody tooth flew from his mouth. The boy slid to the floor, unable to stand, but still conscious.

"Who are you!" Charlie's entire body shook as he pointed the guns at him.

"Uncle Charlie!"

He paid no attention. Shoving the Glock into his waistband, he grabbed the kid's hair with his free hand and yanked it up, forcing the kid to face him. The boy cried out in pain.

"Tell me who you are!"

He refused or was unable. Charlie pulled back the hammer of the remaining weapon.

"Uncle Charlie!" The girl was closer, near the door.

"Where are her parents?" he shouted.

The kid remained silent.

Charlie yanked his hair harder. The boy cried. But that was okay, he'd be out of his misery soon enough. "*Where are they!*"

"A boat," he sputtered through blood.

"Where?"

More resistance.

Another yank, another cry. "I don't know! They didn't find what they wanted! They're going after the partner!"

"Uncle Fredrick?" Jaz shouted. "They're going after Uncle Fredrick?"

The kid gave no answer.

"Where are they now?"

He coughed, half gagging on his blood, but giving no response.

Charlie had had enough. He shoved the barrel into the kid's mouth.

"Uncle Charlie! No! *Uncle Charlie!!*"

He looked up. Saw the horror in the girl's eyes—but not at the gun. At him. She was afraid of *him.*

"Please. He doesn't know! Can't you see, he doesn't know!"

He hesitated.

"Please, Uncle Charlie . . . please."

The animal faltered, blinked . . . then slowly slunk back to its cage.

Angry at his softness, yet full of self-loathing over what had surfaced, Charles Madison pulled the gun from the boy's mouth. "Get up."

The kid hesitated.

"Get up!"

Slowly, with great pain, the boy rose to his feet.

"Step away from the booth." He looked up to Lisa. "You too."

She seemed unsure.

He turned the gun on her. "You too!"

She obeyed.

"Both of you, move to the center of the room."

"What are you doing?" Jaz asked. "What are you going to do?"

He looked to her—the fear in her eyes as painful to him as any bruises he'd received. "Grab some cables. Thick stuff they can't break."

Jaz stared, unsure.

"It'll be okay," he said. "We just need to tie them up."

She still didn't move. Not that he blamed her.

"Get the cables!"

poppa . . .

the wedding plans r going perfect. Kindness and helpfulness seem to be the by-words. with you out of the country and momma gone everyone wants to help. I can't wait for u to get back. Don't get me wrong, aunt deborah and sadie r more than helpful (sometimes way more). Only it's not the same as having u here. hurry and come home . . . but only after u make lots of money, cause this is going to cost u a fortune! Not that i'm planning it that way, it just seems to be happening. still i promise, u will be able to give everything ur usual scrutiny and careful CONSIDERATION! ha! ha!

loves and kisses,
hannah.

Despite twenty-five years of service in the Mossad, a knot formed in Houser's stomach. He stared at the screen a long moment—not because he missed his daughter or because he was anxious to get home for the wedding—

though both were true. As an only child, Hannah had been the apple of his eye. And since Monica's murder she was all he lived for.

But this had not been written by his daughter.

Nor was the code difficult to decipher. In this age of sloppy grammar and Internet punctuation it could have been dreamed up by any youth, and probably was. There were no clever da Vinci decoder rings needed here. No fancy electronics. Thanks to the dumbing down of computer culture, it was simply a matter of stringing together the sporadic use of capital letters:

Kindness . . . **I** . . . **D**on't . . . **O**nly . . . **N**ot
CONSIDERATION

Translation:

KIDON
CONSIDERATION

And that's what made Sheldon Houser go cold.

"*Kidon*" was a death squad selected when an assassination was ordered. Two teams of men remained in perpetual training in Israel, ready upon a moment's notice, should their services be activated. Houser served as a member on such a team once in his life, back when they were "cleaning up" the remaining Palestinians responsible for the Taba bombings of 2004.

That had been a delight. But this . . .

"*Consideration*" meant a trial was about to begin. Two lawyers, one for the prosecution, the other for the defense, would soon present the case before a judicial committee so secret the Israel Supreme Court did not know they existed.

Their purpose?

To determine if the girl, her parents, and now the uncle were a sufficient threat to the State of Israel to be handed over to Kidon for execution.

Eight

Jaz stared at the monitor above the aisle, trying to move the little symbol of their plane faster over Nebraska or Iowa or wherever it was they were.

She glanced to Uncle Charlie in the seat beside her. He looked practically normal now—well, normal for a guy who'd been bashed around. Any trace of the madman with the gun was gone. Whoever or whatever she saw at the lab had disappeared—dissolved back into this guy who, although a major grump, was at least sane.

Most of the trip he'd either been sleeping or faking it. Either way, it only took one time of interrupting him, and practically getting her head bit off, before Jaz decided it was better to catch up on her latest *Cosmopolitan*, *Vogue*, and the required issues of *People*, *Us*, *Self*, and whatever else she had conned him into buying her at the airport.

"Anything to keep you quiet," he had joked. At least *he* thought it was a joke. But Jaz hadn't laughed. It wasn't her fault she was majorly in touch with her emotions and free to express herself . . . or that he was so emotionally constipated he could barely put two sentences together.

Actually, to be fair, he'd done pretty good when they were standing in line at security. Well, not good, but at least he was trying . . .

"What'd you call that thing again?" he'd asked. "'*The Brown Note*'?"

"Yeah." Jaz grinned. "Pretty cool name, huh?"

He shook his head. "It's definitely descriptive."

"Doesn't work on everybody, but the frequencies and harmonics are set to make most people lose control of their bowels."

"So I noticed."

Jaz smiled.

He tried to return it, but with his usual failure. "And your folks dreamed that up?"

"No way. A bunch of college kids did. Should I take these off?" She referred to her earbuds.

He nodded. "Better safe than sorry. We're not out of the woods, yet."

She didn't like it, but pulled them out. It took less than four hours to tie Lisa up with the other guy, travel to San Francisco, and convince some loser, who hadn't bathed in like a month and who owed Charlie some favors, to meet them in a white van at the airport parking lot. There, he cleaned up Charlie's face, gave him a new cell phone and credit card, and handed them both some majorly lame ID.

"It doesn't even look like me," she had complained. "This chick's fat and ugly, and—" She peered more closely. "Are those zits?"

"It'll only be you for a few hours—"

"And what's with the unibrow?"

"Just till we get to Chicago."

"And then Switzerland," she said, pleased that he actually agreed to the idea.

He nodded. "Once we pick up the passports in Chicago."

"More friends with favors?"

He said nothing, which she knew translated as either "*Yes,*" or "*It's none of your business.*"

"Mine's at home."

"Your what?"

She sighed at the obvious. "My passport."

"No, Jazmin Lutzer's passport is at home. You're somebody else now."

"Right"—she referred to her ID—"but not Marlene Murphy. I wanna be like, Nevaeh. I think that name is so hot. It's heaven spelled backwards, you know."

No answer.

"It's one of the most popular names in America right now."

Again, no answer. Well, all right, maybe a little nod. Then, for the hundredth time he grilled her about Uncle Fredrick in Switzerland: Was she sure she knew what city he was in? Was she sure his number wasn't listed? Could she really find his place once they got there?

"Yes!" she sighed. "Yes, yes, yes. I'm not a complete idiot."

"I never said you—"

"What about clothes?"

"We'll buy everything you need over there."

"I'll need plenty," she said, already negotiating.

"I'll take care of it."

Things looked brighter by the second. "And Lisa?"

"What about her?"

"Duh. She's kinda like indisposable at the moment."

"Indisposed," he corrected.

"Whatever."

"We'll call from a pay phone just before we board in Chicago."

"That's a long time to be tied up. What if she has to go to the bathroom?"

"I think you've taken care of that already."

She giggled. "Yeah, I guess."

They had no problems purchasing tickets—Charlie with his new credit card and driver's license, Jaz with her student ID from Saint Something-Or-Other in San Jose.

After that came security.

"Why do you wear those things?" he'd asked, referring to the earbuds she was unthreading from under her sweatshirt.

"Why not?"

"Seems odd if you can't, you know, that is, if you're hearing impair—"

"The word's 'deaf.'"

"Right. Deaf."

"I don't know, mostly fashion, I guess."

He looked confused—one of his more common expressions.

With another sigh, she explained, "Everybody wears them."

"Right . . ."

Another sigh. "And when I've got them in nobody thinks I can't hear, which of course I can't, which is why I wear them so they all think I can."

Charlie frowned.

She shook her head and threw in a good eye roll. How much simpler could she make it?

And now that they were finally on the plane she realized that him being asleep (or pretending to be) might actually be okay. 'Cause, let's face it, it really got annoying having to explain obvious junk to him like a thousand times. Hard to believe he and Mom were actually related. 'Course, Mom could be a pain too. But at least she was a pain that understood how normal-type people act.

She took a deep breath. For the millionth time fears about her parents rose up in her. And for the millionth time she pushed them aside. They'd be okay. They had to be. Uncle Charlie would make sure of it. Emotional retard or not, he'd make sure.

≛ ≛ ≛

"If Allah is so powerful, why are you afraid?"

"I am afraid of nothing," Omar, no last name, said from behind her.

"Right, that's why you're kidnapping scientists and stealing programs—because you're perfectly comfortable with what they'll reveal."

"The truth does not frighten us."

Lisa winced as she contorted her fingers, struggling to slip them out from the thick cables binding her back to back with the young man. "Seems to me if someone found a way to hear God's voice, you religious types would be doing cartwheels."

"Our concern is not about God, but man."

"Meaning?"

"If it was ever legitimate, it has been corrupted."

"Corrupted?"

"This business of Christ's voice being the same as Allah's. Such a thing is blasphemy."

"Blasphemy," she said, making sure he heard her contempt. "Of course."

He answered with a quote: "*There is no God but Allah and Muhammad is his apostle.*"

"So this Program is . . ."

"A way to deceive others into accepting your Western heresies and American immorality."

"American immorality? Listen, pal . . ." She twisted her hand, grimacing in pain. "Despite our faults, America is the most moral country on earth."

"America has sold her soul to Satan."

"Why, because we don't bend down and face Mecca five times a day? Sorry, for some of us that's not exactly the litmus test for morality."

"Your government, your culture, your very lives, all scream of godless immorality."

"We are founded on godly principles that stretch back to—"

"You have sold those principles long ago. Wealth and materialism, those are your gods now."

At last her hand slipped out from under the first set of cables. There were two more to go.

The kid continued. "Look at your Hollywood movies. Your motion picture studios are nothing but factories of porn, violence, and—"

"You're talking Hollywood, not America. There's a whole country out there besides Hollywood."

"That is where you're wrong, my friend."

"I'm not your friend."

She felt the cables slacken around her shoulders, indicating that he was also making progress.

"Your country openly embraces Hollywood and its filth."

"And you know this from reading what book?"

"I am serious."

"So am I. Have you even seen the rest of America?"

He gave no answer.

"No, of course not. You're just parroting what some bigoted zealot—"

"If such indecencies had no commercial appeal, do you think the companies producing them would stay in business? Of course not. Supply and demand. Immoralities are produced because immoralities are purchased."

"Now you're an economist?"

"I am a realist. America has become the Whore of Babylon. She will sell anything, including her god, if it will make her money."

Lisa slipped her hand out from the second set of cables, giving her more room to work . . . until the slack was immediately taken up by his side.

"I need that," she protested.

"As do I."

"I'm just about free here, if you'll—"

He pulled harder.

"Ow!"

Angry and frustrated, she waited for slack then quickly took it. It was his turn to gasp in pain as she tried to slip her hand out from the next band of cables.

"Tell me, Lisa Harmon, do you consider yourself a Christian?"

"I was baptized as a kid. Not that I'm a card-carrying member, but—"

"And how many men have you slept with?"

"How many—that's none of your—"

"How many sins have you winked at because you consider their restrictions repressive and old-fashioned? How many indecencies have you embraced because you are a 'progressive' thinker?"

"Please," Lisa scorned.

"How many times have you turned your back on the poor, the helpless, the unborn because of your idolatry, your pursuit of materialism? Your streets are filled with poverty and lewdness and violence."

"And yours aren't?"

"My sisters walk down any street of any Muslim city—Cairo, Teheran, Riyadh—without fear of being raped or even spoken to in disrespect. Can any of your cities make such a claim?"

"Well at least my sisters don't have to walk around with veils covering their faces and being treated like someone's property."

"They are safe."

"They're in prison."

"It is a prison of morality."

"So we're back to morality. Tell me, what exactly do you call a belief that kills thousands of innocent civilians who have nothing to do with the military or government?"

"You are a democracy. Innocent civilians have everything to do with your government."

"Lots of them don't even vote!"

"Perhaps they should."

"You're one sick puke, you know that? Who do you think you are, choosing who lives and who dies?"

"Their fate is in Allah's hands."

"No. Their fate is in your hands. You and your ilk are nothing but murderers hiding behind your faith. Or, worse, your naiveté is manipulated by others who hide!"

"*In the Name of Allah, the Compassionate, the Merciful.*"

"Your god has no mercy. Open your eyes!"

"*In the Name of Allah, the—*"

"Stop hiding behind verses!"

"*In the name of—*"

"Shut up!"

"*In—*"

"*Shut up!*" Suddenly the cables came loose. They dropped to her waist. And none too soon. She slipped out of the coils surrounding her, as did Omar. Each stood up, shaking them to the floor, their movement firing up the motion sensor lights.

At last Lisa stepped from the pile, rubbing her arms and wrists, taking a moment to size up her opponent.

The kid did likewise. "I would love to stay and chat, but I must be going."

"Sure you don't need a ride?" she asked. "I could contact my friends at the Bureau. It would only take a few minutes for them—"

"I have one other question to ask you, Lisa Harmon."

She sighed wearily. "And what's that?"

His eyes locked onto hers. "Why has *your* government taken such interest in this computer program?"

"What makes you think we have?"

"Have you not been assigned to this case?"

"Perhaps there's another matter we're investigating."

"Is that what they told you?"

She gave no answer, she didn't have to. Apparently, the kid saw it in her eyes.

He broke into a sad smile. "Now, who is being naive?"

Lisa opened her mouth but found no words.

He turned and started for the exit. "I trust the next time we meet, it will be under more favorable conditions." He arrived at the door and opened it.

"Favorable?" Lisa asked.

He stopped and turned. "Yes. Where I have a gun and you do not. Good day, Special Agent Harmon." He gave a nod and disappeared into the hall.

Nine

"Uncle Fredrick!"

Jaz broke from Charlie, her flip-flops echoing down the smooth, concrete tunnel. At the bottom, a pair of tall padded doors stood open to reveal a perfectly round room. Its walls and ceiling were covered in the same black foam as the Cal Poly lab.

Charlie followed. The place was more cavern than room. Sixty feet in diameter and half that high. Circling its perimeter and rising from the floor were a dozen stone or crystal rods of various colors. They were no more than two inches in diameter and reached halfway to the ceiling. At the center of the room, on a black padded bench, much like a doctor's examining table, a shriveled old man lay on his belly, stark naked. At the sound of Jaz's voice he raised his head.

His assistant, a young man, prematurely bald, had been running a tuning fork up and down the old-timer's body. Now he reached for a white towel and draped it over the man's nonexistent buttocks.

"Jaz?" The old man fumbled for his rimless spectacles. "Is that you?" With his assistant's help, he managed to sit up, wrapping the remainder of the towel over him as Jazmin arrived, practically knocking him over with an enthusiastic hug.

"Uncle Fredrick!"

He returned the hug. "What, where . . . What are you

doing here? Where are your mother and father?" His eyes landed on Charlie and he stiffened slightly. "Who are you?"

Jaz gave no answer as she continued clinging to him, her body starting to shudder.

"Child, what's wrong?"

She held him tighter.

Charlie cleared his throat. "I'm Charles Madison . . . Katie's brother."

"But . . . where is Katherine, where is Matthew? And why are they bringing strangers here? They know how sensitive our work is."

"Katie and Matt are not with us."

"They're not?"

Charlie shook his head.

Jaz pulled from the embrace and wiped her face. She took a breath, then changed gears so quickly Charlie thought she'd get emotional whiplash.

"They broke into the lab, some bad guys, don't ask me who, and were looking for the Program. But Mom and Dad knew somebody was coming 'cause earlier they tried hacking into our computers so"—she took a quick breath and continued—"they copied it someplace no one would think of looking and deleted it from our system so they didn't find anything"—another breath—"and then they came to the house looking and of course they didn't find it so they took them instead."

"Them?"

Jaz blinked, then stated the obvious. "Mom and Dad."

"They took your parents?"

"I get there when they're leaving and try to follow but I can't, so I go to Uncle Charlie's like we always say I should if there's trouble. But some guy is chasing me till he gets into a gunfight with the FBI who really aren't the FBI, then the real FBI is there when they attack us at the lab"—another breath—"and say they're coming after you with Mom and Dad, so we came to warn you and find them. And"—she took one final breath—"and I guess that's it."

It was over in thirty seconds. Charlie felt he should add something, but for the life of him he couldn't think what.

The old man had listened carefully, sometimes raising his bushy eyebrows in surprise, sometimes squinting into a scowl. When she had finished he sat a moment, digesting what he'd heard.

"You still into calendula?" she asked, pointing to the tuning fork in the assistant's hand.

The old man spoke and signed to her. "It seems to help my arthritis."

Jaz turned to Charlie and explained. "The Chinese philosopher Lao Tzu, he lived in like 600 BC. He believed we could heal ourselves by retuning our bodies to perfect fifths—that's the interval between notes C and G. He said, like, 'The sound is the *Perfect Universal Harmony* and all other vibrations in the universe align with it.'"

Charlie nodded, pretending to understand.

The old man motioned to his assistant for a nearby terry-cloth robe.

"And not just the Chinese. The Greeks believed it too. They thought music was, like, this supernatural link between heaven and earth. Pythagoras himself found that certain tones produced certain responses in the human body."

Charlie threw a look to the old man.

Jaz spotted it. "You do know who Pythagoras is, right?"

"Sure."

Jaz cocked her head at him.

"Some Greek guy, right?"

She rolled her eyes in disbelief.

The old man touched her arm. She turned to him and he spoke while signing, "I'm afraid I still don't understand how—"

"Of course you do. The entire universe is made up of universal vibrations spoken from higher dimensions down to ours and Pythagoras thought—"

"No, that's not what I meant." He allowed the assistant to help him on with the robe. "Thank you, William." He eased off the table and slipped his boney feet into a pair of orange and red Winnie-the-Pooh slippers. "Would you mind getting some refreshments for our guests? It sounds like they have had a very long and tiresome journey."

"All right!" Jaz exclaimed. "You got chocolate?" Before the assistant could answer she turned to Charlie. "Have you ever had Swiss chocolate? My favorite is Toblerone. It makes American stuff taste like wax." She turned to the old man. "I tried to get him to buy some at the airport, but he was too worried about getting out of there. Do you know we've got, like, fake passports and everything?"

The old man nodded, carefully eyeing Charlie.

She turned to William. "What about it? You got some Toblerone?"

The assistant gave a stiff, cautious nod.

Again the old man signed to Jaz. "Why don't you accompany William upstairs and give him a hand?"

"Sounds good to me." Jaz was immediately at the assistant's side, the two of them heading for the freight elevator with its exposed girders and hardware at the far wall. "So how you been, Willy?"

Charlie looked on, almost smiling. If there was anyone less comfortable with her than he was . . . it was William.

"And now to you, Charles Madison . . ." The old man tightened his robe and turned toward a sitting area near a long console. It consisted of an overstuffed chair, and two couches—all padded in bright blue and green fabric. He motioned for Charlie to follow. "It sounds like we have much to discuss."

"The FBI is not on trial here."

"Well, maybe they should be." Lisa stormed down the third-story hallway of the Federal building in Westwood, just off the 405. Once a showcase building, now everything from its sun-faded wallpaper, to its burned-out fluorescents (at least one per hallway) gave clear signs of its age and their budget cutbacks.

Bernice stayed hot on her tail, her black pumps pounding the worn linoleum tile. "Listen to me, listen to me!"

Lisa came to a stop and folded her arms as Bernie arrived. "You're this far from an OPR review, you know that."

"Under what grounds?"

"Oh, I don't know. How 'bout unauthorized use of a vehicle, for starters."

"Please."

"Aiding and abetting a criminal."

"The man is no criminal."

"Stealing cars is not a criminal act?"

Lisa pushed past her.

"How 'bout lack of candor?"

The phrase brought her to a stop. "What?"

"You heard me."

"You'd file that?"

"You earned it."

"That would get me thrown out of the Bureau."

"You purposefully refused to disclose your location to me."

Lisa shook her head, not believing her ears. Finally she turned and started for the stairway. "I didn't know you were my mother."

"Don't push me. Not on this one."

Lisa whirled around. "What's really going on, Bernie?"

The accusation obviously threw the woman—only for a second, but that was all Lisa needed to know something was up. She moved in. "Charles Madison is no serial bomber."

"You don't know that for certain."

"But you do."

"You saw the reports, the evidence."

"I saw one of four bombs mailed from the Moorpark city post office—*twenty miles* from his house."

"And his work in Special Forces—"

"Your brother was Special Ops."

"And his experience with explosives, and the murder of his entire family, which he holds the U.S. Government responsible for."

"And that makes him a killer?"

"What about the profiler's report?"

"Did you know he was studying for the ministry?"

Bernie came to a stop. "What?" Her look of surprise seemed genuine. "Are you sure?"

"Of course I'm sure. I was in deep cover, remember."

She seemed distracted by the new information. "The reports said nothing about that."

"No, they didn't. And I wonder what else they didn't say?"

Bernie was still digesting the information, but Lisa had heard enough. She turned and headed toward the stairway.

Coming to, the woman called after her. "Since when have you considered religion a positive thing?"

Lisa ignored her.

"Religious folks go nuts too, you know."

"Hey!" Lisa spun back to her. "I'm the one with the preacher daddy, remember? I'm the one he knocked up. So don't lecture me on religious sickos."

"I didn't—"

"I don't care what he believes . . . he's no killer."

Again Bernie seemed to hesitate and Lisa went for broke. "What about the Mossad? They're not even allowed in this country. They get caught, we try them as spies, everyone knows that. So what's so important that they'd risk exposure?"

Bernie had no answer.

"And the terrorist cell? Following that little girl all the way down to his store? Are you telling me that's all coincidence? Are you?"

She glanced down.

"What's going on, Bernie?"

At last she answered, softer. "I don't know . . . not everything."

"But you know something."

She closed her eyes.

"You have me risking my life, going deep cover on a man for completely erroneous reasons and you don't have the decency to tell me?"

Bernie opened her eyes and Lisa saw the helplessness. But it wasn't enough.

"Okay, fine. If you won't tell me, I'll find out on my own." She turned, hit the bar on the stairway door, and flung it open.

"Lisa . . ."

She did not stop but headed down the concrete stairwell.

"Lisa! Lis—"

The door slammed with a resolving *thud-click*.

🕊 🕊 🕊

"Here's your passport . . . Canadian, of course."

"Good." Sheldon Houser took the document from the young *katsa* who sat in the front seat of their rented Citroen. "Canadian is always the best." He flipped the passport to the first page. "And tell me what"—he squinted at the type—"what does *Gerald Elliott Gibson* do for a living?"

"Sparkling Springs Mineral Water," the agent said. He handed Houser a three-page, single-spaced document, typed in English. "You are their sales rep."

Houser scanned the page, taking note of the perts: company headquarters, current size, fiscal growth over the past two years, location of plants. Satisfied, he turned the page to study the personal info. He looked up and smiled. "He's single? No wife or children?"

The young agent grinned. "The office thought they'd make it easy for you."

Houser nodded, grateful that he would not have birthdates and other particulars to memorize. He looked back to the passport, flipping through the stamped pages reading, "Greece, Turkey, Germany, Italy, France—this guy gets around."

The agent nodded. "Third page has all your key accounts as well as the weather and headlines on the days you last visited."

Houser flipped to it and quickly surveyed the info. There was plenty there, but his bad eye started to water and he had to give it a rest. He looked out the passenger window to the lush green hills and the mountains beyond. Leaning back into the seat, he closed his eyes and took a deep breath. Even here on the autobahn everything smelled fresh, and green and alive.

Their *sayan* at the FBI, a reliable source, said the scientist couple was being transported to a lab in Switzerland. The office acted upon this information swiftly. And now, very soon, both the captives and their captors would be met by Sheldon Houser and his newly assembled team.

With eyes still closed, he asked, "And the safe house?"

"Three and a half kilometers from the laboratory. A farm. The owner was a *sayan* from the old days. His wife was a bit more reluctant . . . until we brought up Auschwitz and played the guilt."

"German descent?"

"Second generation."

Houser chuckled. "Sometimes it is too easy."

"Yes, sir."

"And the rest of the squad?"

"Milkner and Brenem are here as you requested. You worked with them before?"

Houser nodded. "Milkner is the best long shooter we have, God forbid we have to use him. And no one is better at recon than Brenem. What of the others?"

"In route by car from various airports. All should be assembled in the next six hours. Brenem already has schematics of the tunnel—rooms, air and exhaust vents, plumbing, entrance and exits."

Houser opened his eyes. "They are accurate?"

"They came from a combatant who managed a company subcontracted to do their electrical."

Houser nodded in satisfaction. To him, combatants were the unsung heroes of Israel. They were just average citizens who agreed to serve abroad for four years—gathering both hard and soft information. For the most part, they were the eyes and ears for harvesting intelligence, though in some Arab countries, they were actually used to plant bombs in bridges and infrastructures they helped build . . . should the time come when such structures needed to be removed.

Unlike the CIA's motto, "*The truth shall make you free*," the Mossad's was a bit more pragmatic: "*By Way of Deception Thou Shalt Do War.*"

Noting the position of the sun, Houser checked his watch. "Why are we heading north? Interlaken is southeast."

"Yes, sir," the driver answered. "We will be turning south in a few kilometers."

"Just making sure we're clean," the other agent explained. "We'll double-back and park to assure we're not being followed. After that we'll be on our way."

Houser nodded. The kids seemed to know what they were doing. He directed his attention back to the document and started memorizing the information. Once the team was in place, there would be little time for such luxuries. Once they studied and devised a plan, discussing every detail and contingency a hundred times, they would strike.

If possible there were to be no fatalities. The trial at home had just begun. No assassination had been ordered. Houser and his men were simply to move in, take the hostages, and move out—though with Charles Madison present he had doubts that it would be quite that simple.

Ten

The visit home would only be a moment. Not long enough to even see his family. Just a ruse. A stopover on his flight to a much more important place: Cairo, Egypt. Even the name made Omar breathe a little faster. And the purpose? He wasn't sure, though he knew it had to do with the scientist couple, since Cairo had always been their ultimate destination. Never Switzerland. That was merely a lie he'd fed the uncle and FBI agent who had both, apparently, taken the bait.

Of course, his work in the States was over. He had been made, his cover blown by the FBI agent. Hence, the quick trip across the border, the flight from Tijuana to Mexico City and now Manila. From there he would purchase tickets to Cairo. If the girl was captured, perhaps they would use his knowledge and personal contact to encourage her cooperation. Then there was the other matter. He'd be representing his Southeast Asian brothers before the Arabs. As far as he knew this was the first time the two *jihad* networks would meet and combine resources. A huge milestone by any definition.

And yet, even now, he could not entirely shake the words of the American from his head . . . *"What exactly do you call a belief that kills thousands of innocent civilians who have nothing to do with the military or government?"*

Of course he'd heard the argument a dozen times, and of course he had the appropriate response . . . but that didn't stop the question from stirring up old embers of doubt, embers that, quite frankly, he had never completely extinguished. Many of them from his own family . . .

"I do not understand your hatred and fanaticism," his father said one evening in their tiny house near the mountains outside Baguio. Omar was home on winter break. His sisters and mother had already gone to bed. Now it was just the two men of the family, sharing the deeper thoughts of men. "Does not the Holy Qur'an itself encourage us to live in peace with People of the Book—even allowing marriage to their women?"

Before Omar could answer, his father quoted:

"The food of those who have received the Scripture is lawful for you and your food is lawful for them. And so are the virtuous women of the believers . . ."

As a respected *imam* in their community, his father knew and understood the Qur'an far better than he. Still, Omar had a suitable reply. "Does not the Holy Qur'an also state:

"Fight against such of those who have been given the Scripture as believe not in Allah nor the Last Day . . ."

"Don't you see?" Omar set his tea on the unsteady bamboo table. "That is the purpose behind *jihad*. Our faith, our very way of life is under attack. We must fight back or be destroyed. We must break the West's stranglehold of immorality until everyone walks in the path of Allah."

"No." His father shook his head, his face glistening under the bare bulb that hung in the kitchen. "You are speaking of *jihad bi al saif*, the holy war of the sword. But it is a different war we must fight—the *jihad al nafs*, the war within our own souls, the struggle against the immoralities of our own flesh."

"Then, tell me," Omar argued, "how do you justify:

"Whoso fighteth in the way of Allah, be he slain or be he victorious, on him We shall bestow a vast reward?"

And so the debate continued—his father insisting upon a watered-down interpretation of the Qur'an, one that only dealt with the war inside a man's heart, while Omar patiently explained the clearer and more literal interpretation that the battle must be waged against real enemies with the sword, or IEDs, or crashing airliners, or dirty bombs . . .

Omar looked out the plane's window. Manila's twinkling lights had just come into view. How he missed his country, his home, his father and mother and sisters. If they only knew the sacrifice he was making for them. But they would. Soon, Allah's way would again rule the world. And, by the looks of things, Omar would be an important servant in bringing that way to pass. He, Omar Atmani, warrior, *mujahid*, wielder of Allah's fierce and holy sword. If he could only rid himself of the doubts.

≠ ≠ ≠

Charlie sipped his Nescafe in the kitchen of Fredrick's farmhouse. He glanced down to the watercolor painting on the table in front of him, something the old priest had been working on. It wasn't a bad representation, but nothing compared to the sunrise he now saw unfolding out the window. Below, in the village of Thun, red-tile roofs had started to glow in the first rays of light. Farther out, the waters of the Thunersee were shimmering. And above the lake, the snow-covered peaks of the Wetterhorn, Schreckhorn, Eiger, and a dozen others blazed with the iridescent pink the locals called, "Alpen Fire."

But Charlie would not allow himself to be drawn in. He'd been seduced by this type of beauty once before, during the family's first and last vacation since his retirement from the military . . .

Brenda's plan had been simple—spend a few weeks at her parents' summer cabin near Estes Park before they got serious and started attending Bible college together in the fall. "To help you unwind," she had insisted.

"I'm unwound."

She literally broke out laughing.

"What?" he demanded.

"You haven't been unwound since the day we met."

Of course she was right. Twenty years of serving in the Special Forces Operational Detachment can make it a bit difficult for anyone to relax. Even during his downtimes he had to remain on *Bowstring*—married to his beeper 24/7, ready to fly out of Pope Air Force Base, adjacent to Fort Bragg, at a moment's notice, prepared to meet and destroy any terrorist, any time, anywhere. It took nearly three weeks of hiking mountain meadows, swimming, reading, fishing with little Amy, playing board games, and late-night rendezvous with Brenda in the hot tub before he started getting the hang of it and began leaving his past behind.

Unfortunately, the past was not something everyone was so quick to forget. He'd made enemies over the years. Dozens of them. In the countries he'd visited, by the men and leaders he'd taken out. And, though the government assured him there would be no reprisals, that his identity was safely protected, they were wrong.

"Daddy, Daddy . . ." He could still hear six-year-old Amy's voice as she ran into the room where he and Brenda were snuggled in front of the fire. "There's someone out back!"

"What?"

"On the porch. With ski masks . . ."

He rose, buttoning his shirt, crossing for his gun.

"Charlie . . ."

"Go to the back bedroom with Mommy."

"What's happening?" Amy's little voice trembled.

"Come to Mommy, sweetheart." Brenda took her into one arm while reaching for the telephone with the other.

"What are you doing?" he asked as he pulled the gun from the top of the bookshelf.

"I'm calling the police."

"Please . . ." he scorned.

"It's what people do."

"Right." He slammed in the clip and headed for the back door.

"Charlie, that's not your job anymore."

He ignored her.

"We're different people now."

"Daddy . . ."

He threw open the screen door.

"You said no more! You made a promise!"

The door slammed behind him. Of course she was right. He had made a promise. The first of many for their new life. But this was his family.

The Syrians were pros. The sound of breaking twigs just beyond the light, a moving branch a little farther out . . . before he knew it, they had drawn him nearly fifty yards from the house.

That's when the screaming began.

First from little Amy . . . which abruptly stopped. Then from Brenda. Hysterical, agonizing wails.

He made it back to the house and dropped the intruders in their tracks. . . but not before they had killed his wife . . . exactly as they had killed and gutted his little girl.

Eleven

"Good morning."

Charlie gave a start and turned to see Fredrick enter the kitchen. The little man was barefoot and wore a long sleeping shirt, right out of the eighteenth century. "You like the view?"

"Very much."

Fredrick shuffled to the stove and reached for the tea kettle. "God had a fine time when he painted that scene."

"How many bunkers like the one under this house are in the area?" Charlie asked.

"Always working, are you?"

"I need to know the options if they come."

Fredrick crossed to the sink. "We have contacted the police. You were outside all night surveying. I have supplied you weapons."

Charlie threw a dubious look at the two rifles propped near the door—a 12-gauge, used for quail hunting, and an AK-47, used for more substantial game.

"Shouldn't that be enough?"

Charlie gave no answer.

The old man turned on the tap. "The bunkers were built to protect Thun's military production facilities from the Germans. Also to defend Lotschberg Pass."

Charlie nodded.

"The one downstairs was used as an artillery depot, hence

the elevator which, thanks to Swiss craftsmanship, works to this day."

"All were disguised as farmhouses?"

Fredrick moved back to the stove. "Or barns or railway buildings or chalets. Most were abandoned in the 1990s or turned into museums. One is even a hospital." He placed the kettle on the burner and reached for a box of matches.

"Are they connected?"

"Some. I know we have one abandoned tunnel beneath us, but it has been sealed for years." He turned on the gas and struck the match. The burner gave a quiet *whoosh*. Putting the matches on the shelf, he shuffled toward the table and eased himself into the wooden chair beside his water-color painting. "You like my art?"

"Yes, very nice."

Fredrick chuckled. "I hope you are a better sentry than liar."

"Jaz tells me you're a priest."

"Yes."

"Odd work for a priest."

"Is it?"

Charlie conceded. "I suppose proving God's existence can be a substantial calling."

"I'm sure it is, though it is not mine."

Charlie looked at him.

"Don't misunderstand me. It is a nice hobby. But what I am created to do, what we are all created to do, well, it is much different."

Charlie waited for more.

"I am called to worship him, to join the rest of creation in celebrating his grandeur and holiness. That, my friend, is what we are all created for."

"Not necessarily."

Fredrick tilted his head, quizzically.

Charlie looked out the window. "Some of us aren't so worthy."

The old man raised his bushy brows. "A Westerner who doesn't think he's worthy of God?" He chuckled. "Usually it is the opposite. Most feel God is not worthy of them."

"You don't know what I've done."

"Nor do I care. Christ died for you regardless of your past. Or mine."

Charlie slowly shook his head.

"What do you think, your sin is greater than his blood? That your actions are greater than his sacrifice?"

Charlie said nothing.

"Then I take it back, my friend. Your pride is no less than any other's." He leaned forward. "If you saw the glory I have seen downstairs, the power, you'd realize there is nothing it cannot do—no one he cannot forgive . . . if we would simply yield to him." He examined Charlie another moment, then sat back in his chair.

Charlie looked down at his Nescafe, then up to the priest. "I can't predict their time frame. If they're traveling by boat as we were told, then you should be packed up and out of here within forty-eight hours."

The priest shifted his weight, obviously disappointed in the change of topic.

Charlie continued. "You have someplace to go?"

"We have a smaller lab south of here."

"South?"

Fredrick looked at him, his filmy eyes sizing him up. After a day and a night in his house, it appeared he still wasn't sure whether to completely trust him. And that was fine with Charlie. The feeling was mutual.

"South," the priest simply repeated.

"Then I suggest you go there . . . if you feel it's safe."

The old man sighed somewhat wearily. "It is as safe as anywhere else."

"How many have access to this information?" Charlie asked. "To this . . . Voice."

"None of us, not entirely. We have the patterns, yes. Mathematical models. But as far as an actual, audible voice?" He shook his head. "A consonant or two, a vowel, a diphthong. But nothing more. That's the Program Katherine and Matthew were working on. And until we have that information . . ." He paused, continuing a bit more quietly, "Until then we are merely children playing with unimaginable power."

"How so?"

"What few sounds we are able to toy with have tremendous impact upon our reality."

Charlie frowned.

"And that's not necessarily bad. Actually, one of my dreams is to open up a healing center."

"A healing center?"

"Do you remember the fad, back in the seventies, when people played music to their houseplants?"

Charlie nodded. "Urban legend says it made them grow faster. At least that's what my pot-growing friends claimed."

"It was no legend."

Charlie looked skeptical.

"But it wasn't the music either. Well it was and it wasn't. There were certain frequencies within the music—imbedded within the harmonics."

"Frequencies of . . . the Voice?" Charlie asked.

Fredrick nodded. "It would only stand to reason. The same Voice that spoke life into existence would have the power to enhance it."

The tea kettle began to whistle. With some effort, Fredrick rose and moved toward the stove.

"So this Voice," Charlie asked, "you're saying it will be able to heal?"

"Yes. Or destroy."

"Destroy?"

Fredrick reached for a mug on the shelf above the stove. "Think about it. If the Voice, this unique pattern of vibrations, is responsible for creation—if it is the building block of our world, and we play it back to our world . . ." He hesitated, then motioned to the watercolor on the table. "Would you mind handing that to me, please?"

Charlie reached for the painting and passed it to Fredrick. Holding the tea kettle in one hand, the priest took the paper in the other and moved to the sink. "This is a watercolor painting, yes?"

Charlie nodded.

"And its base is . . ."

"Water . . . I guess."

"Correct. It is water soluble."

"Okay."

"So. What happens when we take this water-soluble creation and . . ." Without hesitation he poured the hot water from the kettle onto the painting, allowing the excess to flow into the sink. The colors soon smeared into each other. He continued to pour until the kettle was empty. He then set the painting on the counter. Well, what was left of it. Now it was only limp paper and a blur of color.

"That, my friend, is what happens when a creation, whose base is the Voice, is exposed to the Voice."

"Everything material melts?" Charlie asked.

"Not just material, but all of reality. The very laws of physics blur and scramble—space, time, energy, even our thoughts and emotions." He turned the tap back on to refill the kettle. "Just as this paint is water soluble . . . our reality is *God soluble*."

"That could prove dangerous."

"Yes, it could."

"So . . ." Charlie thought aloud, "not only do you have something that creates major theological and political rifts—"

"Jaz has discussed this with you?"

"She said you were at Mount Sinai. That you have no evidence in any of your samples that God spoke to Moses. Which, I'm sure, sets Israel's teeth on edge."

"And ours."

"Because . . ."

"It's one thing to have the patterns of New Testament encounters documented in stones—Yahweh's words to Christ at his baptism, the Mount of Transfiguration in Syria, Paul on the road to Damascus."

"You have all those?"

"Yes. But they were all recorded within a span of thirty years. We have nothing before or after that time to compare them with. And that can leave our findings more than questionable."

Charlie nodded.

"But if we had something from another era—"

"Moses on Mount Sinai."

"Moses on Mount Sinai—then we would have a separate, independent source, something equally substantial that would cause others to take our findings more seriously."

"Looks like folks are taking you seriously already."

Fredrick gave no answer as he turned off the tap and shuffled back to the stove.

Charlie continued thinking aloud. "So, if this Voice can

alter reality, it not only has the potential to heal, but to destroy."

Without looking at him, the man answered, "If misused, there is no end to the damage it can do."

Charlie ventured, "It could destroy entire regions."

"No, my friend." The priest turned to him. "It could destroy entire worlds."

¥ ¥ ¥

Lisa dragged herself up the outdoor steps toward her apartment on Ninth Street in Santa Monica. She wasn't drunk. Just feeling no pain. More and more often she had the good sense to walk away from situations before things got out of hand—no matter how hot the music . . . or the guy. Still plenty of full-on flirting, you bet. But no overnighters. Not anymore. That's what she'd promised Bernie . . . and her shrink. Going on two years now.

"It's how you define your self-worth," the doctor had explained. "Because of your father, you feel it's all you have to offer in a relationship."

Lisa continued up the steps, shaking her head. *Good ol' Dad.* She took a deep breath of the Magnolia blossoming in the courtyard. The sweet smell helped her to clear her mind and relax, just a little . . . until her door came into view. For the second time in as many months her porch light had burned out. But it wasn't the darkness that concerned her.

It was the glow from the kitchen window. It appeared to come from the light over the stove. The light she seldom, if ever, turned on. And definitely not this morning when she raced around like a madwoman getting ready for work.

She reached the top step, tightening the grip on her

keys—self-defense habits die hard. She arrived at the door and hesitated a moment, listening. For what, she wasn't sure. She was about to insert the key when something touched her leg. She gasped, kicking sharply and reaching for her gun . . . only to spot her cat tumbling across the walk with an angry yowl.

"J. Edgar." She holstered her weapon and kneeled. "Baby, I'm sorry."

The cat glared.

"I'm sorry, sweetie. Forgive me?"

Once it was certain Lisa had paid her penance, the cat blinked and sauntered toward her, blessing her with its presence. The fact it was a female had done little to discourage Lisa from giving her the Bureau's ex-chief and leading icon's name. With all those jokes and rumors about his cross-dressing and sexual orientation, it was the obvious choice.

Scooping J. Edgar into her arms, Lisa scolded, "What are you doing out, hmm?" Then, remembering the cat was in heat, she gave a weary sigh. "Oh, wonderful . . ." She'd been meaning to drop her off at the vet's the past six months, but never seemed to have the time. That's why she'd gone to such lengths to make sure J. Edgar was indoors before she left for work this morning. The thought made her frown. She distinctly remembered blocking the cat's escape and locking her inside. So, how did . . .

She let down the cat and rose back to her feet. She moved to the door and pressed her face against the cool metal surface. She heard nothing.

She eased her free hand to the knob and tried turning it.

Locked.

Silently, she inserted her key. She turned it until it gave a dull *click.* She waited, listening.

Still nothing.

As quietly as possible, she pulled back the slide on her Glock. Stepping to the side, she gently pushed the door. It opened with a quiet creak. There was no other sound, no other movement . . . except for J. Edgar who trotted past, meowing to be fed.

She closed her eyes, trying to clear her mind of the booze while adjusting her vision to the waiting darkness. She crouched, taking another breath.

Quickly, she swung into the doorway aiming her gun, checking to the left, then the right, then center.

There was no movement, not a sound.

Still crouching, she reached up to the light switch and turned it on. Brightness filled the room. Everything was as she'd left it—stacked boxes from her move back from Fillmore, two pairs of shoes and a jacket where she'd discarded them this morning in a last-minute change of wardrobe. And, as she rose and peeked around to the kitchen, the same mountain of dirty dishes rising from the sink.

Nothing was different . . . except for that light. And the cat.

She crossed to the guest closet and flattened herself beside it. Taking another breath to clear her head, she reached over and threw it open.

Nothing.

She moved quickly now. Any noise she'd made had signaled her presence. She headed into the hallway and the left bedroom. She snapped on the light only to see the unmade bed and cluttered dresser just as she left them. She checked the open closet. Under the bed.

Then the bathroom. Behind the door. The shower stall.

There was one place left. The bedroom across the hall she used as her office.

J. Edgar strolled into the hallway, meowing, giving little

doubt to anyone who might be wondering about Lisa's position.

With heart pounding, she forced herself to move slowly and deliberately across the hallway. Raising the gun in one hand, she reached for the light switch with the other. She snapped it on and saw . . .

Nothing.

She moved swiftly into the room, throwing a look into the open closet full of stacked books and a filing cabinet. She pivoted around and checked behind the desk.

Everything was clear.

Only then did she exhale. She took another breath and blew out the tension. No one was in the apartment. Whoever was here had left. And that was fine with her. She lowered her weapon and took another breath until J. Edgar suddenly jumped on the desk, causing her to scream, raise her gun, and nearly fire it.

"J. Edgar! Are you trying to get killed?"

The cat gave no answer, but continued to parade back and forth, meowing. That's when Lisa saw it. Next to her computer. A DVD in a white envelope.

She picked it up and turned it over. There was no label, no writing.

Who would have dropped it off? No one had a key to the place. Well, except the landlord. And, of course . . .

A smile crept over her face. There was only one person who could have dropped off the DVD. And, given the covert method in which it was delivered and with no label or identification, there was little doubt what information her best friend had burned onto it.

Twelve

Lisa stared at the computer screen, not believing what she'd read. There was so much they had not included in her file on him, as if they'd purposefully stacked the deck to make her think he was the Postal Bomber. But, in reality, it was just as she suspected, what she had witnessed firsthand. Charles Madison was no deranged serial killer. There was too much goodness. Underneath the tough, silent facade, there was too much compassion. He was going to be a minister for crying out loud—well, all right, maybe there were some problems, but not many.

Then there was the murder of his family . . .

She'd had no idea what grizzly things they'd done to his wife and daughter (a girl who would have been about Jazmin's age now). And, though the government failed in protecting them, it was clear he held one person and only one person responsible for their destruction.

Himself.

So why had the Bureau lied to her? Why this elaborate cover-up?

And why withhold the other information . . . Jaz's parents' work on the voiceprint, the fact that both a terrorist cell and the Mossad had them under surveillance? Alarming, pertinent facts. Yet *none* had been given to her. Not even the attorney's file giving Charles Madison custody of the girl should something happen to her parents.

What was going on? Why was she assigned to keep tabs on a man for reasons entirely different than what she was told?

Then there was the other fact. The one currently up on the screen. The final NSA entry:

> Parents not transported to Switzerland as previously reported.
>
> Arrived Cairo, Egypt 10:35 AM. Currently in hostage situation.
>
> 73 Khairat St.

More alarming still, was the final line:

> Mossad gathering outside Swiss lab.
>
> Lethal armament. Will report results.

"Lethal armament?" And they were doing nothing about it? *"Will report results!"*

As outraged as she was concerned, Lisa rose and headed to her filing cabinet. She dug through the pile on top, the miscellaneous odds and ends she'd not yet filed from Fillmore. Near the bottom she found it. Jaz's card. The one with her e-mail address.

Moving back to her desk, not bothering to sit, she clicked into her e-mail and quickly started a letter. She was no doubt under surveillance, but they had to be warned. She wasn't sure Jaz would get it. But if the child was half the techno geek Lisa supposed, there was a chance she might.

⚔ ⚔ ⚔

"It's a Harmonograph," Jaz said as she adjusted the weights on the pendulums.

To Charlie it was a strange four-legged table with three pendulums hanging through a hole in its middle and almost touching the floor. They were attached to spindles which rose up and through the table at least a foot. Each, in turn, was attached to a gimble arm which held a draftsman's pen that rested on a sheet of typing paper.

Only they weren't resting. As Jaz raised or lowered the weights, the pens circled and spiraled, creating flowing, geometrical patterns. "It helps me see what you hear," she explained. "I can't hear the mathematical patterns and harmonics you hear in music, so this lets me see them. Of course, I could do it electronically, but this is way more fun."

She rose and moved to the papers she'd already etched designs on. "This"—she held up an oval whose circles grew smaller and smaller—"is a simple unison, you know a 1:1 ratio. And that"—she pointed to another drawing with spirals shaped more like wings—"is a lateral octave, 1:2."

Charlie tried to show interest but it didn't matter, she was too engaged to notice.

"But these are the ones that really get interesting. Here's a rotary fifth, 3:2." The pattern was even more complex, filled with hearts and stars. "And finally the fourth, 4:3, with thirds, sixths, and sevenths."

She turned to Charlie. Though completely lost, he did his best to cover. Unfortunately, his best wasn't good enough. Fortunately, before she could give him a good eye rolling, Fredrick came to his rescue.

"She's just showing off," he said, taking Charlie's arm and directing him away. "Don't let her intimidate you."

"She's a kid," Charlie exclaimed. "How could she intimidate me?"

It was another lie and they both knew it.

The priest continued. "It's all patterns and mathematics, my friend—from the pulse of galaxies, to the vibration of electrons, everything can be reduced to patterns, predictable mathematical formulas."

"Including the Voice."

"Which may be the greatest mathematical formula of all."

Charlie nodded. "I need to get back outside. You had something to show me?"

"Yes, it is minor, but you wanted to be apprised of any change?"

"That's right."

"It seems there is a slight shift in air circulation. It is something we try to keep consistent, given the sensitivity of our instruments. But there is a minor fluctuation."

"Any idea why?"

"Remember that tunnel I spoke of? It has been sealed for years. I have not been down it, but it seems to be coming from that direction."

"Show me."

They started across the lab. Adjusting the AK-47 across his shoulders, Charlie couldn't resist asking the question he'd been chewing on since their last conversation. "About this Voice you recorded . . ."

"Yes?"

"Where did it come from, originally I mean?"

"Pardon me?"

"I mean, if it came from outer space, which direction? Where exactly does 'God' live?"

"Oh, I see. No, actually, it came from all around."

"You lost me."

"You and I, we see only 4 percent of what is about us."

"Because the rest is too small—like atoms and things."

"No. Ninety-six to ninety-seven percent of the universe is made up of something we cannot see, touch, taste, or measure. And yet it is all around. We know this by its gravitational pull. For lack of a better term we call it Dark Matter and Dark Energy. We cannot measure it, but we know it is here."

"You're kidding me."

"It is one of science's biggest mysteries."

"And the Voice," Charlie asked, "it came from this invisible, whatever it is?"

"Most likely located in a higher dimension, yes."

"Higher dimension?"

"Physicists today believe we are surrounded by at least seven more dimensions. They are all around us, we simply do not see them."

"I think I'm getting a headache."

Fredrick smiled. "I don't blame you. To put it simply, let us say the Voice, or what or whoever produces it, is as much in this room today as everywhere else in the universe, at any time in the past, present, or the future."

"I'm glad we're putting it simply."

The priest chuckled as they approached the perimeter of slender stone rods. Some rose several feet out of the floor, others only a few. He slowed to a stop, peering at the closest. "Oh, dear."

"Is there a problem?"

"We seem to have a crack. It is hairline, but if you look very closely, you can see it."

Charlie leaned toward the red crystal shaft and squinted. There, barely visible, was a thin black line curving up and through the rod. "What do they do?" he asked, motioning to it and the other rods circling the room.

It took a moment for the question to register. Finally the

old man looked up from the crystal. "These are our, well for lack of a better term, these are our speakers."

"Speakers?"

"Yes. As you may imagine, even though we only have a few of its sounds, playing the Voice through conventional speakers would destroy them."

Charlie hadn't imagined, but it made sense.

"So we use these rods. Each vibrates with a small spectrum of the frequency, just under 9 percent, or one-twelfth, hence twelve rods."

"And they're made of different stones?"

"And crystals, yes. The very type used by the high priest in the Old Testament."

"The twelve on his breastplate?"

"I see you have read your Bible."

Charlie gave no answer.

"Then perhaps you also know of speculation that the stones may have enabled the priest to discern the will of God."

Charlie frowned. "How?"

"We're not certain. However, after careful testing, we have determined that the same type of stones are the best medium for transmitting the Voice. And, should the frequencies ever reach critical mass, creating a dangerous reaction—"

"The watercolor painting," Charlie interjected.

"Precisely. Should we start losing control . . ." He turned to his assistant who stood on a platform before the control console. "William, will you dampen the prime numbers, please?"

The young man entered a few keystrokes on a computer. Immediately, five of the twelve circling rods dropped into the floor with a quiet *whoosh*. Only seven remained visible.

Charlie raised an eyebrow. "Interesting."

"We borrowed the concept from nuclear reactors. Whenever a reaction becomes too hot or cold, they insert or remove the appropriate number of reactor rods to control it."

"That's the only safety measure?"

"Not entirely. Remember how we spoke of our calling—to worship him? It's difficult to explain, but this seems to have an impact as well."

"Worship?"

"Yes, singing in adoration and such."

Charlie gave him a look.

"I don't understand it either. The best we can figure is that it somehow puts us in tune with the other elements of creation—participating, as it were, with similar harmonics."

"Similar harmonics as what—these rocks?"

"As I said, it is a mystery. But Christ himself told the people that if they remained silent, the very stones would cry out his glory."

"Uncle Fredrick! Charlie!" Jaz motioned them to her computer screen. "It's an e-mail from Lisa!"

Fredrick turned to her and signed. "Who?"

"The FBI agent who—"

The explosion filled the lab—its concussion so powerful it nearly threw Charlie off his feet. He stumbled, fighting for balance as he spun around, checking the cavern, looking for the source.

The elevator shaft. Dust and debris poured down it from above, billowing into the lab.

A second explosion followed from behind them, this time knocking Charlie to the ground. He fell, tucking in his rifle to protect it. He spotted Fredrick beside him, coughing, his mouth open in cries Charlie could not hear for the ringing in his ears.

He rolled to his knees and was up and searching. The

second explosion came from the main entrance, the giant, soundproof doors that he'd given strict orders to keep locked. Broken now, smoldering. There was too much smoke to see if they had been entirely breached. It wasn't a bomb. It could not have been planted without his knowledge. A grenade launcher with a high-explosive round? Possibly. An M-72 antitank rocket? Maybe. Both were military, not something terrorists could easily smuggle into the country.

This dramatically reduced his list of suspects while giving him a clue of their professional caliber. He knew a third explosion would follow. But not yet. Not until he and the others regrouped and tried to escape—no doubt, the attackers hoped, directly into their waiting arms.

Fredrick tried to rise, coughing, fighting to catch his breath. Charlie moved to help. That's when he spotted William staggering toward them, holding his chest. Astonishment filled the assistant's face as blood gushed between his fingers. A shard of rock or shrapnel had torn through his shirt and between his ribs. His heart had been punctured. He would be dead in sixty seconds.

"Uncle Charlie!"

He turned, squinting through the dust to see a mound of rubble where Jaz had been.

"Uncle Charlie!"

He raced toward the pile, noticing a searing pain in his right thigh. Glancing down, he saw a bloody hole in his pants. He'd address it later. He arrived and was relieved to see the boulders had not crushed her. She was pinned, mostly clothes, maybe a leg, but nothing serious. He raced around the rocks and dropped to her side.

"You okay?"

She was coughing, panicking. "What's going on? What's happening?"

He grabbed her head, forcing her to see his lips. "Are you okay?"

"Where's Uncle Fredrick?"

Without answering, he began pawing through the rubble. The next attack would come any second. If he did not get her out of the bunker by then, he never would. A large boulder trapped the hood of her sweatshirt. With some effort he rocked it back and forth until it rolled to the side.

She sat up, coughing, demanding, "Where's Uncle Fredrick?"

He moved to her legs. A smaller rock had pinned one. Not smashed, just pinned. Taking advantage of his adrenaline, he was able to lift and heave it away.

"William!"

He turned and spotted Fredrick stumbling toward his assistant. Even through the dust, Charlie could see William's eyes frozen open.

He turned back to Jaz and helped her to her feet. "Can you walk?"

She spotted Fredrick on his knees before his assistant—the pool of blood, the frozen eyes. She started screaming.

Grabbing her shoulders, he shouted into her face, "Can you walk?"

She twisted, trying to look past him, but he held her fast. "Can you walk?"

She stopped and stared at him, eyes wild. "Where . . ."

He turned back to the soundproof doors. Maybe they could escape through them, maybe not. Either way it would be too dangerous. The assault team could still be there waiting. Or preparing another round.

Fredrick yelled, "The tunnel! We can escape through the—"

"No!" Charlie shook his head. "If you know it, they know it!"

"Then where?"

He turned to the elevator shaft, thinking. "Come on!" He grabbed Jaz's hand and half dragged her toward it.

"Where are we—"

"Can you climb?"

"Where are we going?"

They arrived at the elevator, coughing, choking as dirt sifted down, along with the occasional boulder. He pressed against the side and peered up the shaft. It was just as he suspected. The support beams were twisted, blocking any passage of the car.

But not of them.

"Hang on!" He grabbed Jaz around the waist.

"Where are—"

"Up!" He lifted her toward the car's roof. She caught its edge and pulled. Once on top, she turned back down to him.

"Go!" He motioned her up the shaft.

"Not without you guys!"

"We'll follow!"

She hesitated and looked up, then back to Charlie.

"Go!!"

She looked back up. Then, with a breath for courage, she began the climb.

Charlie turned to Fredrick who had risen and was saying last rites over William's body.

"Let's go!"

The old man looked to him. Then, as if for the first time, he saw the remains of the smoke-filled lab.

"Come on!"

He finished the rites. But instead of moving toward Charlie, he turned and limped toward the console, or what was left of it.

"What are you doing?"

"Our work!"

"It's over! It's too late—"

"It is not too late! And that's the problem." He hobbled around a pile of rocks. "There's more than enough information for them to retrieve and duplicate."

Charlie looked up to check on Jaz. She was making good progress. He turned back to Fredrick. The priest had arrived at the console and was already entering keystrokes into the computer.

"We have to go now!" Charlie shouted.

"You go!"

There was a faint whine and dimming of lights. Suddenly the rods that had dropped earlier into the lab's floor rose— but only a few inches before they stopped.

Fredrick scowled and entered another set of keystrokes. The rods remained stuck.

"Come on!" Charlie shouted.

He tried a third time. The rods moved, shuddered, then rose to their complete height of eight feet, joining the other three that remained standing despite the attack. The rest lay broken and shattered on the floor.

The cavern rocked with a third explosion. It came from the far end of the tunnel, the one the attackers had obviously hoped to flush them toward. Dust roiled out of it, followed by voices shouting in Hebrew.

"*Now!*" Charlie yelled at Fredrick.

But the priest remained focused on his task.

Charlie looked back up the shaft. Jaz had climbed the

thirty feet up to the house and was now scrambling out of the shaft and into the library.

"Stop!" a voice shouted.

He spun back to see two . . . three assault personnel appear through the smoke. They'd spotted Fredrick. Not Charlie . . . until he slung his AK-47 around and opened fire.

It had been years since he'd shot the Russian weapon, and he'd forgotten its recoil; the way it bucked in the hands, kicking up the barrel. By the time he forced it back down, the men had leaped for cover and began returning fire.

He pulled back behind the elevator. His rifle had a full magazine. Another clip was in his pocket. He could keep them occupied; long enough for Jaz to get out of the house and run toward the forest as they'd discussed.

The men continued shooting while starting to fan out. He fired alternate bursts, focusing his attention on the two flank men, left and right, trying to slow their attempts to circle him.

Then he saw the center man throwing a canister into the room.

"Close your eyes!" he shouted to the priest. He dropped his head and clenched his own eyes just as the explosion and blinding light filled the room. It was designed to distract and disorient, giving the attackers time to make their move.

The roar reverberated through the cavern, but the light had barely faded before Charlie resumed firing. All attention was focused on him now. No one was threatened by the priest at the console.

But they should have been.

The sound of gunfire began to shimmer; its pops and bursts warbled like a bad tape recording. A roar filled the room. He heard it in his ears the same moment he felt it in his body . . . the same moment he noticed the weapon in his hand feeling wet and sticky. To his astonishment he saw it was melting. And not just the rifle. He looked to the ground. It, too, was melting. Suddenly he stood in several inches of liquid flooring that had been solid just moments before.

But it was more than his weapon and the floor melting. So were his thoughts, his memories. They began to dissolve. Then re-form. Becoming something entirely different. He remembered thirteen-year-old Amy, her mother helping her with algebra on the kitchen table in a house they never owned, living a life they never lived, but had, at least now. He remembered the pain and tears over the arm she broke as a cheerleader. His only child murdered at six, now on the cusp of womanhood.

He spun to Fredrick, but the room had shifted, everything had traded places. The old man and the console were now on the opposite side of the room. The priest's face was filled with fear as he stared at the rods. Not only were the ones still standing glowing, but so were the broken ones on the floor. Even in their condition they seemed to be broadcasting the sound—not completely, but by the looks of things and the expression on Fredrick's face, enough.

The gunfire continued, but it had become mushy drum-beats, a rhythm accompanying the roar. A roar that rose in pitch, higher and higher, until it sounded like singing. But it wasn't singing. At least none that Charlie had ever heard. The notes were rolling, sustained chords, filled with shifting melodies he understood but could not explain.

They came from a light that suddenly appeared floating in the middle of the cavern. But it really wasn't a light. It was more like a slit in the air with an inexplicable brilliance pouring out of it.

And singing.

They were the same. The light was the singing, the singing was the light.

Charlie rose unsteadily to his feet, struggling to stand against the light, the singing, the liquefying floor. He looked back up the elevator shaft. It was changing, flexing, and twisting . . . but not as much as the cavern. The lab's floor, walls, ceiling—everything was glistening, rippling. He slung his rifle to the side. What remained of it flopped like a limp rope. He touched the elevator car. It was soft and gooey. There was no need to leap to the roof and pull himself up. He simply dug his hands into its walls and climbed.

He felt the light and singing soak into his back. He turned, squinting into the brightness. He thought he caught a glimpse of eyes . . . and feathers. He shouted to Fredrick but could no longer hear himself over the music. He saw the light-sound saturating the priest, causing him to glow like the center of the room. The man had lifted his arms, tilted back his head. His mouth was open and he appeared to be joining in the singing.

The floor at the center of the cave buckled under the light, then rolled like a giant wave toward the elevator. Charlie braced himself as it hit the car. But it didn't stop at the base. The wave continued right up the walls to the roof, practically throwing him off.

He hung on and watched as it moved up the shaft, losing its strength.

He looked back to the lab. Another wave was coming. And another after it.

He scrambled up to the nearest girder. It was soft and

spongy, but firmer than the elevator or liquid floor. He clung to it as the second wave hit. He watched with amazement as it rippled through the steel, then his own body, then on up the shaft.

He resumed climbing, working his way to the next girder, then the next.

The third wave hit, but he was farther up and in less danger.

Suddenly the entire shaft rocked. Dust belched up from below. The lab was caving in.

He climbed faster, the girders growing firmer with every step.

Up above, Jaz was in the library, lying on her stomach facing him, shouting down to him. "Hurry! Hurry!!"

The rumbling grew louder. More dust rose.

"Run!" he shouted. "Don't wait, run!"

But of course she didn't. He climbed another eight feet before he was able to grab the library floor. He pulled himself up and onto it. Fire burned all around. Some of the ceiling had fallen. The wall where the bay window had been was blown away. He scrambled to his feet just as the house lurched, seeming to slip from its foundation. He coughed, peering through the smoke until he saw daylight where the wall had been.

Another lurch.

If the enemy was out there, he'd have to face him.

Grabbing Jaz's hand, they half-ran, half-staggered across the pitching floor. They worked their way over fallen bookshelves, around furniture and burning rafters—coughing, barely able to breathe from the smoke.

Once they arrived, Charlie hoisted Jaz up and onto the broken wall. She hesitated then jumped to the lawn below.

Charlie followed, dropping to the ground, rifle up, preparing to fire.

But no one was there.

He grabbed Jaz's hand and they ran across the yard, staying low until they reached a small stone wall. They hopped it and dashed across a single-lane road to the base of a grassy hill.

The air shook with an explosion.

Jaz looked over her shoulder and screamed. Charlie turned to watch.

The remains of the smoldering house groaned and slowly caved in upon itself.

"Uncle Fredrick!" She started back until Charlie caught her arm.

The house continued to collapse, disappearing into its own dust and the bunker below.

"Let me go!" she shouted. "Let go!"

But he would not let go. Instead he threw the sobbing child over his shoulder. Only then did he notice that the strength in his right leg had returned. He glanced to his thigh and saw the bleeding had stopped. The hole in his pants leg gone. Puzzled, he adjusted Jaz's weight and started up the slope. Beyond that was a cow pasture. And beyond that the woods they would hide in. He had scouted it all the night before. Every contingency had been covered and thoroughly thought through.

Every contingency except the Voice.

Thirteen

EGYPT

Jaz was all mixed up. One minute she was crying, the next she was smiling. No wonder Dad called her his favorite schizophrenic. The point was she felt awful about what happened to Uncle Fredrick. She bawled her eyes out all the way to some hotel in Bern and all the next day as they went to the airport and got on the plane to Cairo.

But she was also majorly excited. Her folks were alive. Not only alive, but thanks to Lisa's e-mail, she knew where they were.

Of course, Uncle Charlie had a hard time buying all of it, since he still thought of her as a kid. And she had to promise him like a zillion times that it was true, and if he didn't believe it he could just e-mail Lisa at the FBI and blah, blah, blah.

Long story short, he finally came around. Now they stood in the customs line at the Cairo airport, smiling and pretending everything was cool. Well, not *cool* cool because it was like a million degrees in the big, dingy hall which had obviously never heard of AC. But eventually their time came and they approached the counter. Some sleepy guard, with a uniform right out of an old-time movie, barely glanced at Charlie's passport before stamping it. And he didn't even look at her picture before he stamped hers and motioned them through.

She waited until they were a bunch of steps away before she finally looked up and whispered, "Now what?"

"Don't look back," was all he said.

Which, of course, meant she had to which, of course, was just in time to see some young guy with dark eyes and killer lashes talking to the guard and looking after them.

Jaz spun around, staring straight ahead, then stole a glance to Charlie. "What's going on?"

"Just keep walking."

Heads began to turn in their direction. She guessed someone was shouting after them. She looked back to Charlie but he gave no clues.

More heads turned.

Charlie picked up his pace. He reached down and took her hand.

"What's going—"

"Let's go!" He broke into a run.

She threw a look over her shoulder to see Dark Eyes running after them. She turned back just as they entered a big hall with sunlight pouring in through giant, dust-coated windows. It took lots of swerving in and out not to hit any of the crowd. For the most part they succeeded . . . except for the crippled guy selling peanuts in newspaper funnels.

"Sorry!" she yelled as the peanuts flew into the air.

If he shouted back, she couldn't see.

Up ahead there were these big glass doors with, like, a thousand taxis all waiting outside. The two made a beeline for them and were practically there, when some policeman in an equally tacky uniform stepped in front of them. They put on the brakes, nearly knocking him over.

Jaz shielded her eyes and squinted into the sun to read his lips.

"What is the problem?" he asked.

She turned to Charlie who said nothing. Dark Eyes arrived. The policeman said something to him in a language she couldn't read. Dark Eyes answered in the same gibberish.

She looked back to Charlie who still wasn't answering. Then to Dark Eyes, then to the policeman, then back to Charlie. Finally, unable to stand it, she turned to the policeman. "Look, I don't know what's going on, but we're the good guys here."

Charlie squeezed her hand and she looked up.

All he said was, "Jaz . . ."

But he obviously wasn't helping matters so she kept going. "We're here to save my parents."

Another squeeze. Harder.

She squirmed, trying to slip her hand from his.

"Is this man hurting you?" the policeman asked.

Good, at least he was worried. She could play that. Forcing tears to her eyes—surprised at how fast they came—she sniffed. "No, sir, he's my uncle. He's been looking after me." She gave her nose a swipe. "But there are some real bad men, terrorists or something—"

"*Jazmin!*"

"You will remain quiet!" the policeman snapped, then turned back to her.

Tears streamed down her face. Was she good or what? "They kidnapped my mom and dad and . . ." She took a ragged breath, but before she could continue, Dark Eyes interrupted.

The policeman growled something at him and turned back to her. "You and your friend, you will come with me."

"Are you going to help us? I'm deaf, did you know that?"

The information surprised the man. It usually did. But he recovered and stooped so she could clearly see his mouth. He answered slowly, with unnecessary exaggeration. They usually did.

"Yes . . . I . . . will . . . help . . . you."

He rose, placed a hand on her shoulder, and directed them toward the door.

Jaz was happy with her progress and beamed up to Charlie. She would have been happier if he'd shown the slightest pleasure over her accomplishment. Instead, there was only concern. Deep concern . . . which only increased when two more men without uniforms swooped in from opposite sides.

Bernie fumbled for the car radio and cranked up KUSC, one of the city's classical stations. She turned from the wheel to Lisa and half-mouthed, half-whispered, "What are you talking about?"

Lisa frowned, wondering if someone really had wired the car. And more importantly, why? Now that she had settled back home, they were only resuming their weekly ritual of catching a flick in Westwood—one of Bernie's tactics in helping Lisa swear off the bars and men.

They drove along Veteran Avenue, next to the cemetery, looking for a place to park. It would be a six-block hike to the nearest theater, part of it uphill. But finding a closer spot on Friday night was next to impossible . . . as was justifying the price of a parking lot, at least on their salaries.

Lisa leaned closer and spoke just loud enough to be heard over some concerto. "Look, I really appreciate you taking that risk, but—"

"Risk?"

"Pulling all the information up on your computer and burning me a CD."

"Actually, I pulled it up on *your* computer."

Lisa gave her a look. Bernice shrugged.

"But all you did was tell me the *whats*—what really happened to Madison, what he's really like."

"That's not enough?"

"I don't have any *whys*."

Bernie spotted a place and began to parallel park.

Lisa continued. "Why waste an agent's time with deep cover? Why hide his connection to the voiceprint program? Why—"

An SUV pulled behind them, so close it prevented Bernie from backing up. "Who said there's a connection?" she asked.

"I'm not an idiot."

"You've been doing a pretty good imitation."

The SUV honked. Bernie rolled down her window and waved it around. "Did it ever occur to you that there are some things beyond our jurisdiction, things we *shouldn't* know?"

"But you do."

Again, the SUV honked.

Again, Bernie waved. "Come on, come on . . ."

Lisa repeated. "You do know, don't you?"

"Know what?"

More honking.

"Bernie . . ."

The woman sighed in exasperation. "A little, but not as much as you think."

The SUV pulled around them; a carload of college boys, drunk and swearing with the obligatory hand gesture.

"And God bless you too," she called.

"Bernie . . ."

She looked over her shoulder and started backing the car into place. "I only know that it's related to the DOD."

"We're working with the military? Doesn't that make you the slightest bit suspicious?"

"Will you stop the Big Brother paranoia?"

"Okay . . ." Lisa reached over and snapped off the radio.

"What are you doing?" Bernie spun around and turned it back on.

Lisa folded her arms, having made her point.

Bernie responded, "These are perilous times, girl. Uncle Sam needs all the help he can get."

"Something's still not right."

"Why, 'cause you got the hots for Charlie Madison?" She turned and resumed her parking.

"Because we purposefully set up two Americans, maybe four—one a thirteen-year-old child!" Lisa caught herself and continued, more controlled. "The last I heard, our job was to protect American citizens, not endanger them."

Bernice continued parking.

"The niece, she said the experiments could do things to the body."

"She said that?"

"And gave a little demonstration."

Bernice smiled. "The Brown Note?"

"Don't laugh, it wasn't funny."

Bernie straightened the wheels and pulled the car forward.

"She talked about other things—frequencies that could induce seizures, mind control, weapons of mass destruction—just by using sound."

Concern flickered across Bernie's face.

Lisa saw it. "What?"

"She told you that?"

"What's going on, Bernie?"

The woman hesitated, then reached past Lisa to the glove compartment. She pulled out a pen and a large square pad of Post-it Notes—the type that covered her computer and half her house.

"What are you doing?"

No answer.

"Bernie?"

She began writing. "This is all I know. And don't you dare ask me for anything else." She pulled off the paper and handed it to her, immediately peeling off another five or six sheets, making sure all the imprints were gone. She wadded the extra paper, stuffed it in her pocket, and turned off the ignition.

Lisa looked at the paper. It was a single name:

Dr. Percy Reynolds

She folded it and put it in her jeans pocket. "I owe you for this. Big-time."

Bernie opened her door and stepped into the night. "Just remember that when we're cellmates in Leavenworth."

★ ★ ★

"Please . . . he doesn't know anything . . ."

Omar Atmani stood in the hallway. A blanket had been tacked over the window to darken the tiny room before him . . . and to help muffle the screams.

The man in the black ski mask turned to the girl. "But *you* know, don't you?"

"Please . . ." she whimpered, "please . . ."

He turned from her and swung the pipe hard into the American's back, aiming for his kidneys. He must have found his mark because the man gave an involuntary gasp—the only sound he'd made in the last twenty minutes.

The girl and the American were positioned at opposite ends of the room. It was vacant except for a stained, paper-thin mattress and some scattered newspapers. Their hands were tied and they were on their knees. Well, the girl was on her knees, the man had rolled onto his side vomiting.

"When did they arrive?" Omar quietly asked Sheikh Abdallah Zayd, the elderly leader who stood beside him.

"Two hours ago." Sheikh calmly folded his hands within the sleeves of his long, flowing *galabiya*. "Though Egypt pretends to stand against us, she is full of devout brothers. Many work for the government. Even more for the police."

"And they went to the police?"

"In a manner of speaking."

Omar nodded. It was his second day in Shubra, a slum on the outskirts of Cairo. Nearly a million people were packed into this tiny area, the size of a dozen soccer fields. He had grown used to the noise of constant traffic, as well as the dry oven heat. He had yet to appreciate the choking dust and diesel fumes mixed with the smell of raw sewage that rose from the street below.

The American was struck again. Again the girl screamed. "Please . . . you're killing him . . ."

"How long will this continue?" Omar asked.

"Only a few more minutes. Beatings are worthless when the body grows numb. He will rest, feeling will return, and we will resume."

"And the girl?"

"She will either convince us she knows nothing, or"—he raised his palms—"her fate is in Allah's hands. *Insha'allah*."

"Fate?" There was a concern in Omar's voice that he could not hide.

Sheikh turned to him. "We are not animals, Omar Atmani. See for yourself. We have even allowed her to keep her music." He motioned to the iPod with its headphones on the floor beside her. "We will only use force when necessary."

"What type of force?"

"The mother is still alive and downstairs."

"I have heard her cries."

"Despite her husband's death, she still refuses to cooperate. But now . . ."

Omar waited for more.

"Now she has recognized her daughter's voice. That shall prove most useful in her cooperation."

"In what manner?"

Sheikh turned back to the room. "It is one thing to hear your child scream over the torment of others. It is quite another to hear her scream in her own agony."

"You will not bring them together?"

"Greater images of horror can be conjured by the imagination."

"She is just a child, what do you intend?"

Sheikh Abdallah Zayd turned back to him and with measured tone replied, "Whatever is necessary."

Omar looked away. He'd revealed too many thoughts— several not even his. For even here, with this great man, his father's words still haunted him.

Once again the American was struck. This time in the ribs. It would be a miracle if one or more had not been broken.

"Stop . . ." the girl sobbed, "please, please . . ."

"Perhaps you would like to assist us with the girl," the old man said.

Omar turned to him.

"She is young, so very firm—a tender bud just blossoming into a woman."

Omar swallowed back his revulsion.

"You could be her first."

He looked hard at the floor.

"You find such things disgusting?"

He debated whether or not to answer. Finally he nodded.

"And so you should, my friend. As should all *mujahideen*."

Relief washed over him.

"But there are difficult decisions we must all make. Our battle is to the death, against Satan himself. And there are unpleasant choices every day that face those of us in charge."

Once again the American vomited. Dry heaves now.

Omar felt a gentle hand on his shoulder and looked to the old man. Though his eyes were clouded with milky-gray cataracts, there was no missing their earnestness. "Come, Omar Atmani, it is time to meet the others. As our honored guest, we have much to discuss."

"And the girl?"

"*Insha'allah*." He turned and started up the stairs. "Do not worry. If the time should come, you will not be asked to assist. The streets have many lecherous and willing infidels."

Fourteen

"Hello, Dr. Reynolds." Lisa took a seat and placed her purse and navy-blue windbreaker on the table between them. "My name is Lisa Harmon, I'm from the FBI."

As the orderly had warned, the feeble, old man gave no indication of her presence. He continued staring past her, out the wire-meshed window of the veterans hospital's ninth-floor psychiatric ward.

She pressed on. "I'd like to talk to you about some tests you were running two years ago for the Department of Defense."

There was only the quiet hush of air-conditioning, the occasional clicks from a nearby dominoes game, and the ever-persistent drone of daytime TV.

Earlier she'd run the man's name through the Bureau's database. It was a risky decision but, given the danger Jaz and Charlie were in, she took it. There were one hundred thirty-four Percy Reynolds in the United States. Only three were doctors—an orthodontist in Utah, a chemistry teacher at Florida State, and a physics professor at UC San Diego who specialized in acoustics . . . until he suffered a combination stroke and some sort of mental breakdown twenty-two months ago.

She'd found her man.

"These experiments involved sound waves—the effect

they can have upon the human body, particularly the nervous system."

He kept staring. If anyone was home, they weren't coming to the door.

She glanced around the room and shifted uncomfortably. In many ways the place was a larger version of the retirement home she'd put her dad in, God rest his soul. Same beige walls, similar vinyl floor . . . bathed in the ever-present smell of old people and disinfectant.

"Dr. Reynolds, I know initially you were in communication with Drs. Matthew and Katherine Lutzer, professors up at Cal Poly."

There was the slightest movement in the eyes—so slight she wasn't sure she saw it. She leaned closer. "I have reason to believe their lives are in danger."

Nothing but the stare.

She scooted her chair closer and lowered her voice. "Doctor, listen, you have no reason to trust me, but I think . . ." She tried again. "Records show that all three of you were studying something you believed to be a voice pattern. Something of . . . divine origin." She waited, watching. It was hard fishing without bait, but she continued. "Then, for whatever reason, you quit working with them and began working for the government on your own."

More waiting. More nothing. It was time to go for broke.

"Dr. Reynolds, I believe some people in our government may be doing something very wrong with your work. I believe there are a few loose canons that—"

His eyes moved, she was certain of it—a shifting, back and forth. No, shifting was too big a movement. More like a shudder.

"Dr. Reynolds?"

The shudder grew, spreading around his eyes and into his face.

Lisa's pulse quickened.

His lips began to twitch. She leaned forward and watched as they parted.

"Dr. Reynolds? Is there something you're trying to say?"

He continued to struggle.

"Yes," she whispered. "I'm right here. What do you want to tell me?"

A faint hiss of air escaped between his teeth.

She brought her ear within inches of his mouth.

"*Ssss . . .*" He stopped and took a breath. It began again. "*Ssssi . . .*"

Tiny beads of perspiration appeared on his forehead. The table began to vibrate. She looked down and saw his hand on it, trembling, trying to close, then open, then close again . . . as if grasping.

"Write?" she asked. "Do you want to write something?"

His eyes blinked.

She reached into her purse, fumbled for a white Bic pen. Uncapping it, she slipped it into the man's hand. He had no grip and she carefully balanced it so it did not fall.

Now for paper. She returned to her purse and found nothing but a package of tissues . . . and her checkbook. She pulled the checkbook out and opened it to the registry. She slipped it under the man's hand. The movement caused the pen to fall to the table.

"That's okay." She grabbed it and repositioned it between his thumb and fingers. "Hold it as tight as you can. I've got the paper, you just move the pen."

He gave no response.

She watched, breathlessly. Finally the pen started to

move—first to the left, then to the right, then to the left again. He stopped and for a moment her heart sank . . . until she noticed he had lifted the pen. It was only a millimeter, but definitely off the paper. Taking a guess, she eased the checkbook ahead.

The pen dropped back to the paper. This time it drew a shaky vertical line, straight down.

"Are those letters?" she whispered. "Is that an *s*? An *l*?"

If she was right, he gave no indication. All of his energy was focused on the pen. Once again he lifted it a fraction from the checkbook and once again she slipped the registry forward. Again it touched the paper, repeating the same rough zigzag he had made the first time.

She looked back to him. "*s* . . . *l* . . . *s*?"

His face was wet with perspiration. She wanted to tell him to take a break, but this was too important. He tried moving the pen but could not. It fell back to the table.

"Is there more?" she asked.

Again his eyes moved, the slightest trace of a frown flickered.

She picked up the pen and put it back in his hand.

Summoning what must have been superhuman strength, he made yet another vertical line. Once he'd finished, Lisa started to slide the checkbook forward, but he kept his hand on it. She stopped and watched as, with excruciating effort he moved the pen near the center of the vertical mark and drew a shaky horizontal line across it—either a *t* or an *x*, Lisa couldn't tell. Then his hand relaxed and the pen clattered to the table.

She looked back to him. He had closed his eyes. The shaking came to a stop. She turned back to the checkbook and read the letters:

She waited almost a minute before he reopened his eyes. When he did the lifeless stare had returned.

꙳ ꙳ ꙳

The *shura* met in the upper room—three men, each representing regions committed to worldwide *jihad*. One was an older, heavy gentleman from the Maghreb Arabs. A second, Sheikh Abdallah Zayd, represented what was known as the Core Arabs. The third was a worn, bedraggled Pakistani who represented Bin Laden's al Qaeda. And sitting with them, enjoying the evening's rooftop meal, was Omar Atmani, their brother from the Philippines. Although Omar was their honored guest, chosen for his insight into the American girl and her mother, the men soon penetrated deeper into his heart, looking into his soul. They did not like what they found.

"You are sounding like our wayward brothers," Sheikh Abdallah Zayd said as he spooned the *molokiya*, a goopy green stew, over his rice. "Those who preach compromise with the enemy until they are no different from the enemy."

Omar glanced down in deference. "Then I am afraid I have misrepresented myself."

"Remember, your words are of great importance here," the heaviest of the men said.

"Yes, I apologize."

The lieutenant from al Qaeda spoke. "Perhaps our young brother has spent too long in the West."

Omar turned to him. "Excuse me?"

"The devil's ways are not only deadly, but subtle."

Holding back his irritation, Omar answered, "I am submitted to Allah's will as each of you. There is nothing about the infidels that my spirit finds of interest."

"Your spirit, yes." The heavy man chuckled. "But what of your flesh?"

The men grunted and nodded.

"Please"—Sheikh held out his hand—"let our young friend speak."

Omar took a breath. "The infidels have a saying . . . 'It is better to catch flies with honey than with vinegar.'"

"Ah," the heavy man replied, "but you cannot crush the devil's work with smooth sayings."

"Nor by sleeping in his bed," the lieutenant agreed.

"But . . . are we not even now using the devil's tools?" Omar asked.

The men looked to him. It would be a tricky balance, influencing his elders without offending them. But he must try. "Does not Satan himself exercise brutality . . . detestable acts of violence . . . the slaughter of innocents?"

"There are no innocents," Sheikh corrected.

Omar nodded. "This is true. I often use such arguments, myself." Turning to the old man he quietly asked, "But the rape of a little girl?"

Silence hung over the table. Each knew full well what he meant.

Finally, with grave sincerity, the heavier man answered, "*Insha'allah.*"

"*Insha'allah,*" the lieutenant agreed.

Omar bit his tongue. He had said too much already. These learned men deserved his respect. And he agreed with them. For the most part, he agreed. Now *was* time for action. Now *was* time for force. Had he not argued these very things with his father? And yet, hearing the girl's whimperings downstairs, even as they ate . . . and knowing her future . . .

Ever so gently, Sheikh Abdallah Zayd touched his arm. "Please . . . to do the work of Allah, we must all speak with candor."

Omar held his look. The sheikh nodded in encouragement.

"Yes," the heavier one agreed. "Please, tell us what you are thinking."

Omar looked around the table. These were good men. Wise men. If he was in error they would correct him. If not . . .

He took another breath and began. "We keep saying, if Allah wills, '*Insha'allah, Insha'allah.*'"

The men nodded, their lips quietly repeating the phrase.

"But is that what we really mean? How do we know the difference between Allah's will and our own?"

"We have *Sharia*," the lieutenant answered. "We have the Law."

"But to force people's submission by using the devil's tools? Is this not inconsistent? As we wage Allah's war, will he not use his own tools?"

"I am confused," the heavy man said. "You dare to instruct us?"

"I mean no disrespect."

"I must agree with my brother." The lieutenant nodded. "You sound no different than the Saudi whores."

"No, I'm in full agreement with you. I am merely saying—"

"I know what you are saying and I am disappointed. You were brought here at great expense in hopes that your experience would facilitate the Americans' cooperation. But this . . ."

"Yes," the heavy man agreed. "You speak like an old woman, pleading and cajoling with the enemy."

"Gentlemen, please." Sheikh raised his hands.

The heavy man continued. "Have we not reasoned for these past four hundred years? And now, at this most pivotal moment, you speak weakness. Now, when the Program could force every head to bow to Allah."

"Or be removed," the lieutenant added.

Omar looked to Sheikh Abdallah Zayd in confusion. "I am sorry, I don't understand. I was told we wanted the Program because of its corruption by the West, because they dare claim Allah's voice to be equal to Christ's."

Sheikh nodded. "In part, yes. But those in the scientific community also feel it has the potential of being developed into a weapon of great destruction."

"A weapon?"

"The voice of Allah is all-powerful and all-mighty," the heavy man said.

Omar frowned. "Nothing like this had been mentioned."

The lieutenant leaned forward. "Does such a thing worry you?"

Omar looked up. He hesitated only a moment, but it was enough. The heavy man sighed in exasperation. Gathering his robes, he rose. "We will continue this discussion tomorrow—*after* we have cooperation from our guests downstairs . . . and after our young friend has carefully searched his soul."

"I agree." The lieutenant also rose. "Until tomorrow. *Allah yukaththir khayraka.* May Allah increase your well-being."

"*Allah yukaththir khayraka,*" the others replied as the two men turned and exited the room.

Now, only Sheikh Abdallah Zayd and Omar sat at the table. Unsure what to say, realizing he had said too much, Omar remained silent. Outside, two stories below, the cacophony of street noise continued. Inside, directly below them, the beatings had resumed as the girl continued her screams.

⚑ ⚑ ⚑

With some effort, Lisa unfolded herself from the rental subcompact. The twenty-three-hour drive up from L.A. had taken its toll. But that's why Starbucks was invented. Now if they could come up with an equally potent drug for removing stiffness after a full night and day of driving. It's not that she hated flying, there was just something unnatural about being vacuum-packed in a long tin can with 250 other humans hurtling six hundred miles per hour, seven miles above the earth. Call her old-fashioned, but she enjoyed a lot less stress (and nausea) by taking the extra time to drive.

After stretching her neck and rolling her shoulders, she surveyed the cracker-box house just off 145th NE in Seattle. Though the place was run down, she imagined that in the 1950s it must have been *Good Housekeeping* magazine's version of quaint. Unfortunately, after sixty years, the quaintness had given way to a sagging, moss-covered roof and overgrown rhododendrons.

It hadn't taken much to decipher Percy Reynolds's message—as soon as she realized the *l* was an *i* . . . and that he had a sister. And last night, over the phone, the cordial old woman said she'd have no problem if Lisa wanted to "stop by."

That was the easy part.

Then came the hard. The physical demands of the drive

were nothing compared to the emotions that kept churning and trying to surface. These were her childhood stomping grounds. Just another forty-five minutes up I-5 and you'd find her brother living in his Brady Bunch world. Not that she had anything against him—well, not much, anyway.

It was the man vegetating in the nursing home nearby. The one everybody doted over. It made no difference what he had done. It didn't matter that she had destroyed her own life by blowing the whistle on him. Now that her dad was lost in the labyrinth of Alzheimer's, everyone seemed to think it was their duty to forgive and forget.

Everyone but Lisa. Some way, and she wasn't sure how, but by insisting upon remembering the truth, she'd become its perpetual victim.

She stared back at the house. She'd been debating whether or not to tell Reynolds's sister she was FBI. Had he warned her to be careful of government agencies? How many had visited her in the past? What precautions had the woman taken against them? And, most importantly, how could Lisa succeed in gaining her trust where others had failed?

The questions continued dogging her as she started up the uneven sidewalk, climbed onto the tiny concrete porch, and knocked on the screen door. Eventually, the front door opened and a stooped, fossilized lady in a bright pink coat appeared.

"Hello, Mrs. Brown?"

"Yes?"

"I'm Lisa Harmon, from Los Angeles?"

"Yes?"

"We talked by phone yesterday?"

"Oh, yes, of course." She pushed open the screen. It gave a creaking groan. "Please, come in."

"Thank you."

"I'm afraid I was just stepping out, dear."

"Oh, that's okay, this shouldn't take—"

"But the information you want is right there on the table."

"Information?"

"Yes, from Percy's research."

Lisa looked to the dining room table and saw a large cardboard filing box. "You have"—she coughed slightly—"you have his files? *Here?*"

"Of course, what he asked me to keep. And if you don't mind me saying, you folks have taken your sweet time picking them up. You are from the government, yes?"

Coming to, Lisa blinked. "Yes, ma'am." She fumbled to produce her badge. "FBI."

Without looking at it, the woman started for the door. "Good. Now if you'll excuse me, I have to dash. Just take what you need and throw the rest out."

". . . thank you."

"And be sure to lock up when you're done."

"Yes . . . I'll do that."

"The neighborhood is getting some unsavory characters." She pushed open the screen door. "Bye-bye, then."

"Yes . . . bye . . . bye."

The door slapped shut and she was gone.

Lisa turned back to the table and once again blinked.

Fifteen

"Amy . . ." His mouth barely moved. "I'm . . . sorry."

"Uncle Charlie. It's me, it's Jaz."

But the way he looked at her without seeing, she doubted he even heard.

"I . . . should have—" He coughed, wincing in pain.

The blue-white glow from her iPod display went out. She repressed it and brought it closer to his face so she could keep reading his lips.

". . . sorry . . . sweetheart."

"Uncle Charlie, can't you hear me?" Her voice cracked. "Uncle Charlie, it's Jaz."

He remained lying on the floor at her knees, his nose caked in blood. So was one of his ears. She wanted to wipe it off, but they didn't have water. They hadn't for most of the day. The only way they got some was when they went to the bathroom. And that was majorly embarrassing since it required help, 'cause her hands and feet were both tied with those stupid garbage bag fasteners.

She wasn't sure how long they'd been there, she'd lost track of time. But she knew one thing. She was totally to blame. She was the one who ignored what he said. She was the one who trusted the cop at the airport. She was the reason they were thrown onto the floor of a Mercedes with tape over their eyes and mouths and dragged up here for the beatings.

For some reason, they hadn't touched her, just him. She figured they were trying to make her talk about the Program by making her watch. And she would have. The way they hit him she would have told them everything, except she didn't know anything—at least not the stuff they wanted. But no matter how much she pleaded and cried, they wouldn't believe her.

His lips moved again. "Amy . . ." Sometimes she could make out the words, sometimes she couldn't. But it didn't stop the tears from streaming down her face.

"Amy was your daughter, Uncle Charlie."

". . . I should have . . ."

"No . . ." Her nose dripped and she choked out the words. "It was me, it was my fault."

"Don't cry, Amy . . ."

"I'm not Amy! I'm your niece! I'm Jazmin!"

His eyes were red and puffy from tears. Maybe she was getting through, maybe she wasn't. Again her iPod went out and again she pressed the light.

He began sobbing. ". . . so . . . sorry . . ."

The sight of the big man bawling swelled her heart to breaking.

"Forgive me . . ." His lips barely moved. ". . . forgive . . ." Until they stopped altogether.

"Uncle Charlie?" She shook him. "Uncle Charlie!"

He gave no answer. She cried harder, her whole body trembling until light from the hallway spilled in. She spun around to see the silhouette of a man standing in the doorway. Time for another beating. He stood several seconds, the darkness making it impossible to see if he was speaking.

"If you're talking to me," she croaked, "I can't hear."

The man shifted, then entered the room.

Instinctively, she pulled back.

He continued his approach and she continued scooting away until she was against the wall. He stood over her a moment, then kneeled down. She stared at his mouth, straining to read his words until his face exploded in the brightness of a flashlight.

"Hello, Jazmin."

She instantly recognized him. "You're the guy from California! Where are my parents?"

He grimaced at her volume and threw a glance over his shoulder. This plus the fact he hadn't turned on the overhead bulb told her he didn't want people to know he was there.

"Where are my parents?" she demanded.

"How did you know they were here?"

Her heart skipped. "*Here?* They're *here?*"

"I mean in Cairo. How did you know they are in Cairo?"

"Where are they? Where are my mom and dad?"

The man motioned her to speak softer. "You saved my life in the lab."

"Uncle Charlie was going to shoot you."

"Yes, and now look at him."

"Where are my parents?"

"Listen to me, this is very important—"

"Where are my—"

"Is there anything you know that you haven't told us?"

"I'm not saying another word till I see my mom and dad." If she could move them, she would have crossed her arms.

"You do not understand. These men play very, very rough."

"Really?" She nodded to Charlie, making sure her voice dripped in sarcasm. "I hadn't noticed."

The man pursed his lips in patience. "If you could tell me anything, it would go easier on him and you—"

"I want to see my—"

"And your parents."

Jaz set her jaw.

"The Program, that's all they need. If you would simply—"

"What do you care? It's not the voice of God anyway."

"What?"

"That's what I've been telling them, but nobody's listening." It was a tiny fib but worth a try.

"What do you mean?"

She snorted in contempt.

"What do you mean?"

"I mean what I've been saying about Moses. About the Ten Commandments. There's nothing on the mountain or anywhere near it that has any of God's voiceprint on it. Nothing."

"You are lying."

"Right," she scorned. "It's in all the files you guys stole . . . if you'd ever bother reading them."

He looked at her, still not buying it.

"Fine, don't believe me. See what I care."

He hesitated. "You are telling me the Program shows no sign of God's voice when he spoke to Moses on the holy mountain?"

"Zip, nada. Mount Sinai's got nothing."

"Mount Sinai? You said, 'Mount Sinai'?"

"What, are *you* going deaf now?"

"God did not speak to Moses on Mount Sinai."

"Yeah, right."

"It is a fact."

Jazmin frowned.

He shook his head. "According to our texts, Allah spoke to Moses on Jabal al-Lawz."

"What? Where's that?"

"A mountain in Saudi Arabia, across from the Strait of Tiran."

"That's crazy."

He said nothing, but remained kneeling beside her, thinking.

"Are you going to let me see my parents?"

More silence.

"*Excuse me?*"

"There is nothing more about the Program than you are telling us?"

With a heavy sigh, she looked away, making it clear their little talk was over. If he wasn't going to cooperate, neither was she.

He waited for her to turn back. But he could wait till the cows came home 'cause she wasn't saying another word.

He reached to her. She recoiled, huddling against the wall. He stopped and waited. She waited longer. Again he reached toward her. But instead of touching her, he held his wristwatch in front of her face. Reluctantly, she glanced at it.

It read: 2:14.

He was talking again. Curiosity got the better of her and she looked to his lips: ". . . call to prayer will be sunrise, around 5:00 a.m." He held out three fingers. "That gives you three hours."

She was dying to ask, "Three hours for what?" but she was not about to give him the satisfaction until, suddenly, he pulled out a knife. She gasped and tried scooting away. He grabbed her feet. She tried kicking free but he was too strong. He threw himself on top of her legs. She twisted and squirmed until he sliced through the plastic tie around her ankles.

With the extra mobility, she kicked him hard and scrambled toward the opposite corner.

He came after her.

He kneeled down and grabbed her shoulders. He tried to make her listen, but she would not. His hands slid down her arms. She kicked and squirmed until he again threw himself on top of her. She was about to scream at the top of her lungs when suddenly, with one flick of the knife, the tie around her wrists was cut.

She looked up, startled, confused.

Without a word he rose and moved to Uncle Charlie. He kneeled and began talking to him, words she could not see, words she wondered if Charlie even understood.

Once again the blade of the knife flashed. This time it cut the tie around Charlie's ankles, then around his wrists.

The man rose and walked to the door. He turned and held out three fingers, saying something she couldn't read in the shadows. Then he turned and walked out the door . . . careful to leave it open just a crack.

More than ever, Lisa wished she hadn't cheated her way through physics . . . and chemistry . . . and trig. But she had been the prettiest girl in her dorm back at college, and there were all those geeks more than willing to help. She raked her hand through her hair, looked at the typed file, and tried reading it for the third time. And for the third time she failed. She pushed it aside and reached into the box for the next one. By now she'd grown accustomed to the choking odors of the strip motel just off Highway 99. She'd asked for a non-smoking room and by the smell of things, she figured she was the first to introduce it to its new, healthier lifestyle.

Of course she could have stayed with her brother and his family, but she definitely didn't need the extra questions . . . or emotions. If she played it smart, he'd never know she'd been in the area.

Like the last two folders, the one in her hands had *DOD: Classified Information* clearly stenciled across it. And, like the last two, she opened it with a certain amount of guilt . . . and curiosity. She dumped the contents onto the desk and was relieved to see there were no more reams of paper with single-spaced notes. Instead, there were a half-dozen DVDs, hand-labeled with a black felt pen . . . *Plants, Rodents, Arizona Test Site, Birds, Primates, Pacific Test Site.*

She fired up her laptop and popped in the one labeled *Rodents.* Once it was loaded, she read six chapter listings:

Rats—125–300 grams	Mice –18–30 grams
Rats—325–500 grams	Mice—35–40 grams
Rats—525–600 grams	Mice—45–60 grams

She chose *Rats—325–500 grams*, hit Play, and leaned forward to watch.

Four or five were grooming and milling about in a large laboratory cage. At the bottom of the frame a digital clock ticked off the seconds.

At 00:00:06 the creatures became agitated. They darted around the cage, back and forth, crawling over one another. Some tossed their heads, shaking them from side to side. One or two rose on their hind legs, baring their teeth, then falling, then rising, then falling again. Soon, they had all dropped to their sides—their bodies jerking, their feet kicking. One opened its mouth and bit into its own belly, ripping out chunks of white fur, then bloody tissue. Others followed, their pink and black snouts becoming red in blood and flesh—intestines stringing from their mouths, hanging between gnashing teeth . . . until they slowed to a stop. Except for an occasional twitch, there was no more movement. The cage was filled with only fur and blood and lifeless carcasses.

She glanced to the digital display. To her surprise it read only:

00:00:21

It wasn't so hard getting Uncle Charlie to stand or even helping him down the stairs. And though his mind was really messed up, his feet and legs were, like, on autopilot or something. 'Course, it was pretty dark and the way the wooden steps shifted under their weight, Jaz figured they were making enough noise to wake the dead. Or the living. But somehow they made it to the bottom and outside without a problem.

The night air smelled of warm dust and old urine. A beggar slept curled up next to the door, using his sandals as a pillow. Other than that, the city street, actually a dirt road, was deserted.

But now what? Where was she supposed to go? What was she supposed to do?

A donkey pulling a wooden cart on rubber tires appeared around the corner. She pressed Uncle Charlie against the wall and into the shadows. The driver, who seemed more asleep than awake, pulled up and came to a stop directly in front of them. She glanced about, unsure whether to ignore him or bolt.

He crawled off the cart's seat and hobbled toward them.

She stiffened and looked to Charlie who eyed him suspiciously. But the little man seemed unconcerned. Instead, he moved to Charlie's opposite side and slipped his shoulder under his arm.

"No," Jaz said. "That's okay, we're good."

The little fellow tapped his chest and said something she didn't catch. Then he pointed up.

She shook her head. "Sorry, I don't—"

Again he tapped his chest. He was pointing to a big, old-fashioned cross hanging around his neck. It looked pretty expensive, maybe even with jewels, though they were probably fake.

He spoke again and this time she got it. One word: "Brother."

He pointed to Charlie and then to himself and then to Charlie again. Satisfied that he'd made his point, he shifted Charlie's weight onto his shoulders and started for the cart.

Of course Uncle Charlie resisted.

"Brother," the little guy insisted. Again he pointed to heaven then back to his cross. "Brother."

Jaz still wasn't a hundred percent sure what was happening.

Neither was Charlie.

"Brother." More tapping. "Brother. Brother."

Finally, more in exhaustion than agreement, Charlie allowed himself to be moved. Jaz stayed on his other side as they approached the back of the cart. It had all sorts of junk—old tires, a bicycle frame, a broken-down sofa, a couple computer monitors. Mostly, though, it was full of produce . . . rotting cabbage, tomatoes, and smashed oranges that were growing blue-green mold.

"No way," Jaz balked, "forget it."

But Charlie wasn't so picky. He motioned for them to continue. They helped him up and into the back. He sat in the only empty spot. The little man motioned for Jaz to follow.

"No thanks, I'll walk."

"Brothers," he insisted, pointing to the three of them. Then, shaking his head, he motioned to the street and buildings surrounding them. "*Not* brothers."

Jaz glanced about nervously, then looked back to the cart, then to the little man. He gave an embarrassed shrug and offered his hand to help. Finally, with a sigh loud enough to be understood in any language, she took it and climbed on board.

He motioned for her to sit.

The wood planks were wet and black—from what, she didn't know, probably rotting juice. So, instead of sitting, she chose to squat.

The beggar or priest or whatever he was shrugged again. He produced some gunny sacks and motioned that he needed to cover them.

"*What?*"

"Brothers," the man insisted, again pointing to himself, then motioning to the buildings.

"I know, I know," she muttered, "not brothers."

The man grinned, pleased over their improved communication.

With another sigh and still squatting, Jaz hunkered closer to Charlie and closed her eyes. The man threw the dusty sacks over them and adjusted the material until there was absolutely no chance of getting fresh air. By the time he crossed around to the front and climbed on board, she was already coughing, itching, and regretting her decision.

She regretted it more when the cart lurched forward and she fell backward into a slimy pile of produce.

Lisa stared at the monitor. The image was split four ways. The top left quarter showed a flat-bottom barge with living trees, shrubs, and a large mound of boulders. It floated in what looked like a lake or ocean. Around it, equally spaced, a dozen buoys floated with vertical shafts rising up from them. The other three sections of the screen were closer angles of the barge. They showed a patch of tropical trees and shrubs, a small beach, and a stream that trickled down the face of the boulders into a pond. And, in each of these three closer shots a small colony of chimpanzees could be seen. Lisa spotted two babies, one being nursed by its mother, the other playing nearby. She counted four adults—eating, grooming, and sleeping.

With a certain dread, she reached for the computer, hesitated, then clicked Play.

The digital counter began. For the first several seconds the animals showed no reaction. But, as with the rats, they quickly became agitated. Some started to stagger. Another lifted its hands to cover its ears. Another threw back its head and opened its mouth in what could only be a scream.

The babies took it the worst, squirming, curling into fetal positions, thrashing back and forth. Next came the falling . . . babies and adults. Then the struggle to get back up, then more falling. Two began to convulse. The attacks began within thirty seconds . . . first against each other and then against themselves—pulling out fistfuls of hair, clawing at their faces, one digging at its eyes. The nursing mother snarled into the screaming face of her infant, then violently twisted its head. Lisa could practically hear the neck snap. Instead of sorrow, the mother began thumping the baby's body against the nearest tree. Until she stopped and began feeding upon it.

Nauseated, Lisa nearly punched Stop until something caught her eye. Not the chimps, but the landscape.

At first she thought the DVD was glitching. But no, the trees and bushes seemed to be shifting, melting. She looked to the top left screen, the long shot of the barge. Water between the vessel and buoys suddenly began splashing with life. It rippled white with thousands of fish, even a pod of dolphins. But like the vegetation on the barge, they were changing. A marlin leaped from the water, its shiny scales suddenly fluorescent red, then sprouting giant, feathered wings, as it twisted and dove back into the roiling, living ocean.

Lisa looked back to the chimps. They were nearly indistinguishable from the vegetation, if you could call it vegetation. Because, at the center, everything was melting into a glowing mass of white. Liquid and yet light. Until, one by one, the images from each of the three cameras shorted out and went dark.

Only the distant shot of the barge remained . . . as the white liquid-light spread from its center, rippling out to the edges of the vessel. But not just ripples of light. The boulders were melting and rippling as well. So were the trees, then the very hull. But it didn't stop there. The waves continued to spread beyond the barge. They entered the ocean, changing it first into bright light and then, somehow, dimming and becoming land. Glowing, undulating land that continued to spread. The waves of earth stacking upon one another, rising into hills, then mountains . . . complete with forests.

Finally, the first wave hit the camera, throwing it into the air. There was a brief glimpse of a lightning-filled sky, then everything went dark.

Lisa wasn't sure how long she sat staring. But when her cell rang she practically leaped from her seat. She fumbled in her coat pocket and pulled out the phone. She checked the number, but didn't recognize it. Flipping it open she answered hoarsely. "Yes?"

"Lisa?"

She instantly recognized the voice. "Bern—"

"Don't say anything."

"Wh—"

"Just get home. As fast as you can. But not your place. Don't go back to your apartment, do you understand me?"

"Yes, but—"

"We have to meet."

"Where? What's going—"

"It's time for a little 'come to Jesus' meeting."

"*What?*"

"It's time for a little 'coming to Jesus.'"

And then the line went dead.

Sixteen

Jaz wasn't sure how long she'd been asleep. She knew it was night, she just wasn't sure which one—the night they arrived at the beggar's hut? The next one? Well, whatever time had passed, the rotting produce and acrid smoke of burning garbage were no better. Like the hundreds, maybe thousands of garbage people, the old guy lived right in the middle of the city's mountain-high, smoldering dump. And, like the others, he seemed to make his living by salvaging from the streets at night and the dump by day.

She rolled over on her cardboard mat and saw Uncle Charlie awake. Not only awake, but sitting against a wooden crate talking to the old man.

"Unc . . ." Her voice was so dry she coughed on the words. "Uncle Charlie?"

He looked up. He still wasn't in great shape, but he seemed more together than before. The beggar gave her a nod and rose, ambling across the dirt floor.

"What's . . . going on?" she asked Charlie. "Are you okay?"

Of course the guy suffered from his usual stunted emotions so, instead of answering, he cut to the chase. "We're going back to get your mother."

She struggled to sit up. "My mother? You know where she is?"

"She was downstairs. I heard her calling to you."

"You . . ." Her throat grew tight. "Mom was there? You heard her?"

He nodded.

The news was too good to be true. "And Dad?"

He said nothing, holding her with those steel gray eyes of his.

"And Dad? He's okay too?"

He gave no answer.

Panic stirred. "My dad? Uncle Charlie? My dad's okay too, right? Right?"

His gaze faltered. He looked away, then down to the paper in front of him.

"No . . ." Hot tears burst into her eyes. "He's okay too!" It grew difficult to breathe. "*Right?*" Another gasp. "*Right? He's okay too! Right?*"

The beggar arrived, squatting down with a leather pouch of water. The look on his face said it all.

"No!" She clenched her eyes. "No!" She shook her head from side to side. "*No . . . No . . . Nooo . . .*"

⊭ ⊭ ⊭

"That's just it, I'm not sure." Bernie spoke in hushed tones, either in reverence to the dimly lit sanctuary, or in fear of being heard—by who, Lisa had no idea, since there was nobody present. "Someone's making the Bureau jump through hoops, but no one knows who it is. Somebody high up, though. Real high."

Lisa tried to recap. "So the Jews want the Program 'cause they're touchy about not having the market cornered on God?"

Bernice nodded. "The Muslims aren't crazy about Jesus Christ being God."

"And the West . . ."

"Just wants to play God."

Lisa shook her head. "What I saw was total destruction. No way can something like that be controlled."

"For now. But I suspect once they get their hands on the Program and work out the kinks, they'll figure a way."

" 'They'?"

"That's the billion-dollar question."

Lisa sighed wearily. The red, blue, and yellow lights from the stained-glass window dappled their faces and the pews surrounding them. She was not fond of such places. But Bernie's coded invitation could not have been clearer. Just three years earlier, at Bernie's insistent nagging, the two had visited this church—Bernie no doubt hoping to "get her saved and washed in the blood of the Lamb."

But God had shown little interest in saving Lisa from her daddy as a child, and she showed little interest in trusting him to save her soul as an adult.

Bernice leaned forward. "This is serious stuff, kiddo. You're on the radar screen—you've seen the files."

"How do they know? How did you know?"

"His sister called and complained. Said you forgot to lock the door."

Lisa dropped her head and shook it.

"You sure there was no Program there?"

"Nothing." Lisa looked back up. "So what am I supposed to do, just hide out in a cave somewhere?"

"That would be my recommendation . . . but of course you won't do it."

"What would I do?"

Bernie just looked at her.

"What about Charles Madison?" Lisa asked. "His niece?"

"They're in Cairo."

"*Egypt?*"

Bernie nodded.

"Trying to rescue the parents?"

"The mother. The father is dead."

Lisa swore, then instinctively threw a guilty look up to the cross. Turning back to Bernie, she asked, "Where abouts in Cairo?"

The woman shook her head. "NSA just knows they're in hiding. But once they resurface . . ." She took a deep breath and let it out. "Well, I'm sure their help will no longer be needed."

"They'll be killed." It was more statement than question.

"They'll be a liability, not a benefit." More softly, she added, "Just like you."

"Have you tried contacting them? Warning them?"

Bernie said nothing.

"They're innocent civilians . . . one's a kid!"

"Even if we could contact them, why would they believe us? We haven't exactly proved to be their allies."

"The girl would believe me."

Bernie gave her a skeptical look.

"She did before. If I could just get to her."

"How?"

"I don't know. E-mail's too risky now. I'd have to speak to her, personally, face-to-face."

"What, you're going to fly off to Egypt now?"

"I could. The Bureau's got contacts."

"At this moment you're not exactly on the dean's honor list."

"*You've* got contacts."

Bernice hesitated, then countered, "You hate flying, remember?"

Lisa ignored her. "I'm serious. It's not like my services are needed here. Or wanted."

Bernie said nothing.

"It's better than hiding in some cave. And if the Program is still out there, maybe I could help. You said the Swiss guy was still alive?"

"I said they hadn't found his body."

"So, maybe I—"

"Even if you could sneak out of the country and steal over there, what would you do?"

"I'd . . . improvise. Cross the bridges when I get to them. I'm good at that. You know I'm good."

The woman looked at Lisa a long moment. Then, with a tired sigh, she reached into her handbag and produced a black diplomatic passport.

"What's this?"

She handed it to her. "You know what it is."

Lisa stared speechless. She opened the cover. Inside was a picture of herself, but with an entirely different name.

"Make sure you memorize the information in it," Bernice said.

Lisa looked up, stunned, but Bernie was already reaching into her bag and pulling out two more passports, standard issue this time.

"I'm sure your buddies have probably lost theirs by now."

Lisa took them into her hands. She could only ask hoarsely, "Why . . . why are you doing this?"

"There's only three things I love in this evil world . . . my friends, my God, and the Bureau. And right now, somebody's messin' with all three."

Lisa felt her eyes begin to burn.

"And if that Program is the real deal, if they really have the voiceprint of the Lord God Almighty . . . then *those fools* got no idea what they're dealin' with."

Seventeen

Charlie stooped and checked the grill of the hibachi, then the coals. They were warm, but most likely from the sun's heat. He turned and, remaining low, moved across the roof to check behind the blankets hanging on the clothesline. Then to the water tank in the corner.

All clear.

It had been easy to enter the adjacent building, steal up the stairs to the roof, and hop over the eighteen inches that separated them. Of course every movement brought accompanying pain—he guessed at least one cracked rib and a sprained, maybe broken wrist—but training taught him to ignore these things. For the most part, he was successful.

He scanned the other roofs, looking for activity, anybody who might sound an alarm. But the heat of the day had driven everyone inside. Originally, he wanted to strike later tonight, but every second they held his sister captive was a second closer to losing her. So he decided upon now, mid-afternoon, when everyone was fat and lazy and hopefully asleep.

Silently, without so much as a scrape of a shoe, he moved to the front of the building. Below and across the street, the old beggar busied himself with his donkey and cart. Charlie had no idea who the man was or how he'd come to know they needed his help. But he'd proved invaluable in giving them a place to stay and in securing supplies for the operation.

Sensing his presence, the old-timer looked up to Charlie and nodded. Charlie returned it then dropped lower to watch. The man produced a small lighter and lit the pile of wadded newspapers in the back of his cart. The flame was barely visible in the bright sunlight as he moved to his donkey and calmly led it across the street to the entrance of the building.

Satisfied, Charlie scurried across the roof to the stairway. The metal door creaked as he opened it and stepped into the darkness. Once his eyes adjusted, he started down the uneven, wooden steps. He wasn't sure if Katie was still on the first floor where he heard her cries before he lost consciousness, or if they moved her to the second. He guessed the second, since they'd want her farther from the street should he be foolish enough to attempt a rescue.

He arrived at the landing of the second floor. There were only two doors. The one to his left led to the bathroom, a rotting hole in the floor accompanied by a rust-stained sink. The other led to the room he'd been tortured in.

He paused to listen. There was no sound outside. He frowned. Maybe the cart hadn't ignited. No, that was impossible. He'd soaked the rags in the diesel himself, still smelled it on his hands. But it should have started by now, he needed the distraction.

He heard a downstairs door open, the squeaking of wood as someone started up the steps. He couldn't risk entering the room to his right, not without the diversion, so he backed into the bathroom door, quietly opening it and slipping inside. The smell was rank, but it made little difference. He barely breathed as he prepared for the approaching footsteps.

He heard voices outside the building. The cart had finally caught fire.

Using his good hand, he reached into his waistband and pulled out the steak knife he'd stolen from a café earlier this morning.

The footsteps arrived and a balding man pushed open the bathroom door. He hardly looked up before Charlie plunged the blade deep into his windpipe just below the larynx, making it impossible for him to scream. His breath came out in wheezing gasps as the knife expertly sliced through his trachea and into the carotid artery. The man's eyes widened, his hands gripping his throat to stop the pain.

But the pain would not last.

He continued gasping and wheezing as Charlie pulled him farther into the tiny room—the kicking and thrashing drowned out by shouts from the street.

The killer had returned. The door to the cage had been opened. But not in some wild and savage rush of emotion. This was more frightening. Cold, calculating, methodical. Charlie Madison leaned against the wall and took a breath, slowing his heart, preparing for the next move.

⚡ ⚡ ⚡

Jaz turned to the cart across the street and watched the flames leaping eight, ten feet high. Of course it was just like Uncle Charlie had said—everyone running around, yelling their heads off, and basically going nuts. But she had no time to watch. Instead, she turned and quickly hid the last of the one-liter bottles of Diet Coke. Most were behind posts, inside doorways, or in the piles of rubbish along the street.

When she finished, she walked quickly to her assigned position near the center of the fifty-plus bottles she'd hidden. She glanced to her left to see the old man standing near the middle of the fifty he'd placed.

Earlier, she'd insisted on being part of the rescue. Of course Charlie had refused with the usual excuses of it being too dangerous, and blah, blah, blah. But one of her best talents was talking, and she eventually wore him down. A good thing too. With this plan he needed her help, whether he liked it or not.

All night she'd been preparing the bottles they'd stolen from a truck the day before. She uncapped them, poured out a third of the Coke from each, then carefully taped two candies called Mentos on the inside of each cap before re-sealing them. The only problem came when one of the candies slipped from the cap after she'd closed it. It fell into the soda and, man oh man, did that thing fizz! Uncle Charlie barely had time to get it unscrewed (drenching himself in Diet Coke) so the bottle wouldn't explode.

She looked back to the beggar who was obviously counting, waiting, as the cart across the street continued to burn and the people continued to shout. She could barely stand the suspense and thought *she'd* explode, until he finally turned to her and nodded.

She went to work. Systematically, she raced to each of her fifty bottles, kicking them over, immersing the candy in the soda. A quick glance to the old man said he was doing the same with his fifty. Of course, no one paid attention, what with the flaming cart and all the screaming and everything. But they would. In just a few moments everyone would.

ᴧ ᴧ ᴧ

Charlie stepped over the body and slung down the children's Snoopy backpack he'd scored from the dump. He pulled out a canning jar, yet another courtesy of the garbage mountain. It was sealed with tape and contained the only thing they

Bill Myers

170

had purchased, three dozen Ping-Pong balls, crushed and tightly packed. A diesel-soaked rag stuck out through the tape. He produced a yellow Bic lighter and faced the opposite door. Clicking the lighter, he held the flame to the rag until it caught. Then, gritting his teeth against the pain, he leaned back, raised his foot, and kicked the door. As it flew open, he tossed the jar inside, making sure the arc was high enough to shatter the glass.

He spun around and flattened against the doorway as the jar exploded—though *exploded* wasn't the right term as it mostly flashed—the phosphorus of the Ping-Pong balls as blinding as any flash-grenade . . . and just as debilitating.

He stormed the room, scooting along the right wall . . . as the guard, armed with an AK-47, struggled to regain his sight.

The hostage, he could not think of her as his sister now, lay on the ground to his right, asleep or unconscious.

Unable to see, the guard aimed his rifle at the open door, but of course Charlie was no longer there. Leading with the steak knife, Charlie lunged at the man. The guard didn't know what hit him as the blade slipped easily between his ribs and hopefully into his heart. But the knife was cheap and when the man spun, the blade snapped from its plastic handle. Still, the metal did its damage. He dropped to his knees clawing at the broken knife, gasping through a perforated lung which quickly filled with blood . . . until he fell forward.

A shout from the door turned Charlie to see a kid coming at him—sixteen, eighteen, tops. In his hand was a much more sophisticated blade—an eight-inch, serrated hunting knife. Charlie reached over to the window and ripped down the blanket that had been hanging across it. He flipped the material around his good arm, as the kid leaped at him. He deflected the blow, the knife cutting only blanket. As the boy turned back, Charlie whipped the material around his arm two more times, crouching, ready for the next attack.

The room shook with an explosion. Then another. The cans of diesel in front of the beggar's cart had finally begun igniting.

But the kid was not distracted. Again he lunged and again Charlie was able to deflect the knife and spin out of the way.

More circling. Another lunge, another dodge.

Charlie was beside the window again. He threw back his elbow, busting out the cheap glass. Most of the pieces fell to the street and chaos below, although a couple hit the sill and tumbled inside. One was big enough to use. He scooped up the shard with his bad hand while unwrapping two turns of the blanket from his arm. He slipped the extra material between his bare palm and the glass. Though it protected his hand, the blanket connected his two arms, severely limiting his movement. But it would have to do.

The kid shouted for help, but of course no one heard over the commotion outside. Again he lunged and again Charlie countered, twisting out of the way. Charlie tried using the glass but the limitation of the blanket and the pain in his wrist were too great. So was the exhaustion quickly setting in.

The kid saw it, leered, then attacked again.

This time Charlie dropped the shard and used his blanket as a net, entangling the kid's hand. He yanked hard and the knife clattered to the floor. But the young man was strong. He tore the blanket from Charlie's weak hand and spun behind him, wrapping it around Charlie's neck.

Charlie slipped his hand under the material so he could breathe. For the most part he failed. They dropped to the floor, the kid tightening the blanket with every move. Now it was just a matter of time before Charlie ran out of air and passed out. Until he spotted the reflection . . .

Swept up in the corner with other debris was Jazmin's iPod and earbuds.

He squirmed and kicked across the floor toward them. Though his strength was fading, he made enough progress to lunge and grab them. Unfortunately, this allowed the kid to yank the blanket tighter.

Holding the buds and attached iPod, Charlie threw back his arms once, twice, before he managed to get the wires around the back of the kid's neck. He pulled, praying they would be strong enough.

The startled youth tried to remove them, giving Charlie a moment's advantage. He twisted in the blanket to face the kid, while whipping the cord around the boy's throat. Now he had a garrote. The two faced each other like dancers. They kicked and rolled across the floor, the kid cutting off Charlie's air with the softer, unwieldy blanket . . . Charlie, strangling him with the harder, sharper cord.

But Charlie's strength had left. He could not get enough air and his head grew light. His vision filled with white, darting flecks. Still, he saw enough of the kid's purple face and bulging eyes to know if he could hang on a few more seconds, if he could just keep conscious and tighten the cord another millimeter . . .

The blanket loosened. Charlie took a gasping breath, and then another, all the time tightening the cord. His vision cleared as he saw the youth's jaw slacken, his tongue loll out, his bulging eyes grow lifeless.

Outside, he heard a series of mini explosions, loud "pops" like gunfire. The Mentos and Diet Coke had begun their work. As planned, people began shouting, panicking. Any who had raced out onto the street were now running for cover. The coast would be clear for Charlie to carry the hostage outside and vacate the area.

But he would have just over a minute.

Yanking away the iPod, he untangled himself from the blanket and rolled to his knees. He took another gulp of air as he scrambled toward his sister.

"Katie . . . can you hear me?"

Her hair was disheveled and face beaten. But her lips began to move.

"Katie!"

The outside bottles exploded faster.

Taking another breath and refusing the pain, Charlie lifted her and threw her over his shoulder. He struggled to rise until his legs collapsed under the weight. But this was his sister. He would get her out, an atonement for Brenda and Amy. Shouting with everything he had, he rose back to his feet and staggered toward the door.

There was another burst of gunfire. Louder. Inside the room. So powerful, the impact knocked him off his feet. He turned and saw the first guard, still sprawled on the floor, as the rifle tumbled from his hands. He had used the last breath of his life to take a life.

But not Charlie's. He felt no additional pain. He looked down and saw no holes.

Panic seized him. He turned to his sister on the floor beside him. The left side of her head was missing.

"No!" He pulled her into his arms. "KATIE, DON'T!" He buried his face into her neck—hot tears mixing with warm blood. "No! . . . KATIE!" His body convulsed. And again. He couldn't catch his breath. "Katie . . . no . . . Katie, Katie, Katie . . ."

But it wasn't just Katie. How long he held her, sobbing

over his sister, his wife, his daughter, he didn't know. He didn't see the beggar arrive. Didn't know he was there until the old man tugged on his arm, urging him to come.

Charlie shook his head. What difference did it make?

But the man was relentless, continuing to pull, insisting they must hurry, that they only had seconds.

It didn't matter. Not now. Charlie had failed. *Again.* There was no need for him to continue, no need to go on. Let them kill him. What difference did it make now that—

"Jazmin . . ." The beggar's voice was thick and filled with emotion.

Charlie turned to him.

The old man nodded and pulled, indicating the time. They had to leave now. "Jazmin. Jazmin."

Charlie wiped his face, took a shaking, uneven breath.

Again the beggar motioned. "Jazmin . . ."

Until, at last, he found the strength and, more important, the will to move.

The Voice

Eighteen

"I hate you!"

"Jaz—"

"I hate you, I hate you!" She beat his chest, his shoulders ... wherever her small fists could land. "I hate you! I hate you! I—"

"Jaz!"

"—hate—"

"Jazmin!" He grabbed her arms. Her eyes were swollen, her face wet with tears.

"You screwed up!" Her scream filled the beggar's hut.

"I know."

"I trusted you and"—she took a trembling breath—"I trusted ..." A heaving sob followed. "And you—"

He pulled her into his arms. "I know." His own eyes filled with tears. "I know ..."

She clung to him, shuddering, sobbing. Until suddenly she pushed him away. "NOOO ..." The cry was more animal than human. "YOU KILLED HER!"

He looked at her but could not respond.

She came at him again, arms and fists flying. "YOU KILLED HER!" This time he did not stop her. He simply lowered his head and took the beating, blow after blow. "YOU KILLED THEM ALL!" She continued to scream and beat and wail. "YOU KILL EVERYBODY! EVERYBODY YOU TOUCH! YOU KILL EVERYBODY!!"

Lisa had seen every movie the plane had to offer—another perk of being a single woman on the L.A. scene whose limited income was equal only to her limited social life. Nevertheless, she kept the earphones in and the screen lit—better predictable comedies and superheroes in tights than to acknowledge she was actually flying. The very thought of it put a permanent sheen of sweat over her body.

Unfortunately, there were even larger concerns . . .

What was she doing?

The official answer, of course, was she was heading to Egypt on U.S. Government business. And it was true. The fact the business wasn't exactly sanctioned by the U.S. Government seemed a trifling detail . . . though another reason to keep the movies blasting and the gin and tonic coming.

But there were other reasons, which she could easily name, of equal importance . . .

A precocious deaf girl who had suddenly been orphaned and who everybody in the world was trying to hurt.

A damaged-goods uncle, whose tough facade was betrayed only by a willingness to sacrifice everything for a child he didn't even know. Whatever you said about Charles Madison, he had guts . . . and heart. More than any man she'd met—which kept her staring at the ceiling unable to sleep more nights than she cared to admit.

But there was something else. An ever-present irony lurking just below the surface . . .

Here she was, the one person who had every right to hate God, and yet she had somehow been thrown into a position of protecting him, or at least protecting his power. A power that could create an entire world or, if misused, ruin it. What ate at her was that it was the very same power, misused by another man, that had ruined her. It was a vague, confusing thought and though she sensed a certain logic, she couldn't fully grasp it. More importantly, she couldn't seem to ignore it.

With or without the movies and booze.

"What's the big rush?" Jaz demanded.

The old beggar said nothing but kept motioning for them to hurry down the crowded sidewalk.

She turned to her uncle and demanded, "Why's he making such a big deal?"

Charlie shook his head and glanced away. That's about all their communication amounted to these days. And that was fine with her. Except—and this was what made her mad— it's like he felt as bad about losing her mom as she did. And that was unfair. *Majorly* unfair. It was *her* mom who died. Not his! *Hers! And* her dad! *She* was the one who lost her parents. Not him!

Again, the old-timer motioned for them to hurry.

"All right, all right." Jaz blew the hair out of her eyes and picked up her pace.

The little guy was one strange dude. When they first met him, he couldn't wait to get them to his place and help out. But now that everything went wrong, it's like he couldn't get rid of them fast enough. It was barely morning, before he'd shaken them awake and started jabbering about some cousin who had a hotel in the city. What's with that? Like he couldn't tell them earlier, back when they were sleeping on the floor and hiding under the blankets from killer flies and mosquitoes? And let's not forget those wonderful meals of gruel or whatever it was he fixed. Seriously, the stuff made her gag. Not that she was much in the mood for eating—which was okay, 'cause the way her jeans fit, she figured she'd lost a good three, maybe even four pounds.

"Here . . ." The old man motioned them to stop in front of a tiny, two-story building. "You wait here."

Jaz blew more hair out of her eyes as he entered the building. It was over a hundred degrees and not even noon. The Nile River was just across the street—not that you could see it with all the cars and buses and people. The place was a major zoo, in some ways as dirty as the dump. The only difference was the air. Instead of flies and rotting garbage, it was full of flies and diesel fumes.

She glanced to Uncle Charlie who was doing his usual staring-at-nothing routine. Beyond him, some guy was riding a camel down the street, an honest to goodness camel! Just loping along between racing cars and buses jam-packed with people.

A taxi pulled in front of them and some white chick climbed out. She paid the driver and turned. Only then did Jaz recognize her.

"Lisa?"

She didn't hear.

"LISA!" Jaz ran toward her.

The woman looked up, her eyes widening like saucers. "Jaz?" She barely had time to drop her bags before Jaz threw herself into her arms and started crying. Talk about weird.

Weirder still, she couldn't seem to stop.

⚐ ⚐ ⚐

Lisa waited until they checked into the hotel and entered the room before sharing the news. When she did, Jaz leaped to her feet.

"Uncle Fredrick is alive?"

Lisa nodded. "We think so, yes." Throughout the flight she debated whether or not to tell her. The last thing the child needed was to get her hopes up again only to have them dashed . . . again. Still, some hope was better than none.

It had been nearly an hour since she'd arrived, and for that hour they'd been filling each other in on every detail. Well, Jaz and Lisa had been filling each other in. Charlie was more silent than ever. She knew most of it had to do with the killing of his sister—though she suspected he was also chewing on their recent run-in with the desk clerk/owner downstairs . . .

"What do you mean, no one came in before us?" he had demanded.

The owner, a pleasant man with a gold tooth, smiled politely. "It is a sad fact, but your family has been the only ones to have entered my lobby all morning."

"That's impossible, we saw him go in. He's your cousin."

The man patiently smoothed his moustache. "I have many cousins. Do you happen to have a name?"

Charlie turned to Jaz who shrugged.

"Well, no," he answered. "I . . . he lives in the dump, on that giant mountain of garbage outside town."

The owner's smile wilted. "I have no cousin living upon the mountain, nor any other relative or acquaintance, that I can assure you."

"But . . . that's impossible."

"I am sorry." Without missing a beat, his smile returned and he continued his greeting. "Checkout time is 11:00 a.m. We have coffee and tea available here in the lobby until 10:00

p.m. If you or your family have any questions, my room is down the hall and . . ."

Lisa doubted Charlie had heard the rest. For the first time since she'd met him, the man seemed distracted. Even more importantly, unsure.

"The whole lab collapsed!" Jaz practically danced between the beds. "How could he live through something like that?"

Lisa chose her words carefully. "All I know is they thoroughly searched the lab and found no trace of his body."

"So there's a major chance he's still alive!"

Lisa wasn't sure how to answer.

Unfortunately, Charlie was. "Either way it's no help to us. The Program is gone."

Lisa turned to him and scowled. He sat in a white, plastic lawn chair, off in the shadows. His voice was so soft she barely heard him over the uneven beating of the ceiling fan.

"We have to make everyone understand that the Program does not exist. That the work on it was bogus, unverifiable."

"What I saw on Reynolds's DVD looked plenty verifiable to me," Lisa argued.

He shook his head. "The Jews, Muslims, DOD, whoever we're dealing with—we have to make them see the research was wrong, that the Program, even if it did exist, was not verifiable."

"Why do you keep saying that?" Jaz demanded. "Mom and Dad worked their whole lives on it! You just can't blow them off by saying it's not real!" Her eyes glistened with moisture. "How can you say that? It's real, it's got to be real!"

Charlie wearily closed his eyes. "Every faith believes God spoke to Moses on Mount Sinai."

"So?"

"So, like you and your priest pal said, the Program doesn't verify that."

"See!" The girl raised her chin. "That's all you know!"

"What don't I know?" he sighed.

"Nothing!"

"What are you saying?" Lisa asked.

"Did it ever dawn on you there might be another Mount Sinai?"

Charlie turned to her.

"No, of course not." She wiped her nose with her hand. "'Cause you're too smart for that, aren't you?"

Lisa touched her arm. "What are you saying?"

"I'm saying there are two Mount Sinais."

"Two?"

She gave another sniff. "That's what the guy was telling me."

"What guy?" Lisa asked.

"The one holding me and him." She turned to Charlie. "The one you practically killed in California."

"He's here?" Lisa asked.

Jaz wiped her face. "He said there's like a whole 'nother Mount Sinai, but it's over in Saudi Arabia."

"Why would he say that?" Charlie asked.

"Maybe 'cause it's true. Maybe 'cause it's what the Muslims believe."

Lisa and Charlie traded looks.

Finally, Charlie shook his head. "I don't care what anybody believes. I have to secure your safety. If that means telling the world that the research is not—"

"Mom and Dad died for that Program! They gave up their lives for it!"

Lisa tried to calm her. "Jazmin . . ."

The girl's voice clogged with emotion. "Now we're supposed to what—just pretend it's all a joke? Tell everybody they were fakes, that nothing they did counted, that none of it's real?"

"Jaz . . ." Lisa reasoned. "Sweetheart, all of their work . . . it was used to create a terrible weapon."

"That's stupid! That Dr. Reynolds guy, he's the one that made it a weapon! Mom and Dad had nothing to do with it!"

"I understand, but—"

"They discovered the voice of God! And the Program proves it's real!"

"Except when it comes to Mount Sinai," Charlie corrected.

"Which isn't even the right place!"

A moment passed, until Lisa, feeling more maternal than she liked, asked, "So what would you have us do?"

"Go there, of course!"

She was taken back. "Go to the other mountain?"

"Duh!"

Charlie gave a scornful snort.

"We could," Jaz insisted. "We could go to the real place and bring back some of those rocks. And then we could test them. And then we could show the whole world that—"

Charlie shook his head. "You're not making sense—"

"It's right next door!"

"Saudi Arabia is not exactly a tourist spot."

Lisa turned to him.

He explained. "The place is a fortress. *Nobody* gets into that country."

"Nobody?"

"Not without an official invitation by the Saudi family, or unless you're some big-wig executive, or dignitary, or—"

"A diplomat?" Lisa interrupted.

He looked to her. "What?"

Without a word, she leaned across the bed and pulled the black passport from her purse.

Charlie stared at it in surprise. "Where did you get that?"

Opening it, she checked the information. "As representative for the great state of Utah, Mary Ann Hargiss received this in Salt Lake City on . . . July 9, 2007."

She looked to Charlie and almost smiled at his surprise. It was the first emotion she'd seen all afternoon. But she had more. She reached into her bag and pulled out two other passports. Flipping open the first, she added, "Which was also the same date one was issued to little"—she squinted to read—"Dominique Kay Hargiss." She tossed the passport to Jaz and opened the other. "And to Mary's beloved husband . . . Robert Spencer Hargiss." She closed it and pitched it to Charlie.

He read the first page for himself as Lisa continued.

"Didn't you wonder why I didn't leave mine at the front desk? Why he didn't even ask for yours?"

He looked up, stunned, and maybe a little embarrassed for not noticing. Finally, he answered, "This is insanity. No one will believe this."

"Immigration did." She motioned downstairs. "So does the owner."

"Until he wonders why a diplomat would stay in a dump like this."

Lisa fidgeted. She'd not thought of that.

Charlie continued. "So you're saying we just drop in and visit our pals in Saudi Arabia?" He closed the passport and tossed it on the bed. "No, thanks. It's too dangerous."

Lisa's anger rose. "Really?"

"Really."

"Let me ask you something."

He looked at her.

"What's more dangerous, slipping into a country and hiding out where the borders are protected and sealed ... or flying back to America where it's open season on all three of us?"

"Saudi Arabia is a fortress," Charlie argued.

"To keep undesirables *out*, not in."

Jaz was confused. "Are you saying we'd be safer there, than back home?"

Lisa nodded. "For now, you bet." Charlie shook his head and she pressed in. "Where do you suggest we go? Stay here? How long were you safe in the airport? Two minutes? And you're right, someone will eventually wonder why a hot-shot diplomat is staying in a place like this."

"There's Europe."

"That worked out real good for you too, didn't it?" She continued. "I suppose Antarctica might be okay, though we may have to accessorize our wardrobes a bit."

"Saudi Arabia is Islamic!"

"Which means we'll at least be safe from the Jews and Americans. Two out of three's not bad. And *no* extremists would expect us to go there. At least not *these* extremists."

Charlie faltered.

She continued taking ground, the plan making more and more sense to her. "I promise you, these documents are the real deal. And if Saudi officials ever run a check, the same person who helped me secure them will make sure they're backed up." She wasn't sure about the last statement, but it sounded good and had the desired effect.

Charlie clenched his jaw.

"Uncle Charlie." Jaz approached. "We have to at least try. For Mom and Dad. For all their work. And if it's really safer there, than—"

"Safer? Pretending we're people we're not? Hiding out in a repressive regime? *I promised your parents I'd look after you* and—"

"My parents are dead!" She continued softer, "Or hadn't you noticed?"

Charlie glanced away, swallowing.

Jaz began to pace, growing more and more determined. "I won't let them die in vain. They wouldn't want that to happen, they wouldn't let it happen! And neither will I." She turned on him. "And neither should you."

Once again she approached. "They believed in what they were doing, Uncle Charlie. They died for it. And if all we have to do is swing by some stupid country next door and pick up some stupid rocks . . ." She took an uneven breath, trying to be strong. And then another.

Charlie looked to Lisa for help.

She raised the passport. "We have full diplomatic immunity. And we really would be safer . . ."

He shifted his weight. She could tell he did not like the way the wheels were turning. More importantly, she saw it was unlikely he could stop them.

Sheldon Houser wasn't sure if it was the emotion of the wedding or the wine at the reception. But as he held his daughter, dancing to some American tune he had never heard, it was all he could do not to weep like an old lady. She was so sophisticated; such grace and poise. When had that happened? It seemed only yesterday they were laughing and grossing each other out by showing chewed-up food in their mouths. And now . . . how regal she was, dancing in the very wedding dress her mother danced in when they were married. He closed his eyes, swallowing back the knot in his throat. How proud Monica would be of her little girl, the gangly teen turned elegant lady.

Opening his eyes, he nodded to some family and friends. There was such a richness of life here. Such living. A man surrounded by those he loves in the land he loves. A land intertwined with his life . . . his past, his present, his future.

He reclosed his eyes, letting his mind swim in emotion, until Hannah whispered, ever so gently, "Okay, Dad."

He nodded, continuing to dance.

"Daddy? It's over."

He opened his eyes.

"The song . . . it's over."

He glanced around and saw the guests staring, smiling. Gathering his dignity, he kissed her on the forehead. She rose on her toes and kissed his cheek. Before another wave of emotion could overtake him, he turned and led her off the dance floor to her husband.

The boy took her hand from his. "Thanks, Poppa."

Houser tried not to wince. It was bad enough she'd fallen for this bespectacled child who had barely recovered from acne, the gawky boy with no immediate future of becoming a man . . . but to think they were now related . . . He fought back the shudder with a smile and headed for the bar.

"Sheldon? Shel?"

He looked up to see big Tom Boyer, a friend from the old days. Tom nodded toward a young woman courier who had just arrived at the entrance of the ballroom. She was surveying the crowd, nervously tapping an envelope in her hand.

Houser swore and started toward her. You'd think this time of all times, they could leave him alone. Yes, he embarrassed them with failed attempts in both America and Switzerland. And, yes, they were making him pay the price with more paperwork than he could possibly imagine. But on his daughter's wedding day?

The courier brightened at his approach. "Mr. Houser."

He grunted.

"My name is—"

He took the envelope and turned it over to unlatch the string and open it. To his surprise the second envelope inside was sealed with the emblem of the prime minister.

A cold dread spread into his chest.

He broke the seal, opened the envelope, and pulled out two pieces of paper. The first was an official-looking document. Near the top were two names:

Charles Madison and Jazmin Lutzer

He scanned it quickly, ignoring the legalese until he got to the verdict:

Guilty of actions endangering the
Sovereign State of Israel.

He took a moment to gather his thoughts.

At the very bottom were six signatures. Judges. Beside them, in the lower right corner, was the official seal of the State of Israel. His hand shook ever so slightly as he flipped to the second page. The words were handwritten by the prime minister himself:

Assemble Kidon.
Proceed with extreme prejudice.

Nineteen

SAUDI ARABIA

"You okay?"

Lisa looked up, gave a pathetic nod, then leaned over and puked into the air-sickness bag.

Trying in some clumsy way to comfort her, Charlie reached over and patted her back. It was damp with sweat.

She convulsed again, but with dry heaves. It had to be. This was her second bag.

"Stewardess?" Charlie motioned to the flight attendant who was doing her best to avoid the area. Other passengers had already moved—looking on with compassion, but moving nonetheless . . . during those few seconds when the plane wasn't lunging, dipping, and diving. "Could we have another wet towel, please?"

She nodded and headed to the front of the cabin where Charlie figured she'd be hiding the rest of the flight.

"Here." He took the bag from Lisa's hands and sealed it, adding it to the collection under the seat.

"I'm sorry," she groaned, "I'm—"

The plane pitched violently, followed by a series of shimmies and rattles.

Terror filled her wet, white face.

Charlie lifted the armrest that separated them. "Here . . ." He helped her sit up and leaned her against his chest. The plane lunged and she grabbed him, clinging fiercely. He gritted his teeth against the pain from his cracked rib while managing to pat her clenched hand. "You'll be okay. Just a few more minutes and we'll be on the ground."

She tried to nod.

He glanced to Jaz on his other side. Truth is, she didn't look much better—probably the power of suggestion, or the cabin's hazy-blue cigarette smoke, or the smell of vomit. He reached out and offered his hand. She accepted it without looking.

He'd be strong for both of them, or at least appear to be. But inside he was ruined. He'd hoped saving his sister would be some sort of redemption. He'd lost his wife and daughter through carelessness and sin. By saving Katherine he'd hoped to balance the scales. But he had not saved her. Like the others he cherished, he had destroyed her.

"YOU KILLED HER!" Jaz's accusation still rang in his ears. "YOU KILLED THEM ALL!"

He had no argument then, and he had none now. Except that he was a failure. A failed warrior who lost his edge and destroyed his family. A failed man of God whose sham and hypocrisy brought disaster.

He looked back to Jaz. Despite her erratic mood swings—tears, giggles, rage, sometimes all at once—he was proud of her. She'd been a real trouper during the first leg of their trip, from Cairo to Riyadh. Maybe too real . . .

When the passport official, so young his voice had barely changed, questioned why a diplomat would want to visit an out-of-the-way place like Tabuk, the closest airport to Jabal al-Lawz, Lisa went into her rehearsed explanation:

"Our daughter, our *deaf* daughter here, suffers from a special type of seizure—related to the auditory and nervous system. And, as you are no doubt aware, the Bedouins in that area claim to have a homeopathic cure for such maladies."

"*Homo* what?" the man-boy croaked in alarm.

"Homeopathic. It consists of organic mixtures from various desert plants found only in that region. They seem to have curative properties over such illnesses."

The kid frowned. It was uncertain the bluff was working until Jaz suddenly spoke up.

"Momma?"

Lisa threw her a concerned look. "Not now, sweetheart."

"Momma, I feel one coming."

"What?"

"I think it's all this tension."

"Dominique," Lisa spoke with emphasis, "I really don't think one would happen right now, not when we're—"

Jaz let out a cry and shuddered, "Ahh . . ."

Fighting back the panic, Lisa turned to Charlie. He put his arm around the girl. "Dominique . . ."

"Ahhhh . . ." The shaking grew worse.

It became obvious Charlie and Lisa would have to play along. More so when Jaz rolled back her eyes and collapsed onto the floor.

"Dominique!" Charlie dropped to her side as the girl began to writhe on the linoleum tile.

"Heeeelp meeee . . ."

He was absolutely clueless.

"The medicine!" Lisa cried.

He looked up, confused. "Wha—"

"The medicine! The one that temporarily stops her seizures."

"Right!" Charlie patted his shirt pocket, his pants, looking for something, even a Life Saver. Anything would do.

By now most everyone in the terminal had turned to watch

as Jaz's thrashings grew and her wailings began. She was a natural-born actress and their attention only fed her gifts.

"Here!" Lisa cried. She knelt beside her, pulling a bottle of Midol from her purse. "I have them."

Jaz continued to twist and squirm until Charlie took her head and held it just long enough for Lisa to drop in two tablets.

"There, that should do it!" Lisa shouted. She waited until Jaz opened her eyes then repeated the cue, making sure the girl read her lips. "Those should start working any second!"

And sure enough, the wonder drug took effect. Slowly, the writhing came to an end. Not all at once, but enough to be believable . . . if that term still had any meaning.

"There we go," Charlie said, in case anyone missed the point. "I think she is better now." He was starting to get the hang of this acting thing. "Yes, I think she is. Yes, yes, she definitely is getting much better."

Lisa gave him a look, indicating he might be overdoing it a bit. He frowned. Everybody's a critic.

Still breathing hard, Jaz finally asked, "What . . . what happened?"

"You had another one of those awful seizures," Lisa said.

Jaz nodded. "They seem to be coming more often."

"Yes," Lisa agreed, "and the sooner we find those Bedouins, the sooner we can get you some help."

It was not an Academy Award performance on anyone's part. But the amateurishness must have been lost in translation because, almost immediately, they were given clearance. And now, here they were on the Tabuk flight, riding a pogo stick of a puddle jumper.

To Charlie's surprise, the attendant arrived with the wet towel. He took it and gently wiped the sweat from Lisa's face. He pushed aside the sticky hair and pulled a few strands from her mouth. It was a good face—the one he'd found so engaging in the music store. Strong, compassionate, with just a little childlike vulnerability.

The plane lurched again. She closed her eyes and clung to him. Despite the pain, her closeness felt good, almost natural . . . the way her head rested on his chest, the way his arm wrapped protectively around her. It also felt good to be holding Jaz's hand. In some strange way it reminded him of family.

≝ ≝ ≝

One word.

"Omar Atmani?" The heavyset man of the Maghreb Arabs held him with his eyes. "Did you have anything to do with the American girl and the uncle's escape?"

One word was all that was necessary.

The heavy man, Sheikh Abdallah Zayd, and the lieutenant from al Qaeda, waited. The *shura* had returned to the building where the killing of the two *mujahideen* and the American scientist occurred.

One word and it would be settled. As a respected member of *jihad bis sayf*, he would be believed, no matter his answer.

With a calm resolution belying his pounding heart, Omar looked into the face of each member of the council. If he told the truth, he would be forever banned from participating in *jihad*. His contributions to a cause he so deeply embraced would never again be accepted. But if he were to lie, if he were to betray the truth, the very principles of honesty he held so sacred, he would be able to continue fighting for those principles.

Impossible irony. By practicing what Islam was not, he could continue serving what it was.

"Omar Atmani, we await your answer."

His soul trembled at the contradiction. If the only way to continue in a cause so true was to become so false . . . what did that say of him? What did that say of his cause? How different was this from Sheikh's order to rape and torture a little girl? Or the holy prophet himself, who spoke of peace and tolerance on one hand, and yet commanded to raise the sword in the slaughter of thousands?

"*What do you call a belief that kills thousands of innocents?*" the FBI woman had asked him.

One word.

Through a single lie, he could redeem himself, continue pursuit of the Program, and destroy it so others could not spread its lie and destruction. By practicing unrighteousness, he would secure righteousness.

But even now, he knew such an act would not leave him unchanged. He would cross a line that could never be recrossed. Something inside him would forever become false. Something he held true would forever be untrue.

"Omar Atmani, I ask you a final time—did you have anything to do with the American girl and her uncle's escape?"

Finally, careful to look the man in the eyes, he shook his head. "No."

‡ ‡ ‡

"Taxi, lady, you want taxi?"

Lisa gave a dubious look to the dust-caked Peugeot. There was no sign, no indication it was a taxi—just the perpetual grinning man with yellow teeth. She glanced back to the terminal. Charlie was in there with Jaz doing some last-minute negotiating. Apparently the fashion magazine his niece picked up in Cairo was considered pornography in

Tabuk; contraband—at least according to the nineteen-year-old guard who was trying to confiscate it.

"Anywhere you want, I take you," the driver said. "No tips necessary."

Still a little unsteady on her feet, Lisa adjusted her shoulder carry-on. It was easily 110 degrees in the shade. "You have air-conditioning?"

His grin grew bigger. "Yes." He slapped the hood raising a small cloud of dust. "Best air-conditioning in all Tabuk."

She glanced up and down the street. Only two other cars were there, shimmering before the terminal in the heat. Neither had drivers.

Unslinging her bag, she ordered, "Tabuk Sahara."

The man scurried to her bag. "Yes, Sahara. A very good place." He reached for the rear door while giving its panel a solid punch. It raised more dust, but opened. He grabbed her bag, brushing against her bare leg a bit more than she thought necessary. He heaved it inside, atop a large gas can sitting on the seat.

"Actually," Lisa said, "there are three of us."

"Three?"

"Yes."

He cranked up his grin. "Wonderful. Three." He held open the door, motioning her inside.

Taking her cue, she climbed in and suggested, "You might want to put that bag and gas can in the trunk."

"Ah . . . no. Trunk is no good. Many holes."

"Holes?"

"Yes." He pantomimed things falling through. "*Boom, boom.* No good for luggage."

Suddenly, she had second thoughts. "Listen, maybe we should—"

Charlie and Jaz raced out of the terminal. "Let's go!" Charlie shouted, motioning everyone inside the car.

"Is there a problem?" Lisa asked.

"Let's go, let's go!"

Concerned, she slid across the blistering seat until she was crammed against the gas can. Jaz followed.

"Please." The driver gallantly opened the front passenger door for Charlie.

"Get in and drive!" Charlie shouted.

"What's going on?" Lisa called.

Charlie piled her additional luggage on top of them.

"Ow!" Jaz cried.

"Charlie, what's—"

"His name is Robert," Jaz corrected. "Remember?"

"What's going on?"

The driver, who had moved around the car, slipped behind the wheel as Charlie slammed their door and jumped into his seat. "Let's go!"

"Yes." The driver began grinding gears.

"Go! Go!"

They lurched forward.

"Charlie?"

"Robert," Jaz said.

"Robert!"

"We had a little disagreement with the officials. Riyadh ran a check when we were in the air."

"Disagreement with officials?" the driver asked. He clicked his tongue. "Very bad, very bad."

Charlie threw a look over his shoulder. "Can you make this thing go faster?"

"Yes, of course. But disagreement with officials, that is very bad."

They took the first corner, throwing Lisa and her luggage

into the gas can. Looking out the window, she saw no building over three stories tall. Each was concrete and covered in various degrees of peeling white paint. Nor did she see people. At this time of day, in this type of heat, she suspected all the sane ones were inside.

She glanced into the mirror and saw the driver grinning at her.

Her suspicions were confirmed.

"You say it is bad," Charlie shouted to him. "How bad?"

"It is very bad. I am afraid I must increase your rate."

"So how much is 'very bad' going to cost us?"

"I must charge you twice my normal fee."

"Fine."

In the distance, they heard an approaching siren.

"Plus tips."

"Fine, fine."

Lisa looked out the back window. Through their billowing dust she caught glimpses of an old Mercedes with a flashing blue light on the roof.

"Oh, dear . . ." the driver said. "Things are looking very, very—"

"Triple it!" Charlie shouted.

The driver nodded and took another corner. They slid broadside toward a parked pickup. Jaz screamed as the driver fought the wheel, straightening it just in time to kiss the truck's fender, exchanging only the slightest paint.

Suddenly, Lisa longed for the peace and comfort of air travel. She looked over her shoulder. The Mercedes continued closing in.

"Turn around!" Charlie yelled.

"Excuse me?"

"Turn around, head for the police car!"

"But—"

"Do it!"

"That will be very, very, ver—"

"We'll pay! Do it!"

With a prayer or an oath, Lisa couldn't tell which, the driver cranked the wheel hard to the left—this time throwing the luggage, the gas can, and Lisa onto Jaz.

"Uncle Charlie!"

They skidded to a stop on the sandy asphalt.

"Step on it!" Charlie shouted at the driver.

The driver hit the gas. They spun out and fishtailed, the driver regaining control only as they passed the Mercedes, barely missing it and continuing another 200 yards.

"Uncle Charlie!"

"There's an empty garage!" Charlie shouted. "Up ahead!"

"A garage?"

"Under the building!"

"But—"

"Right there!"

"It is not—"

"There!"

"I—"

Charlie threw his leg over to the driver's side and hit the brakes.

Jaz screamed. Lisa swore. And everyone flew forward as they slid to a stop.

"In there." Charlie pointed to a dark opening to the left.

"It is not my garage. It is not my place to—"

"Now!"

Muttering protests, the driver turned and entered the garage.

"Shut off the engine," Charlie ordered. "Take your foot off the brake."

"This is very much more bad," the driver warned. "Very,

very, much—" He fell silent as the Mercedes and screaming siren passed.

He waited several moments before firing up the engine. Charlie gave no response which he took as consent.

"I truly hope you have much money for this," he said while backing out.

Once in the street, he ground the gears and they resumed their journey.

"How far to Tabuk Sahara?" Lisa asked.

"Change of plans," Charlie said.

The driver threw him a concerned look. "You are not going to the Sahara?"

"Which direction is Jabal al-Lawz?"

"*Jabal al-Lawz?*"

Charlie nodded.

"It is down this road another two, almost three hours."

"That's where we're going."

"But, that is—"

"I know, I know, very bad, very expensive. How much?"

"Now? So much traveling in this heat? And with the authorities' great interest?"

"How much?"

The driver blew air through his pursed lips. "Two hundred and fifty, perhaps three hundred American dollars."

"Fine."

"Robert . . ."

"Plus tips."

"Fine, fine, keep going."

The driver nodded and they picked up speed.

"Robert . . ."

"Yes, dear."

"We don't have that type of money and I doubt he takes plastic."

"Don't worry, dear."

The driver looked to her in the mirror. "How much do you have?" he asked.

"I—"

"Don't worry, dear," Charlie repeated.

"How much?"

"Dear, don't—"

"Just a fraction of that."

The driver turned to Charlie in concern.

"We'll barter," Charlie said.

"What do you have to barter? What do you have that costs three hundred American dollars?"

"We have plenty," Charlie assured him. "Tell him what we have, dear."

"Jewelry?" the driver asked. "Electronics?"

"Sorry," Lisa said, "I'm not into jewelry. But we do have my daughter's iPod."

"I have two already." Once again his eyes lingered on her. And Charlie, always observant, did not fail to notice.

"So . . ." Charlie asked, "what do you suggest?"

Again the driver glanced into the mirror.

"My wife? Do you want my wife?"

"Robert!" Lisa admonished.

The driver said nothing.

"She's a knockout, isn't she?"

The driver pretended to shrug.

Lisa's anger rose.

"But I'd say she's worth much more than three hundred dollars, wouldn't you?"

Again the man shrugged.

"Robert! That's not funny!"

"At least three fifty, don't you think?"

"*Robert!*"

"Or four."

"What are you—" She leaned forward and slugged him.

He continued. "Perhaps the drive to Jabal al-Lawz *and* to the border."

"*ROBERT!*" She hit him harder.

"Mom!" Jaz cried.

Charlie raised his good arm to protect himself. "Sweetheart."

"What are you saying?" She slugged him again. "I'm not some bargaining chip!"

"Dear, please. This doesn't concern you."

"Doesn't concern . . . ?" She hit him again. "*Doesn't concern me?*" She nailed him with everything she had.

"All right, all right!" he protested.

She hit him one last time for good measure then sat back in the seat, fuming.

Charlie turned back to the driver. "So what do you think?"

She gave him another punch.

The driver said nothing, but began slowing the car.

"What are you doing?" Lisa asked. "Why are you slowing?"

The man looked to Charlie. "You have nothing of value to offer me."

"I don't suppose you take checks?"

He eased the car to a stop along the side of the road and turned to Charlie. "You do not have money, you do not wish to barter." Without a word, he started to make a U-turn.

"Where are we going?" Lisa demanded.

"Perhaps the officials will know what to do."

"The officials?" she exclaimed.

Charlie answered, "I really don't think that's such a good—"

"If you have nothing with which to pay, then I see no alternative."

"There's gotta be something we can offer."

"I believe we have covered that. No money. No . . . services." He finished the U-turn, picked up speed, and headed back toward town. "My mind is made."

"Are you sure?"

"Yes." He nodded. "I am sure."

"*Really* sure?"

"Yes. How many times must I say, I am sure?"

"Well, all right then . . ." With lightning speed, Charlie's good hand flew up and struck the man squarely in the face.

The car swerved and Jaz screamed.

Charlie jabbed his elbow into the driver's gut, causing him to double over.

"Char—"

Before the man's head hit the wheel, Charlie's fist again caught his face, throwing him back into the seat . . . out cold.

"Have we lost our minds?" Jaz cried.

"Charlie!"

He pulled the driver's foot off the accelerator with his left hand while steering with the other . . . until they slowly coasted to a stop.

Twenty

Jaz kept slipping in the sand as she traipsed back up the hill to the car. She tried not to let any get between her flip-flops and bare skin, 'cause every grain felt like a red hot coal. And even though she'd only been out there for like three minutes to make a pit stop, she bet the tops of her feet were already sunburned. Then there was the wind. So strong her footsteps disappeared almost before she made them. It felt like someone turned a blow-dryer on high and aimed it at her whole body. The fact that the grit and dust worked its way into her mouth, her nose, and every crease of her body didn't make the experience any more fun. She squinted over to Lisa who had gone down the hill with her. Her scowling and spitting said she didn't enjoy it much better.

To be honest, the wind wasn't a bad change of pace. Before it picked up, everything had been way too still. Spooky almost. She couldn't put her finger on it, but just like she felt cut off from the world by never hearing its sounds, she felt even more cut off by never seeing anything but bare dirt, rocks . . . and mountains of bare dirt and rock. No people, no trees. No nothing.

She still couldn't believe her parents were dead. It's like they were just away or something. Like they'd be coming back any time and everything would be normal. The only way she could grasp they were really gone was if she forced herself to think about it—to imagine what it would be like with no mom to share her secrets, or wake her up three times a morning to make sure she got to school, or no dad to slip her an extra twenty for makeup and junk when Mom was unreasonable. Those were the thoughts that, when she forced them to come, weighed so heavily on her chest she could barely breathe. Then, of course, there were the stupid tears that kept coming at the weirdest times. Like now, as she looked at the lonely nothingness that stretched on forever.

She blinked them back and continued trudging up the hill. Earlier, when Uncle Charlie punched out the guy, dumped him in the passenger seat, and took over driving, she let the jerking and rocking of the car lull her to sleep. Not a sound one. It's hard sleeping soundly with a furnace blasting in your face. (The driver's version of AC was having the windows down.) But after 24/7 with no rest, she took what she could get.

They crested the hill just in time to see Charlie stalking toward the driver who'd climbed out. They'd never got rid of him 'cause they figured he'd just go tell the police. And they never tied him up 'cause, well, where was he going to run?

But now he was shouting, holding one hand over his head and dancing backward in the wind. Charlie was shouting too and definitely not looking happy.

Jaz turned to Lisa. "What's going on?"

Lisa shook her head in disgust.

"What?"

"The guy's got the car keys. He won't give them up."

Jaz looked back. Sure enough, she caught a glint of metal dangling between the man's fingers. And every time Uncle Charlie tried to charge him, the guy danced backward mak-

Bill Myers

ing like he would throw them over the hill and into the current of swiftly changing sand. He probably would too. He was just that crazy.

"Uncle Charlie!"

The driver turned and Charlie took advantage of the distraction by leaping at him. Unfortunately, the guy saw him and had enough time to fling the keys, like a little kid, down the opposite side of the hill into the blowing ocean of sand. Not as far as he'd like, but far enough.

Of course Uncle Charlie finished tackling him, but it was too late.

"Ah-ha!" the man shouted as he scrambled back to his feet, grinning. He pointed at Charlie. "Ah-ha! Ah-ha!" Then in the direction of the disappeared keys. "Ah-ha!" It was either laughter or hysteria, Jaz couldn't tell which. But whatever it was, it didn't take long for his grin to slowly fade as he realized what everyone else already knew.

They were totally screwed.

🥾 🥾 🥾

Sheldon Houser and Secretary Otis Roberts walked the Village, Israel's equivalent to a Hollywood back lot. Like the FBI's facilities in Virginia, it contained fake storefronts, houses, an office building, even a three-story hotel. But today it was relatively quiet. Today the recruits were busy rescuing hostages and killing bad guys at the other end of the compound.

"You are sure you feel up to this?" Secretary Roberts asked. "With Hannah's wedding and all?"

"Now is a perfect time, Mr. Secretary."

"Perhaps."

They continued walking, the silence broken only by the distant burst of Uzis and the single pop of handguns.

"Two missions in a row and two"—Roberts searched for the word—"how should I put it . . ."

"Failures, Mr. Secretary. Yes, I'm familiar with my record."

"Which is why you feel a need to prove yourself?"

Houser cut to the chase. "Sir, I have orders from the prime minister himself. Now if you—"

"If I make one simple call, I guarantee you he will reconsider."

Houser took a breath and reined in his anger. It was foolish to gamble with a man who held all the cards.

"You have nothing to prove, Shel. Not to anyone. You have a record all of us are proud of."

"Yes, sir, I appreciate that."

"And still you feel a need to lead the Kidon."

Houser paused a moment, trying to crystallize his thoughts, the ones swirling in his head these many days. "Sir . . . Israel is my life. She is my soul."

"This from a man who does not believe in God?"

"Israel is what I believe in. She is my religion."

Roberts remained quiet, letting him continue.

"Her ground is soaked with my family's blood. My wife gave up her life for this ground. As did my father. And cousins and friends." He looked down and slowed to a stop. He kneeled and picked up a handful of the dry soil. "This is the history of my family, your family, stretching back thousands of years. And this is their future—my daughter's, her children's, her children's children's."

Roberts remained respectfully silent. Houser rose, dusted off his hands, and they resumed walking.

"And you feel a need to protect that future." It was more statement than question.

"I have a duty to protect it."

They rounded the last storefront of the Village. Not far away was the source of the gunfire. A mock 757 fuselage was burning—full of smoke and a handful of recruits storming it. Nearby, two instructors silently watched video monitors of the inside action.

Giving little notice, Roberts continued. "You have again asked for Milkner and Brenem."

Houser nodded. "They are the best."

"And they have not lost confidence in you?"

"You'll have to ask them."

"And Iserson? He's part of *Al*, safely embedded in the States. The Americans don't even know of his existence."

"I wouldn't be so sure of that."

Roberts frowned. "Our presence is forbidden. If they did know he was there, he would be captured and tried as a spy."

"Or played by the Americans until he fulfilled their wishes."

Roberts's frown deepened. He looked back at the 757. "To pull him is not an easy request."

"His religious devotion will be a good balance for the team."

The secretary nodded. "There are four more necessary to choose."

"At your discretion, sir."

Roberts paused to look at him before finally speaking. "Then come." He motioned them toward the bank of monitors. "Let us find those who may catch our fancy."

Houser followed with a sense of accomplishment . . . and gratitude.

"*Al-salaam alaykum!*"

The voice woke Lisa. She stirred, raising her head from her white, sweat-stained tennis shoes which served as a pillow against the sand. She reached out and pushed aside the blanket draped to the ground and held in place by the car's closed door. It acted as a curtain to block the wind and sand from blowing beneath the vehicle where they slept, or tried to sleep, through the afternoon heat.

She could hear Charlie still working on the steering column. In vain they had searched the shifting sand for the keys. And, like the SUV back in Burbank, the vehicle was too new to simply hot-wire. Without the proper tools it would be impossible to unlock the steering wheel. But that didn't stop him from trying. The man never stopped trying.

The voice also woke the driver. He'd been lying under the car at the opposite end, a good five feet away with the luggage stacked between them as a barrier. "What is it?" he shouted. "What?"

"*Al-salaam alaykum!*" the voice repeated. "*Al-salaam alaykum!*"

"Ah-ha." The driver scrambled out from under the car. "I told you someone would come. Ah-ha!" He rose to his feet and ran off, shouting in Arabic.

Lisa turned to Jaz who was still asleep beside her, sprawled out, her mouth hanging open. Being careful not to wake her, she slid out from the car and into the pounding heat of the sun.

A pickup had joined them. White, maybe yellow, it was hard to tell under the thick coat of dust. Beside it stood a young boy, only a year or two older than Jaz. He wore baggy basketball shorts, some rock band T-shirt, and Converse high tops. The driver approached, giving him a heated earful, but Lisa's attention was drawn back to the pickup. It had tinted windows. Rolled up! A sure sign of AC!

Charlie joined the men and busily presented his own version . . . *in Arabic*. Lisa blinked in surprise. The Arabic wasn't fluid, just enough to remind her that Charles Madison was a man still full of surprises.

She walked toward them, calling, "What's up?"

Charlie turned to her and motioned to their driver. "This guy is giving the kid some nonsense about us hijacking his car." Turning to the driver, he asked, "That's it, isn't it? You say we stole your car?"

"Yes, yes, you know you stole my car!"

Lisa arrived, pulling her hair back from the wind. "Where'd he come up with that?"

The driver flew into a greater rage. "What! What! You know you stole my car! What!"

Charlie shook his head, answering her. "Got me. But it'll be interesting to hear what he says he did with the keys."

The driver exploded, throwing up his hands, motioning wildly as the boy listened. Only when he paused to catch his breath did Charlie take over, giving a much calmer version.

"What's happening?" a sleepy Jaz called as she crawled out from under the car.

Lisa turned so she could see her mouth. "We've got company."

The argument continued to rage as Jaz walked over and joined her. "Now that's *hot*."

Lisa frowned. What was hot, the driver's temper? The blistering sun? Then she saw her giving the boy a smile— brief enough to be modest, brazen enough to say she was interested . . . before she glanced shyly to the ground. Where do they learn this stuff? And at such an early age?

Lisa turned back to the boy and was equally amazed. He'd already taken the bait. Though he pretended to be listening to the argument, it became more and more apparent that he was no longer concerned—well, not as concerned as sucking in his gut and, when Jaz looked back up, giving her a cooler than cool nod.

Lisa glanced back to Jaz who once again dropped her eyes.

Amazing . . . and in less than thirty seconds.

It took a little longer for the men to notice—so what else was new?—but they eventually caught on. As a result, the driver increased his volume and hysteria, while Charlie deliberately stepped back, out of the boy's line of vision, giving him a clear shot of Jaz.

"Uncle Charlie?"

They all turned to her.

She stepped toward them, her movement much more fluid than Lisa had seen in the past.

Simply amazing.

Charlie answered. "I'm trying to explain to this young man that we offered to pay our driver here to take us to Jabal al-Lawz, but that he tried blackmailing us—"

"And threw the keys over in that sand," Jaz said, pointing off in the distance with a helpless pout.

The transformation caught Charlie off guard. "Uh . . . exactly."

Jaz turned back, looking directly into the boy's eyes. "So does he think he can help?"

Charlie translated.

The boy scratched the fuzz on his chin, pretending to think

logically through the situation—though Lisa suspected his decision had little to do with logic . . . or thinking.

Finally, he turned back to the men and spoke soberly—sounding as old as Jazmin pretended to be.

The driver flew into another tirade.

As he did, Charlie shouted to Lisa, "Get in the truck. He's taking us to his father's camp."

"All right!" Jaz cheered as she started for the pickup.

Lisa turned back to the car to grab her luggage.

"Don't bother," Charlie shouted. He strode toward the pickup. "We've no time."

Lisa nodded and joined them.

The boy followed, the driver glued to his side, still yelling.

"How are we all going to fit?" Lisa asked.

Charlie opened the door. Jaz tried to go first, until he blocked her. "*I'll* sit in the middle."

"But—"

"*You* sit on Lisa's lap next to the window."

The boy arrived with the driver still attached. But instead of climbing into the cab, the young man reached back to the bed of the pickup, threw off a tarp, and grabbed what looked like a weed whacker. He shoved it into the driver's hands, then climbed into the cab and shut the door.

The shouts continued but were more muffled. The man banged on the window. The boy turned and locked the door. He reached for the ignition, started it up, and dropped the pickup into gear. They lurched forward.

Lisa watched as the man ran after them, still yelling, still pounding the glass. It took several dozen yards before he wore himself out and slowed, eventually letting them slip away.

"So, what's with the weed whacker?" she asked Charlie.

"Weed whacker?"

She motioned back to the shouting man who now stood all alone with his new possession.

Charlie shook his head. "That's no weed whacker."

"What is it?"

"A metal detector."

Twenty-One

Sheikh Ahmed bin Khalid shook his head. "Such a thing is not possible."

"Why is that?" Charlie asked.

"We are no longer allowed to approach it."

"I don't understand."

From the moment they'd been invited into Sheikh's tent for a meal, Charlie knew this man enjoyed his power . . . as much as he enjoyed flaunting it. If they were to secure any help from this barrel-chested chieftain, it meant appealing to his "greatness."

Sheikh motioned to his son. The boy sat at the end of the table, giggling with Jaz, showing her how to scoop up *tahini*, a mixture of sesame seed paste, oil, and lemon, into her pita bread without it dribbling down her wrist. They were getting pretty chummy and, if Charlie wasn't so intent upon "social engineering" the situation with Sheikh, he would have put a stop to it.

But first things first.

"When Ali was little we would hold our camel races around the mountain. Remember that, son?"

The boy glanced up and politely answered in Arabic before turning back to Jaz and winking, which produced another set of giggles.

"And now?" Charlie asked.

"Now," Sheikh scorned and took a bite of pita, "the military have put a fence around it. The fools have even built a guard shack."

Lisa nodded. "I see why that's a problem for you."

Sheikh stopped chewing. "For me? It is no problem for me."

As the only woman at the table, Lisa's presence was, at best, tolerated. The others, Sheikh's wife and his two teenage daughters, drifted about in their veils, replenishing the pickled vegetables called *torshi,* keeping the glasses filled with mint tea, and performing the usual and expected services of women. But not Lisa. Instead of remaining quiet, allowing Charlie to do his work, she seemed intent upon proving her equality. Maybe an acceptable trait in America, but definitely not appreciated here. "Why would they build a fence around it?" she asked.

Without looking at her, Sheikh answered, "Only Allah knows."

She pressed in. "It's just rock and dirt—like everything else around here."

Sheikh closed his eyes, seeing no need to repeat himself.

Charlie eased them back to topic. "So, if you wanted, you could deal with the guards?"

"If I wanted I could deal with the entire army." He plucked a date off a silver tray. "*If* I wanted."

Charlie purposefully let the phrase hang. The ceiling of black goat hair rippled from the outside wind. Beneath his feet was a purple and violet carpet with Arabic patterns of blue and gold. At the far wall sat a plush sofa covered in sheepskin. On the opposite wall, a forty-two-inch plasma TV was hooked up to an outside satellite dish. Like the two million Bedouin who roam the Saudi desert, Sheikh Ahmed bin Khalid was a proud man, fiercely independent and honorable. Attributes Charlie hoped to cash in on if Lisa would let him do his work.

"And why," she asked, "are you so certain this is the real Mount Sinai?"

Sheikh looked to Charlie, then to Lisa, then back to Charlie again. He seemed perplexed at her continual participation.

Charlie shrugged. He wasn't perplexed, just frustrated.

Lisa scooped up another gooey rice ball and plopped it into her mouth. "What evidence do you have this one's the real deal, compared to, say, the more traditional Mount Sinai?"

"Evidence?"

"Right." She began licking each of her fingers. "How do we know your location is more accurate than ours?" She looked up just in time to see the man swallow back his anger. She stopped mid-lick.

"*Evidence?*"

Charlie caught her eye, scowling at her to back down.

But she continued. "It just sounds like one person's hearsay versus another's."

"Hearsay?" Sheikh's voice grew louder. "*Hearsay?*"

Charlie lowered his head.

"Well, yeah, I mean where are your facts?"

"*Facts?*" The big man was all bristles. "I will tell you *facts*."

"Please." Lisa sat back in her chair and folded her arms, waiting for him to present his case.

Charlie groaned quietly.

"Should I first speak of the natural land bridge under the Red Sea? The one stretching from Nuweiba to the Saudi-Arabian coast?"

"Why's that important?"

"*Why is that* . . . ? To facilitate the Jews' crossing, of course. When they were pursued by Pharaoh's army."

Lisa shrugged.

Sheikh leaned forward. "Or perhaps I should speak of Al Bad with its twelve springs between the Red Sea's crossing and our holy mountain. The very same twelve springs of Elim described in the book of Exodus. Not eleven springs, not thirteen springs. Twelve!"

"Impressive, but not exactly—"

"Or the giant altar at the base of the mountain!"

"Altar?"

"Once again described in Exodus."

Lisa started sounding impressed. "An altar is still there?"

"With the ancient inscriptions of bulls still carved into it."

"Bulls?" Lisa said. "You don't raise cattle out here."

Sheikh smiled tightly. "Precisely. The bulls would have come from wandering nomads who traveled from a land that did raise cattle . . . such as Egypt."

Charlie stepped in. "Those are very impressive facts."

Sheikh nodded in satisfaction.

"Or coincidences," Lisa added.

Charlie closed his eyes. Was she purposefully sabotaging them?

"Coincidences?" Sheikh sputtered. He turned to his son in disbelief. "*Coincidences?*"

The boy shook his head, then replied in heavily accented English, "Tell them about the top, Father."

"The top?" Charlie asked.

"Yes"—Sheikh nodded—"the top of the holy mountain." He turned to Lisa. "The entire top of Jabal al-Lawz, which is completely burned."

"Burned?" Lisa said. "What, like brush and trees and stuff?"

"Do you see any 'brush and trees' in this part of my desert?"

"Well, no, but—"

"I am speaking of the rocks themselves. All of the rocks atop the holy mountain of God are burned. Entirely black and melted."

Lisa started to respond, but he cut her off.

"And no, these are not volcanic rocks. There are no such rocks in this region. What I am speaking of is a summit completely scorched, melted by intense heat."

"I don't . . . understand."

Sheikh smiled and turned to his boy. "Tell her the verse, my son."

The young man rose and recited in heavy accent:

"And Mount Sinai was altogether of smoke, because the Lord descended upon it in fire: and the smoke thereof ascended as the smoke of a furnace, and the whole mount quaked greatly."

When he finished, he sat down, looking for Jaz's approval. He got a smile and returned it with a modest nod.

"That's . . . incredible." Finally, Lisa seemed to be showing the proper respect. Fortunately, it was not lost on Sheikh.

Unfortunately, it did not last. "But," she sighed, "we'll never really know, will we?"

Sheikh scowled. "Why do you say that?"

She shrugged. "You said yourself, it's a military complex."

"The military does not own our mountain."

"Right, but it's not like you can just stroll on up and—"

"I can do anything I wish."

"But they're military. They've got guns." She pantomimed, "Bang, bang."

Charlie grimaced.

"They've got real soldiers with real—"

"I have guns. I have soldiers. How dare you say I cannot visit our own mountain."

"I'm sorry, but—"

"Tonight."

"Pardon me?"

"Tonight. Rest until it is dark and then my men and I, we will take you to the mountain. We will show you its top." He wiped his mouth, tossed the napkin on the table, and rose from his patio chair. Apparently the meal was over.

"What about the soldiers?" Lisa asked.

"They are no match for us."

"Are you sure, because—"

"Tonight. Rest and then you shall see."

"Listen, you don't have to prove anything to me. I just—"

"Tonight!" Turning to Charlie he touched his forehead, his lips, and his heart. "*Allah yukaththir khayraka.*"

Charlie gave a low nod, repeating the phrase.

The man turned to Lisa, nodded coolly, then gathered his robes and strode out of the tent.

Charlie sat stunned, not believing what he'd just witnessed.

Lisa reached for more *torshi*, flashing him a quick smile.

Amazing. She'd known what she was doing all along. In spite of himself, Charlie shook his head.

꙳ ꙳ ꙳

"It is decided?" Omar asked.

"Yes." The oil lamp flickered on the table, highlighting every crease in Sheikh Abdallah Zayd's weathered face. "The girl and her uncle, there is word where they may be heading."

Omar remained silent, listening intently.

"*Shura* has met and chosen you to pursue them. They know you best. Perhaps they will now listen."

"The others, they believe me?"

"Every man makes mistakes. And every man has the obligation to correct them. That is the path of Allah."

"And once I find them?"

"You will persuade them."

Omar shifted. The cane chair squeaked under his weight. "But . . . how likely will they listen?"

"You will persuade them."

"And if I can't?"

"Then you will have no other choice."

"No other choice . . ."

"But to silence them."

Omar held Sheikh's eyes a moment, then slowly nodded. He understood. It was part discipline, part test of loyalty. In both cases, the man was right. He had no other choice.

Twenty-Two

Maybe it was the desert stars, so close he could reach out and touch them. Or the absolute stillness; a silence broken only by the crunch of gravel under his boots. More likely, it was the fact that Charlie Madison could very soon be standing on the ground where God himself spoke to Moses. An event so powerful, so terrifying, that according to the Bible, any person who even touched the base of the mountain would die.

At Sheikh's orders, they'd left Lisa and Jaz behind in his late-model Hummer. There, under Ali's watchful protection, they would remain hidden in a slight dip a kilometer from the fence.

"The mountain, it is not a place for women or children," he had explained.

Of course Lisa argued. "I'm just as capable as any—"

And of course Sheikh cut her off. "No."

"You don't understand, I can help out by—"

"*No.*"

"You'll need someone to—"

"Woman, I order your silence!" The command was so fierce it even intimidated Lisa . . . for a moment.

"I appreciate your concern, but—"

"Shh!" the man hissed.

"I—"

"*Shhh!*"

Again she opened her mouth but stopped as he pressed his finger to his lips and closed his eyes.

She threw Charlie a look, asking for help. But he shook his head. She slumped back into her seat with the same pout he occasionally saw on Jaz's face.

Only Charlie, one armed bodyguard, and the sheikh would approach the base of the mountain. From there, Sheikh would send them on the climb while he waited for their return. Since, as he explained, "My breath does not return as quickly as it once did."

Earlier, two of his men had arrived at the guard shack and distracted the soldier with their latest DVD player, along with a pirated version of some kung-fu flick. Once the diversion was in full swing, the sheikh's bodyguard quickly cut a hole in the hurricane fence and they stepped through. Within minutes they came upon a solitary pile of boulders, rising twenty feet high and stretching sixty to seventy feet in length.

"The Altar of the Golden Calf," Sheikh proudly stated.

"But," Charlie said, "those boulders, they're at least five, ten tons apiece. How could they possibly be moved to build an altar?"

"Are these not the same people who built the pyramids?"

Before Charlie could answer, he motioned them forward. "Come, let me show you the bulls."

They moved closer. Soon he spotted what looked like crude etchings of cattle. For the most part they were tucked between the rocks, safely out of the elements. Charlie counted four, then five, then six of them.

"Egyptian bulls," Sheikh explained, "from their Apis cult. In all Arabia, these pictures are found only at this place."

Almost against his will, Charlie reached up to touch the rocks. What had happened here? If the Scriptures were right, despite all the power and all the glory the people had witnessed, they still turned their backs on God. They still chose to build an altar and worship their old, false gods. And yet, according to the Scriptures, God remained faithful to them. Even in their disobedience, he refused to give up on them. As always, Charlie's own failures rose before him—the faces of those he had loved and forsaken . . . and killed. Only this time they were accompanied by another thought. Was it possible? Despite his unforgivable failures, his gross disobedience, was it possible God still refused to give up on him?

"Come." Sheikh touched his arm and they started off.

It was not a big mountain, probably a two-hour climb at best. But instead of starting up it, they circled around to the west.

"Where are we going?" Charlie asked.

"There is something else you must see."

Forty minutes later they came upon a giant rock pillar rising from a hill of rubble. It stood eight stories above the desert floor and was split in two near the halfway point. Sheikh climbed the small knoll of loose stones surrounding its base.

"Come," he ordered. He stooped down and touched the smooth, polished rocks. "Feel."

Charlie climbed to join him. He arrived and kneeled down to the stones. They were as smooth as river rock. In fact, all the stones they stood upon looked like they were part of some ancient riverbed. A riverbed that stretched down to the desert floor . . . and up to the split in the rock.

"I don't . . ." Charlie frowned. "I don't understand."

The Sheikh softly quoted:

"Behold, I will stand before thee upon the rock in Horeb; and thou shalt smite the rock, and there shall come water

out of it, that the people may drink. And Moses did so in
the sight of the elders of Israel."

Charlie looked to him in surprise. "You believe . . . you believe this is the rock of Horeb?"

Sheikh only smiled, indicating the riverbed that stretched up to the split rock before them.

Charlie felt himself breathing just a little faster.

"Now you go." Sheikh signaled to their bodyguard. "Go climb God's holy mountain, my friend. Perhaps he will speak to you as he has to others."

Charlie held his look.

The man gave him a nod. "Go."

"*Nobody* loves the Bureau more than me!" Special Agent in Charge Harold Petersen snapped.

Bernie leaned toward his desk. "Then why can't you see we're being used? Why aren't you paying attention?"

"Paying attention? *Paying attention!*" She thought the big man was going to blow a vessel. "Like noticing your rendez-vous with Agent Harmon?"

"We're friends, you know—"

"Or the information you've been passing to her? Reyn-olds's work with the DOD?"

"You knew I was—"

"Or your illegal requisition of three separate passports?"

Bernie swallowed. "You knew about those?"

"Nobody loves the Bureau more than me."

She sat back in her chair, unsure what to say.

"And that's why I'm asking for your resignation."

"My . . . resignation?"

"Or your suspension. And given your list of offenses, I'd say you certainly deserve the latter."

"But, I—the Bureau is my life."

"No, Agent Wolff. God and country are your life. And apparently so are your friends."

"Shouldn't they be the same?"

Petersen gave no response, but she saw the agreement in his eyes. After eighteen years of working together, she saw the agreement.

"We've put a BOLO out on Agent Harmon. As a member of the Bureau she will be apprehended and brought back to the States to face an OPR review, suspension, and most likely criminal charges."

"Sir—"

"There's little I can do about that. If she would have resigned first, it would be a different matter." He leaned forward, making sure Bernie didn't miss a single word. "If Agent Harmon had tendered her resignation, she could have left the country to help any friend she chose—especially those who may be in over their heads in matters they don't fully understand."

Bernice frowned.

The man paused, waiting for her response. Was he saying what she thought he was saying?

Finally, choosing her words with equal care, she responded. "What help could she or any agent offer if they resigned and no longer had access to priority information?"

Satisfied they were on the same page, Special Agent in Charge Petersen leaned back in his cracked vinyl chair. "Because of the paperwork, it's not unusual for access codes of resigned agents to stay active for up to two weeks after they've left the Bureau."

Bernice stared at him. The decision before her was heart-breaking. But given what they had on her, and given Lisa's situation, what other choice remained? She took a deep breath.

Petersen waited.

She cleared her throat. "Sir . . . I'd like to discuss the possibility of tendering my resignation."

Holding his hands before him, placing one fingertip against the other, he answered, "I think that's an excellent idea, Agent Wolff. And given the serious nature of your offenses, I would suggest the sooner you do so, the better. Say, by the end of the day."

She looked at him, startled. Then glanced down. Finally, she began to nod.

"Good . . . good." He returned to the paperwork. "I'll expect it on my desk before five."

Bernie remained sitting, unsure if she could stand. Eighteen years was a long time.

Without looking up, he asked, "Is there anything else?"

She swallowed back the ache in her throat. "No, sir." It was a half-whisper, half-croak. She pushed herself out of the chair and onto her feet. Numbly, she turned and started for the door.

"Oh, and Agent Wolff?"

She turned back.

"Once you resign, you may want to take a few days to rest and unwind."

"Sir?"

"Ever been to Europe? Rome is beautiful this time of year."

She frowned.

"You have a brother in the military, right?"

"Retired, yes. Special Forces."

"It might be good to make it a family affair."

Not fully understanding, but knowing she would, Bernice answered, "Yes, sir." She started to turn, then hesitated. "And sir?"

He looked up.

"Thank you."

"Nobody loves the Bureau more than me, Agent Wolff. Nobody."

The climb was slow. There were no trails, just fanned-out washes that narrowed into promising paths which only became dead-end walls that they had to scale or circumvent. Sometimes the ground was bare rock, sometimes loose gravel that slipped under their boots.

It was nearly 4:00 a.m. when Charlie noticed there were no more bluffs above them, just one last outcropping of rock. Wedging his feet into a crevice, he pushed while dragging himself up with his good hand. At last he made it over the final boulder and onto the summit. He lay there on his belly catching his breath. Then he turned and reached over the outcropping to pull up his bodyguard. The man's M-16 clattered against the rocks as he joined him.

Together, they rose, both breathing hard.

A thin strip of pink spread across the horizon. In that faint light, other colors appeared—the taupe of surrounding mountains, the navy-blue shadows of their creases and folds, and the beige of a desert floor that lay beyond and stretched out forever.

To Charlie's left, in the distance, there was a black line that could only be the Red Sea.

And at his feet?

He looked down. Unlike the rest of the mountain which

they spent the last ninety minutes climbing, these stones were jet black, their surface smooth and shiny. He surveyed the summit. They were all that way. His pulse quickened as he knelt down. Slowly, almost reverently, he reached out to touch a stone. It was as slick as glass. So were the others. Like black obsidian. Many were strangely shaped, like slabs of partially melted butter.

Like slabs of partially melted rock.

He picked up one, rubbed his fingers over its glazed surface. Something very strange had happened here, there was little doubt. Something had changed the surface. Again he looked around. And if the account was accurate, that change came from the presence of God himself. Much the same way the Voice changed the laboratory in Switzerland, his presence had changed these stones. Rough, hard stones dramatically changed. And if his presence could change stone . . .

I will remove from you your heart of stone and give you a heart of flesh. The verse leaped to mind before he could stop it.

He snorted in quiet contempt. It was that very thinking that had destroyed his family in the first place. The presumption that God had somehow touched him, changed him. Wasn't that his claim? Wasn't that why he wanted to be a minister of the gospel—to help others experience the change he thought he'd experienced?

But he'd only fooled himself. When push came to shove, it was the old Charlie that surfaced, the one that killed his sister and wife and daughter. Changed? He hadn't changed. He could babble all the Christian bromides he wanted, talk about being "born again" till he was blue in the face. But the fact was, it had not happened. He was still the same old Charles Madison. He always would be.

And nothing, not even God, could change that.

An idea flickered. He rose and crossed to another rock the size of a small football. He scooped it up. It was slick and black like the others. He hesitated then raised it high over his head and smashed it to the ground. As he hoped, it broke into several pieces. But to his surprise, the inside was different. Instead of smooth and black, it was like the rest of the mountain . . . beige and taupe. He picked up a piece and turned it over. Only the outside was burned and glazed. The rest of the rock was unchanged.

Again he thought of his life. He'd been so sure something had happened. From the moment he'd given God control, he'd been so sure something had changed. And the more time he spent in prayer and study, the deeper that change became. Not completely. Inside, he was like this rock. Inside, he was still a man with weaknesses, wrong thoughts, selfish behavior. But . . .

A tightness filled his chest. The rock was still a rock and yet the presence of God had changed it.

Began to change it.

How long had God remained here? An hour, a night, a day? Who knew. But, just as the Voice in the Swiss lab played longer and longer, changing more and more reality, the same must have been true with this rock. The longer God's presence remained, the deeper the change.

How long ago had Charlie made his commitment of faith? A handful of years? Like the rock, his change wasn't complete. He couldn't expect it to be. Not yet. When then? A decade? A lifetime? He didn't know. And there seemed little he could do to speed it up . . . certainly not by deciding to become a minister—his dead wife and child proved that. And certainly not through works of atonement—Katie's death proved that.

No, the only thing he could do to speed up the process

was to remain in God's presence. Like this rock. And, like the rock, he suspected some part of him would always be a man, always made of clay. But clay that was slowly being changed.

Charlie's eyes welled with moisture. He lowered his head. Soon, tears fell onto the stone. How could he have been so stupid and thick and unbelieving? But, of course, the answer was the same.

He was a man.

He felt a rifle tap his shoulder. He looked up to the bodyguard, who motioned off in the distance. Slowly, he rose to his feet. In the southeast, far, far away, a thin trail of headlights was approaching.

Approaching from Tabuk.

He guessed the cars to be an hour away. Enough time for the two of them to grab some rocks, climb down, and get out of there. At least that's what he hoped.

At least that's what he prayed.

Twenty-Three

It was nearly dawn by the time Charlie and Sheikh appeared over the ridge. Lisa was grateful for their arrival but not for their news.

"Soldiers!" Charlie shouted.

"What?"

"From Tabuk!"

Waddling toward the car and gasping for breath, Sheikh motioned. "Get in!"

Lisa slid off the Hummer's hood where she'd been keeping watch—not so much for Charlie and Sheikh as over Jaz and her friend. For a young boy, Ali seemed to know all the moves. And for a young girl, Jaz knew all the appropriate responses—well, appropriate for her "R-rated" generation; not so appropriate for Lisa's . . . at least that's what she told herself . . . at least on the first date.

It's not that the couple was doing anything out of line—with an FBI agent for a chaperone there wasn't much they could do . . . when she was awake. But it was the progress they made whenever she dozed off that concerned her.

As Sheikh arrived, he shouted to his son. Ali leaped to action, motioning for Jaz to follow while racing to the back passenger door of the vehicle.

"What's going on?" she asked Lisa.

There was no need to answer as headlights suddenly appeared, bouncing over the top of a not-too-distant hill.

"Hurry!" Sheikh yelled. He threw open the driver's door as Charlie and the bodyguard raced to the other side.

Jaz ducked into the truck and the boy followed, until Lisa's maternal instincts kicked in. She blocked him and climbed in between. Not that it made much difference. In the next couple minutes they'd be arrested, anyway. Or killed.

Doors slammed and Sheikh started the Hummer. For a moment the tires spun in the loose sand until they caught and the vehicle lurched forward. Lisa turned to look out the rear window. The lights were fifty yards away. Two trucks and a car.

The Hummer rocked and bounced, picking up speed. Sheikh continued yelling but he didn't sound angry. Lisa saw his reflection in the mirror and could have sworn there was a twinkle in his eye. Charlie shouted something back to him in Arabic and both men broke out laughing.

Laughing! Those were some serious headlights behind them carrying some serious consequences and they were laughing?

Seeing her concern in the mirror, Sheikh shouted, "Just like the old days!"

Charlie shouted something and again they laughed . . . until he turned and caught her icy glare. His smile faded and he looked straight ahead. Lisa shook her head, raking back her hair. There was far too much testosterone for her taste. Unfortunately, it didn't stop with the men . . .

Ali rolled down his window and shouted in Arabic.

"Ali, no!" Sheikh yelled.

Again the boy shouted, pulling up his gun. He stuck it outside and fired a burst into the air. The sound was deafening.

"Ali!"

Ignoring his father, he screamed and fired off another burst.

Lisa turned to the mirror, catching Sheikh's eyes. "Teenagers." The man shrugged. "What to do?"

It might have been amusing if it wasn't for the returning gunfire. Only they didn't shoot into the air. A series of *ker-plinks* and *ker-plunks* hit the back end of the Hummer. Sheikh pressed the accelerator to the floor.

Ali gleefully returned fire, relishing the opportunity. Only now he didn't shoot into the air. Now he aimed for the trucks.

Meanwhile, up front, the bodyguard was climbing over Charlie to join the firefight. As he did, Charlie turned to Lisa and Jaz. "Get down! Down!"

The Hummer slid hard to the right, throwing Lisa into the girl.

More shots struck, this time catching the left fender. Lisa grabbed Jazz's head and, despite the girl's protests, forced her to the floor, covering her with her body.

The bodyguard leaned out his window and began to fire.

Sheikh angrily yelled at his son, who angrily yelled back. A family squabble, interrupted only by Ali's intermittent firing.

The car hit a series of ruts, tossing Lisa every direction.

"Hang on!" Charlie shouted.

"If you say so!" she yelled.

Suddenly the car was airborne. Jaz screamed and Lisa tightened her hold on her. When they landed, they hit hard, scraping the Hummer's undercarriage and bouncing several times before leveling off.

"Everyone is okay?" Sheikh hollered.

Lisa raised her head. "What happened?"

"We're going off road!" Charlie shouted.

Lisa spun to the back window and saw the vehicles hitting the same jump. One, two, three—hitting hard and leveling off. Well, two leveling off. The third, the sedan, lost control and suddenly flipped, rolling over and over until it exploded in flames.

"That's one!" Charlie shouted to Sheikh.

"Yes!" Sheikh beamed. "Two to go!"

"Sure you don't need help?" Charlie yelled.

"Thank you, no. The time has been long, but like riding a bicycle, one does not forget!"

A series of bullets blew out the back window, throwing pebbles of glass inside.

"Sorry!" Sheikh shouted.

"What are we doing? Where are we going?" Lisa demanded.

"I have a cousin, on the coast. He owns a boat."

"How far is that?" Charlie shouted.

They hit another series of bumps.

"By this route, not far."

"How far?" Lisa yelled.

Ali pulled his head in to reload as the bodyguard took advantage of a clearer view and fired several bursts.

Sheikh shouted over the roar, "An hour!"

"What!" Lisa yelled.

"Perhaps, two."

"Two hours!"

Ali finished reloading, stuck his weapon back outside, and resumed firing.

"This is insane!" Lisa cried.

Sheikh shouted back. "Insane?"

More gunshots.

"No, my friends. It is an adventure!"

Another spray of bullets caught the roof and everyone ducked.

"All right," Sheikh admitted as he rose. "Insane. But only a little."

The phone rang at 5:51 a.m.

Sheldon Houser lowered the barbell onto the bench-press stand, took a cleansing breath, and slid from under the weights. A sheen of sweat covered his bare chest and arms. And for good reason. At his age, he had to work twice as hard just to maintain his strength and agility.

But it wasn't for him.

He threw a towel around his neck and started for the phone. The terra-cotta tile was cool under his calloused feet. As he passed the living room window he caught a reflection of himself. A bit thicker than he preferred, with a slight bulge where there had once been an impressive six-pack. Still, he was in pretty good shape.

But not for himself. It had never been for himself.

He scooped up the receiver on the fourth ring.

The voice was soft, but curt. "Houser?"

"Yes?"

"It is time."

"They have been discovered?"

"The operation is go. Assemble your team zero, seven hundred at Sde Dov Airport."

"Yes, sir."

The other end quietly clicked. Houser lowered the phone. He would start paging the rest of the team in a moment. But for now he paused. This would be his final mission. He knew that. Success or failure, it made little difference. He would be asked to step down and retire. It was a bittersweet truth, but a truth nonetheless.

Still, even that was acceptable. Because, like everything else it would be for his beloved country.

"Yee-Haw!"

Charlie turned in surprise to the bodyguard. Not only had the Bedouin given a good ol' boy shout, he'd done it in a near perfect accent. Glancing out the back window, Charlie saw the reason. One of the two remaining trucks chasing them was slowing to a stop, steam billowing from its radiator. Somehow, no doubt through sheer accident, a bullet of theirs had actually struck the vehicle.

And a good thing. Because, despite Charlie's warnings, the man's enthusiastic firings were quickly draining them of ammunition. The boy had already used up his last clip. The guard's would shortly follow.

Then there was the gas.

"Not to worry." Sheikh motioned to the switch for the reserve tank. "It is an excellent option. You Americans, you have Hummers too?"

Charlie nodded.

"Necessary for freeway driving, I hear. Especially Los Angeles."

Charlie glanced over to see the man's grin. Jokes were coming faster—either because Sheikh was relaxed, or because he was trying to get Charlie to relax.

Thirty minutes earlier they had raced through the tiny village of Al Bad. The sifting sand of the wadi briefly gave way to blacktop before returning to rock and sand . . . but not before they passed a John Deere tractor, the only vehicle on their entire trip.

"Rush hour." Sheikh laughed.

Over time they managed to pull ahead of their pursuers by a hundred yards. Now, it was mostly a matter of endurance.

Earlier, the old man had produced a satellite phone from the glove compartment. He called his cousin asking him to prepare his boat. The conversation was brief, less than a minute, before he hung up.

"What did he say?" Charlie asked.

"He says no problem. It should be fun."

Charlie nodded.

"He also says strangers have arrived."

"Strangers?"

"Italians, he thinks."

Charlie scowled.

"Not to worry. If they cause problems, my cousin will handle them. With me at his side, we can handle all of Europe!"

And so the race continued. From time to time the truck behind them would fire, but of course their shots were futile . . . which of course meant the bodyguard had to return double the amount . . . equally as futile.

Charlie looked back to Lisa. She held Jaz in her arms, both looking the worse for wear.

"We'll be okay," he assured them. "Just a little while and we'll be there."

Lisa watched his eyes and nodded. It was clear she trusted him which made him even more uneasy. Others had made the same mistake.

"Ah, here we are now."

He turned and saw several whitewashed houses. Behind them a series of multiple-story condos.

"Welcome to Al Maqnah," Sheikh shouted. "Only city in all the north with a regulation Olympic-sized swimming pool. Oh, dear."

Up ahead, a late-model BMW had pulled in front of them to block the road.

"It is al-Shurta."

"Who?"

"The police."

Sheikh began honking his horn. He stuck his head out the window and shouted in a dialect Charlie didn't understand.

The policeman, who had been climbing out of his car, stopped. Sheikh slowed slightly, but continued shouting. They were thirty yards away and rapidly closing the distance.

The officer seemed to hesitate.

Sheikh kept shouting, until the man hopped back inside and quickly pulled his car out of the way . . . just as the Hummer raced by.

"What did you tell him?" Charlie asked.

"That he had a lovely car which I did not wish to spoil."

More gunshots came from behind. Charlie looked over his shoulder. The truck had taken advantage of their slowing and quickly gained ground.

Sheikh cranked the Hummer hard to the right then straightened out and accelerated. "It is here!" he shouted. "Just ahead!"

They bounced into a parking lot containing two dust-coated cars. A small dock lay just ahead. Moored to it was an old twenty-foot cabin cruiser. He slammed on the brakes just a few feet from the dock, sliding the vehicle around to expose his side to the approaching truck.

"Everyone to the boat!" Charlie shouted.

The group piled out on the dock side.

"Go! Go!"

The women stayed low, racing along the dock toward the boat. The bodyguard took position over the hood and began firing as Charlie turned to help Sheikh. The old man was halfway across the seat when a bullet shattered the driver's window and hit his shoulder. He cried out and fell forward.

Charlie scrambled inside and grabbed the man, pulling him to the passenger door. From there he eased him outside and down onto the pavement. An obvious veteran, Sheikh gathered the material of his long galabiya and used it to apply pressure to the wound.

Ali came to his side, shouting in hysterics.

Sheikh assured him he would be okay, insisting he join the others at the boat. But the boy would have none of it.

More shots were fired.

Charlie rose to take a peek. It was just as he expected. One of the two soldiers was breaking away from the truck, fanning out . . . until a spray of bullets caught him in the chest and threw him backward—killing him instantly.

Charlie turned to see the bodyguard at the hood whoop in success. But his triumph was short-lived when he discovered he was out of ammunition. Cursing his luck, he removed the clip to double-check. And in that moment of distraction, a bullet snapped back his head. Another pierced his neck.

He fell to the pavement, joining his victim in eternity.

Once again the boy cried out. He scurried to the bodyguard who lay on the ground behind the front of the vehicle.

The remaining soldier at the truck fired another burst, then waited. Then fired again.

"Go!" Sheikh shouted at Charlie. "Go!"

"What about you!"

"Not to worry!"

Incensed at the bodyguard's death, Ali rose over the hood, brandishing his rifle, shouting oaths. He had no ammunition, but that didn't seem to be the point.

"Get down!" Charlie ordered. "Down!"

The kid paid no attention.

Charlie raced to him and, staying low, pulled his arm. "Get down!"

The boy would not listen. He broke free and stepped out in front of the hood, screaming at the soldier in defiance. Charlie lunged at him, tackling him hard to the ground. The kid struggled, trying to scramble free.

More shots fired. Charlie felt the spray of sand and asphalt. And still the kid fought him. With no other recourse, Charlie reached back and hit the boy hard in the face. Instantly, the kid went limp. He picked him up. Wincing in pain over his wrist and ribs, he stayed low and raced back to the safety of the Hummer, bullets exploding all around.

He arrived at Sheikh's side and laid the boy down. "Sorry."

The old man shrugged. "What to do."

Meanwhile, the soldier, who by now suspected they were out of ammunition, rose behind his truck's door and yelled.

"Go!" Sheikh shouted at Charlie. "Go! Go!"

"What about you two?"

"Allah is merciful, he will protect us."

"But—"

"And if he is busy . . ." Sheikh pulled out a German Luger from his robes. He smiled but the weight of the gun was too much for his weakened arm. It slipped from his hand and clattered to the ground.

The shouting soldier stepped out from behind his door, rifle poised.

Charlie grabbed the Luger. He chambered a round and hurried to the back of the Hummer.

Still shouting, the soldier moved closer. He was twenty yards away.

Charlie dropped to the ground and scooted just clear of

the back tire, using the vehicle's shadows to his advantage. Supporting his arms on the ground he carefully lined the Luger's sights on the soldier's head. He had no idea how accurate the weapon was, but Sheikh appeared to have taken good care of it.

The soldier continued his approach, cautious.

Charlie took a deep breath, then exhaled so the throbbing pulse of his body would not spoil the shot. He paused a moment, feeling for wind from the sea. There was some but not enough to compensate. Still, just to be safe, he lowered his aim to the chest. A bigger target.

The soldier was fifteen yards away.

Charlie tightened his finger on the trigger, took another breath, and partially exhaled. Then, for a reason he could not explain, he glanced back up to the soldier's face.

He was in his early twenties. Young and, yes, frightened. Very frightened.

Ten yards.

Charlie focused back on the chest. He had a clear shot, could drop the young man where he stood. Everything he was, told him to take the shot—his training, his years of experience. And yet . . .

He looked to the soldier's eyes. So young and terrified. If he wasn't married he was the age where he soon would be. And with marriage would come children and an entire lifetime.

Seven yards away. He was still shouting. Still frightened.

Charlie dropped his aim lower—first to the man's kneecap, then up slightly to the fleshy part of his thigh. This would stop him. And, if the bullet was true, it would not cripple.

Once again he inhaled, partially exhaled . . . and fired.

The solider screamed, dropping his rifle as he grabbed his leg and fell to the pavement.

Charlie scrambled to his feet and raced back to Sheikh.

"Go," the old man insisted.

He laid the Luger in his lap. "You'll be okay?"

"My cousin has many friends."

Charlie nodded. Then, touching his hand to his head, his lips, his chest, he said, "*Salaam aleikum.*"

Sheikh returned the gesture. "*Salaam aleikum.*"

Charlie turned and started for the boat. Even now he marveled at his actions. For the first time he could remember *he had not fought back*. Not returned evil for evil. Stepping onto the dock, he reached into his vest pocket and felt the stones he took from the top of the mountain. Stones only partially changed, but changed nonetheless. He continued toward the boat. Not proud by any means. But not ashamed. Because, despite his failures, he was changed. Even here, even now.

Rifle shots rang out. Their impact slammed into his back. He gasped as he stumbled forward and fell. Even before he hit the dock, he heard different shots. A Luger. Abruptly halting the rifle.

From the sun-baked wood he looked up and saw two men running toward him. They came from the boat but did not appear Arab. As they approached, his vision grew white, overexposed. He faintly heard Jaz screaming, "Uncle Charlie! Uncle Charlie!"

And then he heard nothing at all.

Twenty-Four

ITALY

Consciousness drifted in and out, fleeting and blurry. At one point Charlie was sure he heard the Muslim call to prayer until the sound focused and he recognized the clear ringing of church bells. With the focus came the headache. Every cell in his brain throbbed. Then there was the searing burn in his back and gut. For a moment he thought he'd died. Then doubted it. There couldn't be that much pain in hell.

Lisa's voice floated in. "They say you refused the morphine." With the recognition came a certain comfort. And determination. He concentrated on his eyes, using all of his strength to pry them open. The stabbing brightness did little to help his headache.

She sat to his left, her body outlined by a window. He tried to smile and ease her concern. He doubted he pulled it off.

"Here, take a sip." She brought a straw to his lips.

He took a long, cool drink of water.

"You should really take it. The morphine drip, I mean."

He shook his head, exploding any remaining synapses that hadn't fired their pain. "Dulls . . ." He forced the words through a leather-cracked voice. ". . . senses."

"I told them you'd say something stupid like that. But I think we're safe now. I think we're all right."

"Where . . ." He coughed.

"Italy. Near Rome."

"Jaz . . ."

"She's with her uncle Fredrick."

"The priest . . . alive? How?"

"Something about worship. I didn't ask. He and Jaz are at a lab not far from here, putting those little rocks you nabbed to the test."

"The boat . . . the men?"

"More priests. From the Vatican."

"Vatican?"

"Can you believe it? They're actually the good guys for once." She gave him another sip. "According to Fredrick, they've bankrolled this whole project."

He stared at her.

"What?"

"You look . . . good."

She was caught off guard, at least for a moment. Recovering, she responded, "And you look like crap."

He nodded and closed his eyes. This time he did smile. The pain was still there, but more bearable.

‡ ‡ ‡

"There we go. See?"

With the iPod buds in her ears, Jaz leaned over Uncle Fredrick to look at the computer screen. Earlier, he'd shown her all sorts of charts and figures and junk. And, as usual, she drank it in like a sponge.

Now in front of them were four graphs in four different colors. The blue was labeled Baptism, the green, Transfiguration, the red, Damascus Road, and the black, Cosmic Background Radiation. Each went their own direction . . . except in the center. Here, all four came together, running perfectly parallel to one another. Jaz had seen this before, back in California. As far as she was concerned, it was clear evidence of God's voiceprint.

But now a fifth graph was forming. Yellow. Like the others, it had its own pattern. It started on the left and slowly, way too slowly, worked its way across the screen.

The lab was basically like the one in Switzerland—underground, with twelve stone rods that could be raised and lowered. The only difference was this one lay underneath a church which meant they had to go through the building, and pass a bunch of statues and stuff. Actually, the church was pretty cool. It was the cemetery next door that creeped her out. How weird to know that just beyond the lab walls hundreds of dead people were buried. Not weird. Gross. Of course she tried not to think about it, which meant most of the time that's all she thought about.

On the nearby counter the little Molecular Resonance Analyzer was humming away. It looked a lot like a microwave oven, complete with a front loading door. Inside, a paper-thin slice from one of the rocks Uncle Charlie had retrieved from the mountain was being studied.

Uncle Fredrick tapped her on the arm. "Jaz . . ."

She turned back to the computer screen. He seemed pretty excited and for good reason. Halfway across the screen the yellow graph had begun perfectly lining up with all the other colors.

The two didn't talk. They didn't move. Jaz doubted she breathed. Eventually Uncle Fredrick reached out to take her hands. Both of them. Because, like his own, they were ice cold.

The clanging church bells rankled Omar's nerves. Such cacophony, such vanity. Unlike the *adhan*, the call to prayer, their noise only drew attention to themselves, to the power behind those who ordered their ringing. As far as Omar could tell, they did nothing to glorify Allah.

Fight against such of those who have been given the Scripture as believe not in Allah nor the Last Day . . .

Standing in the center of St. Peter's Plaza, he closed his eyes against the sound. And against the tourists and pilgrims who bustled about him. Some came to visit the museum with its thousands of forbidden graven images. Others came to worship a man, a single old man, surrounded by a massive empire of marble, politics, man-made saints and a dead, bleeding god hanging from a cross.

He placed another pistachio between his teeth and lifted his face toward the sun.

Every man makes mistakes. And every man has the obligation to correct them. That is the path of Allah.

And here he was, at the very heart of Christendom, to correct his mistake. Arrangements had been made to meet others. He was no fool. He knew they would be there as a precaution in case he should again become weak. But he would not. Even if it involved the killing of innocents such as the girl—

There are no innocents.

Even if it involved the killing of others, then so be it. *Insha'allah.*

The only reward of those who make war upon Allah and his messenger and strive after corruption in the land will be that they will be killed or crucified . . .

And yet, even now, the hypocrisy was not lost on him. The lie he spoke to the *shura* so he could return to the path. The fact he must soon disguise himself as an infidel, the very enemy of Allah, to accomplish the holy work of Allah. Still, it was not the way of Islam that was imperfect. The problem lay with man, with his imperfections, his sins, his rebellion. And to stop man, Omar Atmani must use the sword of man.

Of course those like his father would never understand: *"You are speaking of jihad bi al saif, the holy war of the sword. But it is a different war we must fight—the jihad al nafs, the war within our own souls, the struggle against the immoralities of our own flesh."*

But Omar did understand. He did not always approve of the methods, and such thinking was his weakness, but he understood.

"David Riggs?"

He opened his eyes into the bright sun. The silhouette of a young man wearing the robes of a priest stood before him.

"Dr. David Riggs?" It was the assigned code name.

Shielding his eyes, Omar saw the speaker was of Mediterranean descent, slight in build. "Yes?"

"You will come with me, please?"

Omar nodded and reached for his backpack. He rose and followed as the two threaded their way through the plaza.

Whoso fighteth in the way of Allah, be he slain or be he victorious, on him We shall bestow a vast reward.

The bells continued to ring, but he barely heard. *Insha'allah*, he repeated to himself. *Insha'allah . . .*

Twenty-Five

"I hear there's good news?"

Fredrick looked up from his computer. "Ms. Harmon, I am glad you could join us."

"And actually pull yourself away from Uncle Charlie," Jaz teased.

Lisa ignored the dig. "It's all I could do to convince him to stay behind. He's already making plans to be transported from the hospital to our hotel."

"Under a nurse's care, I hope," Fredrick said.

"I wouldn't be taking any bets."

"You know," Jaz said, "you really shouldn't be throwing yourself at him like that."

"I beg your pardon?"

"Mom says if you're interested in a boy, you should let *him* chase *you* . . . at least until you catch him."

"I see."

"It's true. Take it from me, never let them know you're desperate."

"*Desperate?*" Lisa laughed. "Who said anything about desperate?"

"Okay"—Jaz shrugged—"in love. It's all the same."

"Listen, I don't know where you get your infor—"

"Ladies . . ." Fredrick interrupted.

"Well, it's true, isn't—"

"But there are some things you might not be such an expert—"

"Ladies, please." Fredrick held up his hands.

Lisa came to a stop. She was surprised at her reaction. Taking a breath to compose herself, she returned to the topic. "So these stones, they're the right ones? Their molecular whatever, it's the same?"

The priest nodded and referred to the screen. "They are *precisely* the same."

"So there you have it."

"Yes. Well, except, of course, for the Program."

"But you'll get that."

He looked up from the monitor and sighed. "Perhaps . . . in time." Removing his glasses he rubbed his eyes and turned to Jaz. "I still find it difficult to believe your parents left no clues as to where they may have hidden it."

The girl shrugged. "They left nothing at the lab, I can tell you that. Not when they knew people were coming after us."

"And they gave you absolutely no hints."

"Nothing. They came home, said they'd made a big discovery people would want to get their hands on, and that was that."

"With no instructions where to look should something happen. No envelopes, no safety-deposit boxes, no—"

"Forget safety-deposit boxes," Lisa said. "It's the first place the Bureau would check."

"It was just like every other night," Jaz said. "'Cept we went out for Chinese. I love Chinese, 'specially now that I'm an expert with chopsticks. You know it's important to rub them together first in case there are, like, splinters and stuff."

Fredrick nodded. "Nothing else?"

"Nope. Well, this." She held out her iPod. "I'd been asking

for one for, like, a thousand years and I guess they figured we'd finally be able to afford it. They made a big deal about not letting it out of my sight 'cause lots of people like to steal them and everything."

Fredrick thought a moment. "May I see it?"

"Sure." She pulled the buds from her ears and handed the unit to him.

He took one earbud and listened to it.

"She uses it to fit in," Lisa explained.

"A fashion statement," Jaz corrected.

Fredrick nodded, then tried the other bud. Glancing up, he asked, "You don't mind if I look inside, do you?"

Jaz shook her head. "I already thought of it. There's no room to slip in papers or microfiche or anything."

"I understand." The priest sounded just a little breathier as he reached into a nearby drawer and dug through it.

"It's just for playing music," Lisa explained.

"Yes. Of course." He continued to dig a bit more urgently.

"Or Podcasts," Jaz said. "Or . . ." Suddenly lights started coming on. "Or TV shows . . ."

"Yes." He was growing more excited. "Yes . . ."

Lisa turned from one to the other. What was going on?

He continued. "Or anything else that can be recorded on an electromagnetic medium, including—"

"A computer program!" Jaz leaped off the stool. "Of course! Why didn't I think of it!" She joined his side, hopping from one foot to another.

"Do you think . . ." Lisa played the calm skeptic, or tried to. "You think the Program could be in there?"

Pulling a soldering gun from the drawer, Fredrick grabbed a handful of cables and his magnifying glasses. "We shall soon find out."

Sheldon Houser adjusted the vinyl headphones, damp with sweat. They had matted his hair and, over the hours, begun pinching his ears. But it was evening. Madison and both women were in the hotel together and every word counted.

He looked across the darkened room to the window where Brenem had carefully positioned a tripod. It held what looked like a small telescope. From it a nearly invisible laser beam shot across the street and struck the hotel window thirty meters away. It left a red circle on the glass no bigger than the eraser of a pencil.

Directly beside Houser another tripod was set up. It held another device with a telescopic rifle sight atop it. The scope was trained on the red dot. Now the ultra-sensitive receptors in the unit below the scope were recording every vibration of the dot, no matter how slight. In short, they had turned the entire window of the hotel room into a giant microphone allowing Houser and the team to hear everything from flushing toilets to clinking glasses to human conversation.

"Congratulations."

It was great to hear some life back in Charlie's voice. Although exhausted from his move out of the hospital, he was in good spirits. He'd already shooed away the nurse for a few hours and was sitting up in the easy chair. He was clad in a white terry-cloth robe, with ribs taped, and a stainless-steel IV stand beside him.

"And," Jaz said, pirouetting from foot to foot across the

room, "he'll have everything going before dawn. In just a few hours it'll be operational."

"Operational?" Charlie asked.

Jaz was too busy dancing to see his lips.

Lisa caught her attention and motioned to Charlie.

"Operational?" he repeated.

"That's right." She resumed spinning. "Now we'll be able to hear everything. The *whole* voice of God."

"But isn't that . . ." She wasn't watching so he turned to Lisa. "Isn't that dangerous?"

"He has those same control rods you mentioned he had in Switzerland."

"And," Jaz added, "he's got the *whole* Program so he can finally control it."

"So that's good news?"

"Yeah . . ." Jaz slowed to a stop near the window, hesitated, then turned to face them. "Can we talk? Grown-up to grown-up?"

Lisa and Charlie exchanged glances.

"Sure," Lisa said. "What's on your mind?"

Jaz stepped closer. "I've been giving this a lot of thought lately."

"What's that?"

"I mean, it's cool we got the rocks and the Program and everything. But now what?"

"Now what?" Charlie asked. "You've got the actual voice of God, kiddo. The very thing your mom and dad gave their lives for."

"Right"—she plopped down on the nearby sofa—"but nobody cares."

Lisa replied, "From what I've seen, *everybody* cares."

Jaz threw back her head. "Not really." She sat back up. "I mean, they do and they don't."

"Meaning?"

"Meaning people only care about it if they can use it." She rose and started dancing again, keeping her eye on her reflection in the window. "Those creeps in Egypt, they just wanted it 'cause it messed up their religious stuff."

Lisa nodded. "And . . ."

"And those Israel guys, they just wanted it 'cause you said it messed up their politics." She turned back to Lisa. "And even the good guys—we just want it to scare people into doing what we want them to do."

"So what are you saying?" Charlie asked. He waited until she saw him and repeated, "So what are you saying?"

Jaz slowed to a stop and shrugged. "I'm just saying if everybody's using it to get their own way . . . is it really that good of a thing?"

Charlie scoffed. "It's the voice of God."

"Right."

"That's like saying . . . if everybody uses God, is *he* really that good?"

Jaz cocked her head, as if he'd just made her point.

Lisa frowned, thinking. Wasn't that the whole purpose of believing in God in the first place? To have someone you can turn to? Wasn't that why she'd walked away from her faith, because he wasn't there when she needed him?

"Whatever . . ." Jaz broke into another series of pirouettes.

Lisa watched, continuing to think. That was the whole purpose of Christianity . . . wasn't it? To have God there whenever you needed him, whenever you wanted him?

Or was it?

The question left her just a little unsettled.

Jaz came to a stop. "What's this?" She started toward the window. "Guys?"

Lisa barely heard.

"Somebody better check this out."

Lisa looked up and rose to join her. "What's what?"

Without answering, Jaz pulled back the curtains to reveal a red dot of light on the window.

≛ ≛ ≛

"Down!" Houser hissed to Brenem. "Shut it down!"

Brenem was too slow. By the time he reached the power supply, the woman had not only arrived at the window, but was grabbing the girl and pulling her down.

Houser pressed his lapel mic. "We're made! Move in! Move in!"

Twenty-Six

"What are you—"

"Surveillance!" Lisa shouted as they hit the floor. "Across the street!"

Charlie knew the drill and, despite the danger of reopening his wounds, he struggled to stand. If they could see through the window, they could shoot through it. With more staggering than walking, he threw himself at the wall switch near the door and caught it before sliding to the ground, dragging the IV stand with him.

"Charlie!"

He kept the pain out of his voice. "I'm okay!"

"What's going on?" Jaz cried.

"Stay down!"

"What's—"

"Stay down!"

Someone slammed into the door.

Charlie reached for the IV stand.

They hit it again, this time splintering it open. Light spilled in from the hallway, revealing a pair of legs in black trousers. Charlie swung the stand hard into the legs. The intruder tripped and, cursing in Hebrew, fell. Charlie raised the stand to strike again, but his pain and weakness betrayed him. He'd barely lifted it before it fell back to the parquet flooring.

The intruder scrambled to his feet.

Charlie had no strength in his arms, but he had plenty in his legs. He spun around on the floor until his feet found the wall's baseboard. He pushed off, sliding, reaching out and grabbing the man's legs. The intruder tried kicking him away but only succeeded in losing his balance, once again falling.

This time a gun clattered to the floor.

Trusting that Lisa heard it, Charlie focused on the man's legs. He clung to them for all he was worth. Despite his efforts, one foot slipped from his grasp and kicked hard, missing Charlie the first time, catching his face the second. Pain shot through his nose, but the foot was back within reach and he grabbed it.

More twisting and kicking until the intruder reached down to disengage himself—exactly as Charlie had hoped. Releasing his legs, he lunged forward, grabbing the man's arms. Of course he was no match for the intruder who freed his right hand and delivered a series of expert blows.

But fighting was not Charlie's purpose. Giving Lisa time to find the gun was.

The beating continued as consciousness began slipping away.

"All right!" Lisa's voice brought him back. "That's enough!"

More punches.

"That's enough!"

The blows stopped.

Charlie either released the agent or he slipped away. In either case, the intruder was breathing heavily as he rose to his feet.

Jaz had risen too. "What's happening?"

"Get away from the window," Lisa ordered.

Unable to see her lips, the girl repeated, "What's going on?"

Lisa turned to her. "Get away from the—"

That was all the distraction the man needed. He leaped at Lisa. Only then did Charlie see the glint of steel in his hand. She fired the gun once, twice, lighting up the room, but not stopping the attack. She cried as the knife plunged into her.

It took a third shot to drop him to the ground.

"Lisa!"

She sank to her knees.

Charlie crawled toward her. She held the right side of her neck just above the clavicle. Even in the dim light he could see her fingers growing wet with blackness. The knife had either nicked or sliced her jugular or carotid.

"Keep your hand there!" he shouted. "Press it!"

Jaz continued shouting, but he did not answer. He reached to the easy chair and pulled down the paper-thin blanket that had been covering him. Shoving it toward Lisa, he shouted, "Hold this! Hold it tight!"

Lisa kept her left hand on the wound while reaching for the blanket with her right, the one holding the gun. Her eyes widened as something caught her attention just over Charlie's shoulder. He saw her face the same instant a shadow filled the doorway. He dropped and rolled, giving Lisa a clear shot.

She took it. The room exploded with two more flashes of light and a second man tumbled to the floor.

Jaz was screaming now.

"Here!" Charlie shoved the blanket at Lisa and took the gun. "Can you move?"

She nodded.

Using the chair for support, he struggled to stand, trying to raise Lisa with him. He could feel the wounds in his back tearing open. Finally he made it to his feet.

"Where . . ." She choked.

"A doctor. The hospital."

She shook her head. "There will be more . . ."

"We've got a gun."

Again she shook her head. "I'll slow you. Take Jaz."

"No!" There was more feeling in his voice than he intended. "We're not leaving you!"

"Take Jaz—"

"We'll go back to the hospital!" The emotion continued rising. "A doctor! We'll find a doctor! Jaz!" He waved his arm in the darkness, hoping she'd see. "JAZMIN!"

No answer.

He carried Lisa across the room toward the door. If there was pain, he couldn't feel it—not through the adrenaline, the emotion, the memory of past failures.

They reached the wall. Fumbling for the light switch, he turned it on and flooded the room with brightness.

Jaz was cowering in the corner—hair disheveled, face wet with tears.

"Come on!" he ordered. "We have to go!"

ᴸ ᴸ ᴸ

"You ever fire one of these things?" Bernie's brother tossed her an M-16. It was heavier than she thought.

"Actually, I'm a Sig girl, myself," she said.

"Yeah, well your toys might not be enough this time around." He glanced to his two buddies who snickered.

Doing her best to be cool, Bernie checked the sight, then the clip.

257

The Voice

"Just remember that baby has a bit more power than you're used to."

"Meaning?"

"Make sure it doesn't knock you on your fat butt."

Jaz had to admit, it wasn't so easy moving Lisa down the hall. Uncle Charlie tried to help, but let's face it, the guy was having a hard time moving himself. And his mind wasn't so clear either. 'Fact, when they got to the end of the hallway, instead of going down the stairs, he headed for the elevator.

"What are you doing?" Jaz shouted.

He said nothing, just hit the button and leaned against the wall, catching his breath.

But Jaz was no idiot. She'd seen enough movies to know that taking elevators was exactly what the bad guys wanted. As soon as they reached the lobby, the doors would open and there would be two men in trench coats with guns to blow them away.

"We've gotta take the stairs!" she said.

He shook his head. "The extra movement—she'll lose too much blood."

The elevator doors opened.

"Come on!"

Reluctantly, Jaz moved Lisa forward, but, to her surprise, Charlie blocked her.

"Not yet." He reached in, pressed the top button, something like eleven or twelve, then he hit another button for another floor and stepped back out.

"What are—"

"*Now* we'll take the stairs."

Yes sir, he was definitely losing it. But at least they were back to taking the stairs. They hobbled to the door. Jaz held Lisa against her and managed to open it. Uncle Charlie hung back a sec, double-checking the hallway. Then he joined them and they started down the steps. Each one was like a major trauma—Jaz clinging to the railing, holding Lisa on one side. Uncle Charlie trying to do the same on the other.

But they'd only gone one flight, before Uncle Charlie pointed to the door. "Here," he wheezed. "In here."

"But we've only—"

"They think we've gone to the roof. We can take it from here."

Jaz rolled her eyes. And they call women fickle.

The three entered the hallway and barely got to the elevator before the doors opened. Apparently this was the other floor he'd pushed.

They helped Lisa inside and Jaz hit the button to the lobby. The doors closed and they started to drop. Uncle Charlie braced himself against the back wall. It took both hands for him to raise the gun toward the doors. Even at that, he was shaking.

The elevator sighed to a stop. After what seemed like forever, the doors rattled open. Jaz held Lisa, waiting for the worst. But to her surprise, there was no shoot-out. The coast was clear.

Charlie grabbed Lisa and they moved into the lobby. It must have been a sight, the three of them limping through the fancy place. Of course Jaz did her best to smile at the concerned faces, assuring them, "We're good, it's cool, everything's okay," but somehow she doubted they bought it. Maybe 'cause Uncle Charlie was still wearing that ugly robe and was barefoot. Either that or it was the blood-soaked blanket they held to Lisa's throat.

In any case, when they arrived at the revolving door, all

three of them crammed into one section and staggered forward until they stepped out into the night air.

"Find a car . . ." Charlie gasped, "with keys."

Jaz nodded. She leaned Lisa and Charlie against the building and started on her hunt. The first three cars were a bust which was too bad. Two were Mercedes, another a fancy red sports car. She scored on the fourth—something called a Renault. Definitely boring. And yellow was definitely not her color. But it would have to do.

"Over here." She motioned. "Here!"

Charlie tried to move with Lisa, but by now he was so weak he practically fell.

"Hang on!" Jaz ran to their side. She grabbed Lisa and half walked, half dragged both of them toward the car. Once they opened the back door, they sat Lisa inside. She was so out of it she toppled over.

"That's okay," Charlie said as he climbed in beside her. "Just . . . drive." He barely moved his lips.

"What?"

He turned to her, eyes closed. "Drive."

"Me? I've never—"

"The . . . hospital. Hurry."

"But—"

He reached over, trying to shut the door, but couldn't.

"I don't even have a permit!"

He didn't answer, but leaned back in the seat, eyes still closed.

"Uncle Charlie!"

No response.

"Uncle Charlie!!"

He motioned for the door.

"You're not listening!"

Again he motioned.

"Great," she scorned, "just great!" She slammed the door. Hard. She looked around, searching the sidewalk for help. There was no one except some old couple shuffling toward her. They'd have to do.

"Excuse me?" She raced to them. "Excuse me?"

They looked up, startled.

"Can you tell me where the hospital is?"

They frowned, pulling back. It was obvious they didn't understand. She tried again, with greater exaggeration. "*Hospital. Where is?*"

They shook their heads, looking even more afraid.

"HOS—PIT—AL!"

The old man stepped in front of his wife to protect her.

"Great," Jaz muttered. She turned and ran back to the car. "Uncle Charlie!"

His eyes remained closed.

She banged on the window. "How am I supposed to know where the hospital— Uncle Charlie!!"

He did not answer.

She ran around to the driver's side and stood on the threshold, searching the streets for somebody, anybody. There were no other pedestrians . . . well, except for the two men racing out of the hotel lobby. Two men who appeared to be searching for something . . . until they spotted her and began shouting and running.

"Great." She ducked into the car and fumbled with the ignition. "Just great!"

Twenty-Seven

Charlie was fading.

His wounds had opened. He could feel the warm stickiness of the soaked gauze and the heavy wetness of his robe. Only when the car jerked or swerved did he wake enough to make sure he still had his hand pressed against Lisa's throat. The blast of passing horns and Jazmin's screaming also helped. Lisa had already lost consciousness. He hoped and prayed he wouldn't.

Suddenly, squealing brakes and the sickening crunch of metal threw them to a stop.

"Jaz—" He tried to shout but it turned to coughing.

He heard the creaking of the driver's door as she pried it open. "Uncle Charlie!" A moment later his door opened. But instead of Jaz, men's hands reached in and pulled him out.

He tried fighting them.

"It's okay!" she yelled from behind them. "It's all right."

They got him outside. Instead of hospital personnel, he was surrounded by men in robes. Priests! A half dozen. Because of the bright lights illuminating the church, he couldn't make out their faces, but they were definitely priests.

"No!" he shouted. "A hospital! We need—"

"It's the lab!" she shouted. "Uncle Fredrick can help."

Charlie closed his eyes. By the time the priest found them a hospital, it would be too late. He turned back to the men pulling Lisa out. "Her neck! Put pressure on—"

"*Si, si,*" a hooded priest answered and shouted to the others, "Neck! *Il collo! Il collo!*"

There was another screech of tires, some fifty feet away. And then another. Car doors opened. A voice shouted, "*Polizia! Fermati! Polizia!*"

But they were not police. Charlie knew that. Apparently, so did the priests . . . which would explain the AK-47s suddenly appearing from under their robes. His eyes widened in surprise. This made no sense.

It made even less sense when they opened fire.

The newest arrivals took cover behind their cars.

"*Rapido!*" the first priest shouted. He motioned them toward the church. "*Rapido!*"

Two men had retrieved Lisa and were carrying her up the church steps. A third was half carrying, half pulling Charlie.

Catching a glimpse of Jaz's face, Charlie coughed. "The hospital . . . why didn't—"

"I didn't know where it was!"

He understood. He didn't like it, but he understood.

"Remember your leg—how it got healed?"

He glanced at his leg, remembering how even the hole in his pants had disappeared. He recalled his discussion with the priest about healing, remembered how the man had somehow avoided destruction at the lab.

He turned back to her and shouted, "Tell him to fire it up! Now!"

"It might be too early! He said the Program wouldn't be ready until—"

"If he doesn't do it now, she won't live!" He broke out coughing. "Tell him!"

Jaz nodded and raced up the steps.

Chips of marble steps exploded at Charlie's feet. The pursuers had opened fire from behind their cars.

The accompanying priests spun around and returned their own bursts of fire.

"Who are you guys?" Charlie shouted to the man carrying him.

The priest did not answer until they entered the large double doors and stood inside the church. Only then did he remove his hood and turn so Charlie could see.

It was Omar Atmani, the kid he'd beaten up at Cal Poly.

⚔ ⚔ ⚔

"Move it!" Houser shouted. "Move it! Move it!" His team broke from the cover of their cars and started for the church . . . and apparently the lab. He guessed the Americans had raced to it for protection in what they hoped to be a repeat performance of Switzerland.

But not this time. Houser had learned his lesson. This time no one would escape.

He glanced over to see Milkner and Brenem already circling to the back. He motioned to the two newest recruits to enter through the side door. He and Iserson would take the steps.

In a matter of seconds they reached the front doors, locked and loaded. He'd already lost two men, he would not lose another. Certainly not to a handful of priests.

⚔ ⚔ ⚔

The steps down the narrow staircase were slick from centuries of use. Only the flicker of an occasional fluorescent reminded Omar they were not descending into some Inquisition dungeon. Behind him was the sporadic pop and crackle of gunfire . . . Islamic-owned AK-47s versus Jewish

Uzis, inside a Christian church. The irony was not lost on him.

As he dragged the semi-conscious American down into the dank coolness, he focused on the task at hand. The past arguments with friends, his father, even the intellectual gymnastics of the *shura* . . . everything had to be forgotten. Now there was only his training and the success of the mission.

Stepping from the stairway into the cavern, he dumped the man onto the floor. He was impressed with the lab's size. Like the one at Cal Poly, it was covered in tiles of large, sound-absorbent foam that clung to the walls and ceiling like shark fins. Although similar to the one in California, there were differences—particularly when it came to the center of the room. It was completely empty, encircled by what appeared to be a dozen small discs on the floor.

The girl was already across the room at a long console, shouting at the scientist/priest who stood beside her. The old man seemed surprised. Who wouldn't be? His fellow clergy had just been replaced by gun-toting *mujahideen.* Omar and his team had arrived only minutes before the Americans. During that time they'd safely escorted the real priests off to a tiny side chapel . . . wedging one of their bloody crucifixes through the door handles to lock them in.

"No." The scientist was shaking his head. "No!" He looked across the room to Omar and demanded, "Who are you people?"

The girl did not quit. "Uncle Fredrick, she's going to die!" She spun back to Lisa Harmon, the FBI agent Omar had been tied to in California. She'd been carefully laid on the floor next to them.

The scientist repeated, "I said, who are you?"

Omar signaled his number two man, Rashid al-Madani, to approach.

"Uncle Fredrick, *please!*"

"What does she want of you?" Omar demanded.

"*I* want to know who *you*—"

Rashid arrived and slammed the butt of his rifle into the priest's gut, doubling him over.

"Stop it!" the girl shouted. Moving into Rashid's face, she yelled, "Stop that right now!"

Rashid threw a look to Omar who forced an amused shrug.

The girl spotted it and turned on Omar. "Do you think that's funny?"

He gave no answer.

"Do you?"

"What do you want him to do?" Omar asked.

"Who?" she demanded.

"Him." He motioned to the priest. "What do you want him to do?"

"Heal her, of course."

Omar could not hide his surprise.

"Jazmin—" The priest rose stiffly.

"Is this true?" Omar asked.

"We're still testing it," the priest said. "There's no way to know for—"

"Is this true?"

"I don't . . . know."

"Uncle Fredrick, *please!*" The girl was in tears. "She's lost a lot of blood! So has Charlie!"

"How would such a thing happen?"

There was no answer . . . except the muffled explosions and gunfire upstairs.

"*Uncle Fredrick . . .*"

The priest looked away.

Frustrated, she turned and answered Omar. "If you put

them there"—she motioned to the center of the room—
"and bring up the rods—"

"Jazmin!" the priest snapped.

"—stuff happens. At least it's supposed to."

"*Stuff?*" Omar asked. "What type of *stuff*?"

"I just told you!" She blew the hair out of her eyes.
"Doesn't anybody listen?"

Omar took a guess. "They become . . . healed?"

"Give the man a cigar."

Omar frowned. It was one thing to destroy a computer
program that brought dishonor to Allah, but if that program
could heal—*In the name of Allah, the compassionate*—if it
could bring people health, then surely, such a thing should
not be feared.

Turning to the girl he asked, "Where are these . . . rods?"

"There." She pointed at the twelve discs on the floor.
"They come up from those holes."

He looked to Rashid. Their orders were to capture the
people and the Program. Nothing was said against first ob-
serving what it could do. *In the name of Allah, the compassionate.* Surely, this was acceptable.

Rashid gave a nod. He was just as curious.

"All right," Omar agreed. "Let us see this healing."

The girl spun toward the console.

Omar motioned his men toward the Americans. "Move
them. Put them in the center."

They obeyed as the girl began working the controls . . . and
the priest reluctantly joined her.

With a series of quiet hisses, thin rods of stone rose
from the floor. They were different colors and transparen-
cies, some as clear as diamonds, others opaque rock. Black,
speckled, jade green, bloodred . . . they rose, creating a circle
eight feet high with the American couple in the center.

Houser ducked as a burst of bullets splintered the pew directly beside him. It was an ignorant shot, full of emotion, but he didn't complain. It allowed him to pinpoint the shooter's location at the front of the church. He dropped to the floor and sprayed a line of fire, just inches off the stone floor. The scream indicated he'd gotten at least one of the legs. Maybe both. Not as rewarding as a direct kill, but for their purposes just as useful.

Houser rose and raced forward. Iserson was on his feet doing the same from his right flank.

It had taken little time to realize that the priests were not priests. These were no amateurs. That's why he'd resorted to the grenades. Sloppy business, he thought. No one likes blowing up a house of worship . . . unless, of course, it's a mosque . . . or two.

The good news was they'd already taken out three men. From Houser's count that left four, tops.

He pressed his lapel mic. "Milkner, position?"

The answer came through his earpiece. "Nothing in back. Moving in."

He arrived at the front row of pews, his right eye twitching and watering. He spotted a smear of blood leading behind the altar. He pointed the location to Iserson who pivoted out to the right as Houser moved in.

Two meters from the altar he stopped and signaled Iserson.

Iserson nodded and slapped the nearest pew with his hand.

The diversion worked.

The "priest" opened fire, giving Houser plenty of time to

approach from behind and shoot a burst into his back. The man collapsed onto the stones. For good measure, and a little revenge, Houser fired another round directly at his head. He brought the muzzle closer and fired yet again.

He might have continued, if he'd not spotted Brenem. The agent had arrived from the back and was signaling to a side room. Houser nodded and approached with Iserson. Milkner appeared and joined them.

But it wasn't a side room they found. It was a stairway.

The Voice

The first thing Lisa felt was the heat about her throat. Not a burning heat, as when the knife had cut into her, but a soothing warmth. With it came a tickling, a rapid little vibration. It started at the wound, but quickly spread down her torso and up into her head until it filled her entire body.

But it wasn't just her body. It was also her mind.

Somehow the vibration began seeping into her thinking. It seemed to shake her ideas, her very memories—as if loosening her thoughts—forcing them to fall into one giant tumbler where they were all mixed.

But that was only the beginning . . .

To her astonishment, the thoughts came back together again. But in an entirely different order. Now they had a cohesiveness to them. Random thoughts and memories began forming an intricate mosaic, an understandable pattern of logic and reason.

It was like a thousand random jigsaw pieces coming together to form a single . . . portrait.

Smaller memories, like falling off her skateboard at seven, failing her driver's test at sixteen, the Rudolph-like pimple on her nose at homecoming. Bigger issues—her marriage to Kevin, his drug abuse, her acceptance into the Bureau . . . this trip. All thoughts, all actions and experiences had been shaken loose and were coming together again in an alignment. A *perfect* alignment. The mystery behind them was still there, but somehow they made sense. Somehow, even though she didn't fully comprehend, they were forming a logical and beautiful pattern. More than beautiful. They were forming a masterpiece.

She sat up and felt her throat. There was no blood. No trace of a wound. Only the vibration which she now realized had started outside her body. It had been a distant thunder, but quickly grew into a deafening roar. As it increased so had her sense of order . . . and peace. Now, try as she might, she could not find a single thought that failed to align itself with the vibration. Those nagging fears and doubts that always nibbled away at the back of her mind? Gone. Those concerns that made her lose sleep? Disappeared.

Everything was coming into perfect order.

Even her father's actions. The despicable things. Yes, they were still despicable. Yes, they would always be. But now she saw them with deeper understanding. Now she saw a sick man with a crippled soul struggling as best he could with a sickness he inherited from his father. Was he to blame? Yes. By resisting the vibration. Yes. By refusing to allow it to align and heal his abhorrent illness. Absolutely. But now she understood the logic. Everything she thought and did resonated with it.

As did the stones of the floor she sat upon. Stones that were quarried from the earth . . . that were created from the vibration . . . whose atoms still vibrated in perfect resonance to that vibration.

As did the acoustical foam above her. Coming from the oil of decayed vegetation . . . that was created from the vibration . . . whose atoms still vibrated in perfect resonance to that vibration.

Even her body of clay . . . from the vibration . . . its atoms still resonating.

"Lisa . . ."

She turned to see Charlie sitting beside her. The look on his face said he experienced the same understanding. And peace. The pain in his face was gone and she knew why. He had been healed just as she was. And, like her, it did not stop with his body.

He reached his hand out to her and she took it. Together, they rose. There was no longer a need to hide her feelings from him. He knew them. As surely as she knew his.

Then the gunshots began.

Charlie spun to the console. Jaz and the old man were working the Program. Not far away, the armed "priest" he had nearly killed at Cal Poly dropped down and was taking cover with two associates. Charlie followed their eyes across the lab and saw the reason.

Four Mossad had entered from the stairway, their guns blazing.

It felt like someone had thrown ice water in his face. One minute Charlie was experiencing unimaginable peace—the next, unbelievable brutality. Of course the peace wasn't entirely foreign to him. A long time ago there had been fleeting moments of it, during his deepest times of prayer and worship—back when he prayed and worshiped. And the ice water? That's where he spent the rest of his life.

He turned back to Jaz and Fredrick. "Down!" he shouted. "Behind the console! Get down!"

They didn't have to be told twice.

"Charlie . . ."

Lisa pulled him back to the stone floor where they surveyed the scene.

The Mossad were spreading across the room, firing as they took cover. Behind Lisa and Charlie, the "priests" were doing likewise. Multiple times he heard the double pop of bullets as they passed just overhead.

"What do we do?" Lisa shouted.

They lay in the center of the room, no-man's land. The closest cover was the console behind them. A good twenty feet away.

He motioned toward it. "Go! I'll follow!"

She nodded and started off. He followed, inching his way across the floor. Mossad and mujahideen were intent upon one another and paid little attention to the couple. Charlie approached one of the stone rods—a ruby crystal. He reached out to touch it. There was no vibration or sound. He imagined Fredrick had shut the system down at the first gunshot to avoid a repeat of the Swiss disaster.

They continued forward and had nearly reached the console when an excited Jaz spotted Lisa and cried out, "Your throat!"

"Stay there!" Lisa ordered.

The girl could barely contain herself. "Your throat! Your throat!"

Lisa arrived and lifted her chin to confirm the gash was completely gone.

"You're healed!" Jaz shouted. Then to Charlie, "And your back?"

He joined them. "Everything's okay."

"All right!" Jaz squealed, giving him a high five.

"What do we do?" Fredrick shouted.

Again Charlie surveyed the room. The two forces had spread out equal distance from one another.

"Is there another way out?" Lisa yelled.

The priest shook his head. "Just the stairs!"

"What about this?" Charlie motioned to the console before them. "Can't you stun them or something? Like Switzerland?"

"You saw what happened there."

"But you've got the Program now. You can control it."

"In theory, yes, but—"

"Charlie, the gun?"

He turned to Lisa.

"At the apartment. I gave it to you."

He reached to his back waistband and pulled out the 9mm Glock. In the excitement he'd forgotten, though he'd been too weak to use it anyway. He checked the magazine. It still had several rounds, enough to do serious damage.

Looking back to the shooters, he was about to propose a plan when, suddenly, another thought formed—the promise he'd made to God so long ago of putting away this old life and starting anew. Maybe it was residue of the peace he'd just experienced in the center of the room, maybe not. Whatever it was, he couldn't shake it.

Lisa saw it in his face. "Charlie?"

He thought again of the peace. The vibration. The Voice. The knowing there was something far greater than the conflict before them.

"Charlie . . . what's going on?"

He turned to Fredrick. "Can you crank this thing back up?" he asked. "Only hotter? Do to everyone here what you did to me and Lisa?"

"Yes, but the dangers—"

"You've got a gun!" Lisa shouted.

He turned to her.

"Drop the nearest one! I'll grab his rifle and we'll fight our way out!"

He frowned. "But . . . the Voice."

"They're killing each other! And when they're done, they'll kill us!"

A bullet glanced off the console and they ducked.

She motioned to the Glock. "Use it!"

He looked at the weapon.

"Uncle Charlie?"

He turned to Jaz. In the light she almost looked like his sister . . . and in some ways his baby girl.

"Charlie!"

He turned back to Lisa. Her patience was gone. And he fully understood. He fully agreed. Yet there was his oath, his sister, his family . . . those partially charred rocks from the mountain.

"Here then!" She grabbed the gun from him. "*I'll* pop the closest one and *you* grab his rifle." She chose the nearest shooter, one of the priests. Rising, she rose and leaned against the console, taking careful aim.

Instinctively, Charlie checked the room and spotted another priest watching her.

"Lisa, no!"

The priest spun his rifle toward her.

With no time to think, Charlie leaped to his feet to pull her down. "Lisa—"

A line of bullets fired up his spine and exploded the back of his skull. Charlie Madison was dead before he hit the floor.

Twenty-Nine

Lisa dropped and rolled from Charlie as she fired at the shooter. Her first two rounds missed. There was no need to fire a third. A Mossad across the room did it for her.

"Uncle Charlie!" Jaz scrambled to him. "Uncle Charlie!"

But he was gone and nothing could bring him back.

Emotion knotted Lisa's throat. She swallowed, forcing it back. The loss would break her heart . . . but later, when she allowed it.

Right now there were other matters. The fallen priest lay too far away for her to secure his weapon. That meant she would have to find and kill another. Jew, Muslim, it made no difference. She took a quick survey of the room. There were four active sights of fire—two partially exposed. The closest knelt a dozen feet away.

Jaz was screaming at Fredrick, trying to convince him to crank up the Program for another healing.

But it was too late. Lisa knew too much damage had been done.

Crouching and leaning against the console, she took careful aim at the closest gunman. She held her breath, lined him up, *Hello, boys, there's a new girl in town,* and dropped him with the first round. His Uzi fell to the floor, a tantalizing eight feet away.

She quickly rechecked the room, expecting to draw fire. She wasn't wrong. The other exposed gunman repositioned himself and shot an obligatory burst in her direction. She ducked behind the console.

As far as she could tell, Jaz and Fredrick were temporarily safe . . . though the old man was taking risks by giving in to Jaz's demands. He had reached up and was trying to reactivate the console by feel. Lisa could warn him, but doubted he'd listen. Not with Jaz shouting in his ear.

She stole another look at Charlie, or what was left of him. Grief choked her, tightened her chest, making it difficult to breathe. If she didn't act now, she'd never be able to.

Once again, low rumbling shook the room. She glanced to Fredrick working the console. She turned back to the Uzi on the floor. It was risky, but it still might save them. She forced a breath then rolled out from the console and fired shots at each of the hot spots—a precautionary measure to force them back into cover. That's when she noticed the stone rods. All twelve had started to glow.

The rumbling grew louder, stronger. As before, she felt it vibrating through her body, into her mind. With it came the same ordering of thoughts, memories, emotions . . . and that all-consuming peace. But this time she had to fight it. She could not let it have its way. She crawled for the Uzi.

The stones under her knees and elbows grew soft, then gooey. She looked down. They were melting! But not from heat. They began flowing into one another. Soon there were no longer any cracks between them. Instinctively, she knew what was happening. They were returning to the same giant slab they'd been before they were cut and quarried.

She looked over to the walls. The acoustical foam was also changing. Like the stones below her, the foam seemed to be returning to its original state—first, runny tar and dripping oil, then into an even-earlier version . . . vegetation. Before her eyes, the walls grew vines and leaves. Prehistoric ferns began sprouting. Tropical flowers appeared. As she watched, the feeling of peace and order grew stronger by the second—so strong that it was all she could do to continue crawling, to remember who she was fighting, and why.

She looked ahead to the rifle. It was also changing—first to a bar of steel then, as if the refinery process had been reversed, to raw ore and stone . . . mixed with vegetation where the resin and plastic handgrip had been.

The same was true with the Glock in her hand. She stared in disbelief.

The rumbling became a roar. Deafening. There was no other sound—certainly not gunfire. Apparently, the soldiers' weapons had met the same fate as hers. A twenty-first-century version of swords to plowshares.

The peace continued consuming her until finally, slowly, she rose to her feet. There was no longer any fear, no need to escape. How could there be? Now there was nothing but the roar. And the sense of order. Once again thoughts and memories filled her mind. But not just memories of the past. Memories of the future. A clumsy kiss by Charlie on a moving train . . . the birthing of a child, and another . . . a husband whose face she could not see . . . the funeral of her father as she wept over the loss. She knew she could resist these images, just as she could resist the vibration. But why, when they were so perfect and ordered?

Finally she let go and dropped whatever walls of resistance remained. As she did, the vibration rushed in. She started to smile, then grin, then laugh. Slowly she raised her arms, allowing the power to fill every cell of who she was, of who she ever would be. She sensed others around her doing the same, being filled with equal awe and peace and wonder.

Bernice Wolff, recently retired FBI, followed her brother and his two Special Ops buddies down the church steps. They'd just freed the priests who'd been locked up in a side room. Now they raced into the basement laboratory with their rifles ready.

Except it was no longer a lab, more like an exotic garden. And they were no longer holding rifles. As soon as they entered the room their weapons began changing. Now they held chunks of iron, rock, pieces of plants.

Then there was the sound. So powerful it sent her staggering backward . . . until she felt it entering her. She'd experienced something like this only once before, and on a much smaller scale. Back when she was a little girl. Back when Brother Thomas healed her appendicitis. Of course no one believed it was possible until they opened her up and saw a perfectly normal appendix with no sign of infection. And, of course, they'd chalked it up to misdiagnosis.

But even then little Bernice knew better. Even then she knew what she'd felt.

And she knew what she felt now.

The sound was like a waterfall, like a dozen waterfalls. And woven amidst the roar was the music of horns—trumpets. Deafening. But the intensity did not hurt her ears. Like everything else, it seemed to pass *through* her, entering her body, her head . . . until everything she was vibrated with its power.

As she allowed it.

She glanced to her brother. Instead of the peace and power that saturated her, she saw a look of terror.

"Timmy!" she shouted. "Let go!"

He turned to her, teeth gritted, starting to shake.

"Don't fight it!"

He tried to speak, but could not. The shaking grew worse.

She ran to him and grabbed his shoulders, shouting into his face. "Let go!"

His eyes searched hers.

"Give in to it! Let go!"

He closed his eyes.

"LET GO!"

Finally, he nodded. The muscles in his face started to relax. So did the rest of his body. The shaking came to an end and he opened his eyes. He started to smile. But not a mindless smile that lacked understanding. This was a smile *full* of understanding.

Bernie turned back to the garden. Above and at its center a slit of bright light appeared. It spread, filling the lab with unbearable brilliance, brighter than any sun, than any hundred suns. She squinted against it, catching glimpses of crystal-like substances. But they were not crystals. They were creatures. Hundreds of them. Human in form, but bigger. As the slit grew, they continued appearing until the entire garden was full of their light, full of them.

"NO!"

The scream startled her. She spun around to see one of the Mossad not far from her. He was on the ground squirming, clinging to a stone that had once been a rifle.

"Don't fight it!" She ran toward him. "Let go!"

The writhing grew worse.

She knelt down. "Listen to me!"

He began rolling from side to side.

She pinned his shoulders forcing him to look at her. "Listen to me!" That's when she recognized the scar across the left side of his face and the ruined eye. Sheldon Houser, head of the Kidon team.

"You've got to let go!" she shouted.

He seemed to understand. As he did, the scar, like his rifle, began to melt, to dissolve.

But only for a second.

"NO!" He resumed thrashing.

"Let go!"

He convulsed. "NOO . . . NOOOO . . ." Until, suddenly, his body ignited.

Bernie leaped back at the *whoosh* of flames. She staggered to her feet as his entire body caught fire. The writhing slowed to a stop until there was no longer any movement . . . except for the flames as they crackled and popped and hissed.

She watched with sadness. But she understood. The sound filling her body helped her understand everything . . . including his hatred of the sound and his resistance to it. It wasn't the sound that killed him. It was his resistance.

She understood something else as well . . .

Everything she'd experienced, the light, the sound . . . it was all a preamble, a wake coming before the real force. A breath taken before speech. No sooner had the thought formed, before a Voice began. It started with only one word. One syllable. But with a roar so forceful, so powerful, that it threw her across the garden and into the wall of vegetation:

I . . .

Jazmin understood the word as surely as if she'd heard it. It was a single sound that vibrated through the people, the lab, through every atom and subatomic particle around her. If ever there was proof of the superstring theory, this was it. A universe not made of matter, but of vibrations. No, not of vibrations, but a Vibration.

A single, solitary Voice. All of creation, the lab, her body, the light . . . everything was simply a part of that Voice.

But she had little time to marvel at the thought before it evaporated. The Word dissolved it. Every other thought and idea she ever had became unimportant. All that mattered was the Word. The Word that was with God, the Word that was God.

Like so many others in the room, friends and foes, she lifted her arms. It wasn't a plea, and it wasn't forced. Instead, it was a spontaneous response to the greatness filling the lab. A yielding to it. A submission.

Others still fought it. A handful shook violently, trying to scream. They dropped to the floor writhing and convulsing . . . until they suddenly burst into flames. The explosions startled her. And they made her sad. But she understood. The men refused to submit, to vibrate with the Frequency of the rest of creation. Instead, they insisted upon creating their own sound, their own harmonics. And the results could not be more disastrous. The dissonance between the two frequencies created such friction and heat that they simply combusted.

But, just as some had dropped and burned on the lab's stone floor, others who had been shot and killed were rising to their feet. With sudden hope, she twirled around to where Uncle Charlie had fallen. Sure enough, he was also standing, raising his arms . . . his face glowing with the same peace she felt.

"Uncle Charlie!" She raced to him and he caught her in his arms, lifting her high into the air, grinning the biggest grin she'd ever seen. And laughing! A first for him. Big-hearted laughter that made her break out laughing.

He spotted something and gently lowered her to the ground.

She turned to see the leaves and vines of the far wall begin to part as people stepped out from behind them. They wore strange clothes from different times—some fifty years ago, others a hundred, others several hundred. And they were all grinning just as big as Uncle Charlie. Grinning and smiling and laughing as they passed through the wall that was next to the cemetery.

Jaz stared in wonder, feeling no fear. With all the joy and peace, how could she?

She turned to the middle of the room, where the light was the brightest, nearly impossible to look at. At its center some sort of shape had appeared. She held up her hand, shielding her eyes from the glare. It was the shape of a person. No, two persons. Standing side by side. A man and a woman. She squinted, refusing to turn from the brilliance. Her pulse quickened, her breath came faster ... until she was absolutely certain. And then her heart nearly exploded!

"Mom! Dad!"

They grinned. Even in the glare she could see the love in their eyes. And the joy. She wanted to race to them, but instinctively she didn't. Just as surely as she felt the love and joy, she sensed a separation that could not be crossed. Not yet. In time, but not yet. And that was okay. Surrounded by such peace, everything was okay.

"I'm all right!" she shouted. "Me and Uncle Charlie, we're all right!"

They nodded, grinning more broadly.

She looked up to Uncle Charlie who stood beside her. The big man also stared, his eyes filling with moisture. She took his hand and turned back, but this time she saw another couple in the light. A woman and a little girl.

She felt Charlie's grip tighten, heard him gasp. She looked up and saw that it wasn't a gasp. More like a sob. His entire body convulsed. And then again. But they weren't sobs of sadness, they were sobs of joy. He raised his hands to his mouth, like a child not believing what he saw, tears spilling onto his face. No one spoke. No one had to. The vibration and light filling them said it all . . .

Until the Voice sounded again. It was another single Word. Just as short. Just as powerful:

. . . AM

A sentence! Immediately Jaz understood. Together the two Words formed a statement! The same statement Moses heard when he asked God who he was. The same statement Jesus made when they asked him.

The effect was overpowering—the light, the sound, the joy, the realization. It was the last thing Jaz heard as the vibration entirely consumed her. Consumed everybody. Like Uncle Charlie, like everyone else in the room, she crumpled to her knees, the only response to such awesome power . . . before she fell forward onto the ground, losing all consciousness.

Epilogue

"So you're saying all trace of the Program is gone?" Charlie asked.

Fredrick wiped the alfredo sauce from his mouth with the white linen napkin. "The Program, my work on mineral fluctuations, all pertinent data has been erased."

Lisa eyed the priest carefully. The best she could tell, he wasn't lying. She wondered if he was even capable of it—if any of them were capable of it after all they'd experienced.

Omar Atmani leaned across the table. The veranda above their heads cast a series of stripes across his face from the afternoon sun. "You are not saying this because you fear me? I give you my solemn word that what I have witnessed, it will not be passed to my brothers." Turning to Iserson, the Mossad member who sat beside him, he continued. "Not because I believe we are wrong, but because there are many wolves in sheep's clothing."

Iserson nodded. "The same is true for me and my people." With a sad shake of the head he added, "Besides, who would believe us?"

Charlie pressed Fredrick. "But you could re-create the Program if you wanted?"

"No. And that is the strangest thing of all. I know I have done the work. I know I have spent years of research, but for the life of me . . ." He shrugged sadly. "I cannot remember any specifics. It is as if the data inside my own head was erased as well."

Silence stole over the group. There was only the chirping of a lark and a distant truck lumbering up the mountainside. Lisa thought a moment of Dr. Percy Reynolds, the mental vegetable she'd interviewed at the veterans hospital. She wondered if, in some way, his condition and the priest's were related.

This was their second day together and their first meal—Charlie, Jaz, Bernie, Fredrick, Omar, Iserson, and the others she had not yet met who sat farther down the table, engrossed in their own conversations. They were eating supper in the courtyard of a small monastery just outside Cuneo. Priests from the church in Ostia Lido had helped them escape from what remained of the lab. And, under Fredrick's instruction, brought them here to rest and recover.

"Doesn't it make you mad?" Jaz asked Fredrick.

"How is that?"

"Having all that information just get wiped away?" Unlike the others, Jaz had experienced no healing. A mystery Lisa knew she wasn't entirely thrilled about, though at the time, in the Voice's presence, it had made complete sense. During those moments everything had made complete sense. Although her deafness remained, Jaz now claimed she could "hear" thoughts and "sense" feelings. Lisa smiled at the teen's obvious need for attention. Yet another part of her wondered if it just might be true. After all they'd experienced, little would surprise her.

Fredrick smiled with his answer. "No, it does not make me angry, child. Not in the slightest."

Bernie spoke up from the other side of the table. "I'm betting it's like the Tower of Babel."

"How's that?" Iserson asked.

"We built what we shouldn't have built. We tried to be God."

Fredrick continued her thought. "And . . . just as God confused their thoughts in speech, he has erased mine regarding his Voice."

Iserson joked, "I guess he does not like the competition."

Lisa shook her head. "I'm not so sure that's it." She felt their eyes turning to her. Especially, Charlie's. She was always aware of his eyes. "I've seen what the Program can do in the wrong hands. I'm wondering if your mental block . . . I'm wondering if it's more out of compassion for us than fear."

Omar nodded. "A father not letting his children play with dangerous toys."

The group seemed to agree and returned to their pasta. A woman, no more than thirty, modestly dressed in a green wool skirt and white blouse, approached with a decanter of red wine. She began refilling the glasses.

Jaz stretched hers out until Charlie blocked her. "No *grazie*," he said.

"Uncle Charlie."

"*Grazie*, no," he repeated.

"This is Europe!"

"*Grazie, no.*"

Jaz thumped her glass on the table in a perfect pout. "Okay, fine."

The server bowed and moved off.

"Are they all here?" Bernie asked, nodding toward the departing woman.

Fredrick took a sip and answered. "There were nearly three dozen, those closest to the laboratory wall. We've relocated them to several monasteries for their safety until they reacclimate."

"And none of them will speak of their experiences?" Iserson asked.

Fredrick shook his head. "It is almost as if they have taken an oath."

Lisa added, "Or, like the Voice, they know we'll abuse the information."

Fredrick mused, "I wonder if the first-century saints in Jerusalem did the same?"

"This has happened before?" Omar asked.

The priest softly quoted: "*The tombs broke open and the bodies of many holy people who had died were raised to life . . . and after Jesus' resurrection they went into the holy city and appeared to many people.*"

"That's in the Bible?" Jaz asked.

Fredrick nodded. "Apparently the energy released at the moment of Christ's crucifixion was similar to what we experienced with the Voice."

Omar politely corrected, "*If* you believe Christ was actually crucified."

Jaz looked surprised. "You guys don't believe that?"

"The Qur'an clearly states that Allah did not kill Jesus on the cross, but that he was supernaturally saved from such shame."

Lisa noticed a trace of uneasiness in the group. Maybe the effects of the Voice were already wearing off. She hoped not. She stole a glance to Charlie who was frowning.

"You okay?" she asked.

He looked at her a moment, then cleared his throat. "I'm just curious . . ." The others looked to him. "Why did some of us survive the encounter and others didn't?"

"Yes," Omar asked.

"An excellent question," Iserson agreed.

Fredrick slowly chewed a bite of bread before answering.

"I am not entirely certain except . . . those who resisted the Voice are the ones who did not survive. While those who joined in, well, here we are."

Lisa added, "And those who joined in immediately"—she motioned to the priest—"you not only survived, but you didn't even lose consciousness."

"In many ways it was similar to my experience in Switzerland." He nodded to Bernice. "And your experience, it was similar?"

Bernice grinned. "Just like church, but a thousand times better."

Lisa turned to her in surprise. "You didn't pass out?"

Bernie shook her head.

Charlie continued the thought. "So it's what you told me earlier—about the power of worship."

"Perhaps."

Iserson ventured, "And the quicker we aligned ourselves to that Voice, to that"—he searched for the word—"*truth*, the less trauma we experienced?"

"That is my best guess, yes."

"But, how can that be?" Omar asked. The group turned to him. He motioned to Iserson. "How can he and I"—he turned to Fredrick—"or you, for that matter—how can we all be followers of the same truth?"

"I didn't say you were followers of the truth . . ." The priest picked his words carefully. "I simply agreed that you were less resistant to it."

Another moment of silence, a bit more uneasy.

Finally, changing the subject, Bernie asked, "And now what? We all go home and pretend like nothing ever happened?"

"I'm not sure that's possible," Iserson said.

Omar agreed. "Things may be difficult for all of us."

"Yes," Fredrick said. "Unless we rest in the pattern which we all felt—that overarching logic."

They turned to him.

"Our experience, somehow I expect it will fit into each of our lives as perfectly as all that has happened to us in the past. Not that we'll understand it, at least for now. But we will always have the opportunity to rest in it; to align it with the truth we experienced . . . and to rest."

The group nodded in silent agreement—each returning to their meal, each losing themselves to their own private hopes and fears.

‼ ‼ ‼

"You sure you'll be okay?" Charlie did not look at her, but busied himself checking out the train platform, then the train, then the platform again.

"What, are you kidding?" Lisa grinned. "A few review boards, a day or two in court, I'll be good as new."

"You'll let me know if there's any way I can help?" It was way over the top and he busied himself with the train and platform again.

"What, you going to come in with guns blazing?"

"No, I just . . ." As usual he found himself struggling for the right words around her.

"Don't worry, I'll be fine. Besides"—she turned to Bernie beside her—"you're putting in a word to the Man Upstairs, right?"

Bernie nodded. "Every chance I get."

He felt Jaz give him a poke. She was obviously encouraging him to make his move, the one they'd discussed the night before.

"If you like her, you gotta tell her," she'd said. "We may be a lot smarter than you guys, but we're not mind readers."

He ignored her then, and he ignored her now. He re-checked the platform and train. Nearly everyone had boarded.

"And you?" Lisa asked.

"I'm sorry, what?"

"You two, you'll be okay?"

"Oh sure." He forced a grin and set a clumsy hand on Jaz's shoulder, wondering if he looked as uncomfortable as he felt. "We've got a few issues to work out. After that, it's back to the music store."

Jaz poked him again, harder.

"Well, if you need help," Bernie said, "I know a couple gals who just might be looking for employment."

"*Salire su,*" the steward called to them from the train. "*Subito.*"

"Well, all right then." He reached out and clumsily shook Lisa's hand.

Jaz let out a sigh of frustration. He ignored her and reached for Bernie's.

"Oh, please," the woman said and threw her arms around him. He tried his best to return the gesture.

"Okay, well, we'll see you later, then," Lisa said.

"All right," Charlie said.

There was an awkward silence. Jaz filled it by clearing her throat.

"*Signora!*" the steward called. "*Per favore.*"

"Right." Lisa turned and started toward the train.

Bernie gave Jaz a helpless shrug and followed.

"Unbelievable," Jaz muttered. Charlie looked down at her as she shook her head. "You really are clueless, aren't you?"

The women boarded the train, Bernie first, followed by Lisa who hung back on the steps. The car gave a little jerk and they started forward.

Stuffing his hands into his pockets, Charlie strolled beside her.

"You be good now," Lisa called to Jaz.

"You know me." Jaz smiled.

"That's what I'm worried about."

The train picked up speed. Lisa hesitated, gave one last nod to Charlie, then turned and bumped into Bernie who was directly behind her.

"Uh . . ." Charlie cleared his throat, unsure what he wanted to say. He picked up his pace to stay at her side.

She turned back.

He broke into a trot.

She looked at him, waiting. But, as usual, he'd run out of words. Suddenly, he reached out to the handrail and pulled himself on board.

"What are you doing?"

He had no idea. Even less when he leaned in and gave her a quick kiss. She was startled to say the least and pulled back. Not that he blamed her. It was a stupid, clumsy move. So what else was new? He glanced down, unsure how to apologize, when suddenly she pulled his head toward hers for another—longer, warmer.

The whistle blew.

"Uncle Charlie."

They separated. He turned to see Jaz several yards behind them with the distance growing by the second. He looked back to Lisa. She smiled and gave a shrug. It was louder than any words and he appreciated that.

With rising confidence he turned, then back again to give her another quick kiss, then turned and jumped from the train to the platform. It should have been an easy jump; the train was traveling less than ten miles per hour. That's why it surprised him when his ankle gave out and he crumpled to the platform.

"Uncle Charlie!"

"Are you all right?" Lisa called.

He nodded holding his foot, pressing away the pain, wishing he could do the same with his embarrassment.

Jaz's arrival didn't help. "Smooth move."

Lisa called, "You look after him, all right?"

"I'll try," Jaz shouted. "But no promises."

"Good-bye," Lisa shouted.

Jaz looked up and waved. So did Charlie. Sort of.

The train continued pulling away as Jaz helped him to his feet. "Very uncool, Uncle Charlie, very uncool."

"Tell me about it," he muttered.

"And it's about time." As usual, he didn't know what she meant. They turned and started toward the terminal. "But don't expect me to help you out forever. I got my own life to live, you know."

"I'll keep that in mind."

They entered through the glass doors of the terminal and he noticed a group of teen boys watching. Only it was more like leering. And certainly not at him.

"When we get back, the first thing we're doing is buying you some decent clothes," he said.

She'd also spotted the boys, which explained her completely ignoring them. "Clothes?"

"Clothes. Something that doesn't make you look like a hooker."

"Uncle Charlie!"

"Why bother to buy pants if you wear them so low it doesn't matter."

"These are my favorite jeans and I'll wear them however I want."

"Not on my watch."

"Says who?"

"Says me."

"You got a lot to learn about raising women, you know that?"

"And you got a lot to learn about being one."

"Right, and you're going to teach me."

"Listen, I'm not any more thrilled about this than—"

She looked away. "I'm not listening."

"You *will* listen."

No answer.

"Jaz, look at me."

"I'm not listening." She threw a look over her shoulder, making sure the boys were still watching.

"Jazmin!"

And so the two continued through the terminal as Charles Madison, who'd fought and beaten some of the world's most ruthless terrorists, began to suspect that his greatest battles lay ahead.

"Jaz? Jazmin, answer me. Jazmin!"

About the Author

Bill Myers is an author/screenwriter/director who has sold over eight million books and videos and whose work has won over forty national and international awards. He holds a degree in theater arts from the University of Washington, studied filmmaking at the Italian State Institute for Cinema in Rome, and was awarded an honorary Doctorate of Theology from the Institute Theologique de Nimes in France, where he taught. When not writing and directing, he enjoys voice-over work (he's the voice of Jesus in the NIV Audio Bible), speaking at schools and campuses, and working with young adults in his church. You can visit him at www.Billmyers .com.